I0417888

Yesterday Was Long Ago

Mary Ann Nocera

Little Classics Publishing

Cover design by Mary Ann Nocera

Publication date September 2017

Yesterday Was Long Ago is a work of fiction. Names, characters, places and incidents, included therein are products of the author's imagination. Any resemblance to actual persons is coincidental. Names of places, actual or real are used fictitiously.

ISBN-13: 978-0692910658
ISBN-10: 0692910654

For My Sons
David and Joseph

CHAPTER ONE

ɷ

Cheryl softly closed their apartment door, and whispered, "Bye Zach." No warm body to cuddle with tonight. One glass of wine on the tray. One toothbrush in the holder. They both felt a trial separation would decide the uncertainty about their love. Does it need rekindling or has it slipped away? I hope in the end we both have the same answer.

Behind that closed door Zach was alone. Cheryl had been his life since the first day at Northwestern, nine years ago. So vivid was his memory seeing her come out of the book store when her bag, full of books, split and spilled on the walkway. She needed me. *Quantum Physics,* scary. Oh, those hazel eyes. She laughed with them. They spoke. Anxiety widened them. Care softened them. She carried it all in her eyes. Her tousled, dark blond hair framed her classic face. So pretty, today, just like that day.

They had gathered her books and he walked with her to the dorm room. I took her for ice cream and asked her about that scary book. She was all science. So long ago, so much has happened.

He walked across the room and gazed out the front window, his thoughts clouding the view of the park across the way. Her doctorate. I felt every twist and turn as she struggled through those harrowing equations and formulas. She was my lifeline when my mother passed. I love her, but how, as a friend? I still want passion in my love. Somehow we have to get our relationship back on track. It can't be over.

He turned and looked at the packed boxes. Shirts, trousers, Hemingway's and a few Follett's with the Rachmaninoff's and other CD's ready to be transported to their new home. Their message, the trial separation starts today.

ꟹ

The light snow had turned to sleet. Fat, gray clouds were hanging around making the morning look more like twilight than early in the day. A mix of seasons when winter had not let go and spring was only on the calendar.

As Cheryl drove into the city her thoughts were trying to find a way out of the maze. A future without Zach. Dad's heart attack. My career — holography — could end quickly. We could accomplish what Dr. Seigbahn wants or it could end in a failure. If Zach and I don't get back together, should I go to New York? But Mom might need me with Dad sick. I might have to make some serious decisions soon. But today I have to put my personal problems on hold and think, what did we accomplish in the holography lab this week? As team leader she was required to prepare a report each Friday.

The car almost drove itself into the lot of Colburn Scientific Laboratory. Shivering, she stepped into the raw mixture. Her all-weather black coat and boots were warm, but the wind flipped the hood back and the cold curled around her neck making her shiver even more. Her long strides could appear as if she were tall but she was not, just average height and trying to avoid Mother Nature's wrath.

First to Billow's Coffee Shop to meet friend and colleague, Kimberly. They met every morning for their daily chat before going to the lab. Kim worked in micro-biology. Cheryl was in the new division that Dr. Seigbahn had added to his laboratory a few months ago, holography.

Kim was at their usual table talking on her cell. Cheryl dropped her coat, sat down and waited. When Kim looked up her expression was telling, but she asked, "Cheryl McAndrews, did you sleep last night?"

Cheryl answered without expression or emotion. "Not much. Today is our separation day. I left Zach to move his things to his father's. He's going to stay there for now."

"I didn't think this would happen. I'm so sorry for both of you. It's a lot of years to throw away."

"We both are trying to be sensible and get this uncertainty out of our minds before we get married. We already had our honeymoon last year in Paris. Regardless what happens in the future we had a wonderful time." Her words brought a smile.

"If everything works out your relationship will be stronger," Kim was reassuring.

"I would like to have just gone off by myself today, but Dr. Seigbahn needs his weekly report. It's part of what I have to do. The other four days in the lab working with my colleagues is the best part."

"Holography is a world away from my thinking. I can understand using it for medical records, even insurance registering, but sending an image to another location is beyond my comprehension."

"As you know, I was reluctant to leave my physics lab, but we have a great group. Eight is the right size. We all agreed if we run out of ideas we would go back to our old divisions. Doesn't look like that's going to happen soon, but we don't know."

As Cheryl talked, her demeanor became more natural and some of the sadness fell away.

"Should I ask, are you two coming for dinner tomorrow?"

"Zach mentioned. We will. We are not enemies, just confused. He can drop me off at the apartment."

"I hope it won't be a farewell dinner."

"No… I don't…. It will be a date."

"Are you sure you don't want to go home?" Kim asked. "You look so tired."

"No — after more coffee I'll feel better for a while. It will get me through my notes so I can get this report written. After work I'll go to the gym and work out a little. Go home, have a salad and sleep." She paused. "How did your Petri dish look yesterday?"

"Dangerous. I put it in the oven and started over. Something accelerated the growth."

"When I was in high school I thought about

micro, but when I went into Mr. Everson's physics class, micro was left behind. That seems long ago."

After a few more sips of coffee and a few more words about their career choices, they decided it was time to make their way to Colburn.

Cheryl settled into her office and immediately checked her e-mail and calendar for next week. She thought of Zach. Can't expect a call or text — he knows it's report day and I need to focus. Emptying her mind of personal thoughts, software open, she began to put the notes for the third week of March, 2013 in order.

Moving through the morning, the clock and stomach said lunch. She unwrapped the chicken salad sandwich that Zach had made for her and took a bite. Lunch at her desk was part of the Friday report writing.

Four o'clock, the last revision was complete and she was relieved to hit Send. It would be waiting for Dr. Seigbahn Monday morning. She took a deep breath and opened her office door.

Jack was passing, and asked, "Cheryl, how are things? Good report today?"

"Good as I can get out of the week's effort."

"Going to happy hour?"

"No, to the gym, after I stop by the lab, if anyone is still there."

"Either way it's a good release. See you Monday."

Gathering her things, Zach's presence was again in and out of her mind. Alone, an empty apartment. Coat on, gym bag with lots of supplies, her purse strap over her shoulder, she walked down the hall to the lab.

Entering the outer office, she noticed that the monitor screens were on, but the chairs were empty.

They're in the test lab still working on their new digital time equations. The overhead lights were dim and the computers anchored the room. In between hung an emptiness, like the space between thunder and lightning, like the no-man's-land of war.

She walked across the room to the lab where blue and red beams were intersecting with white, where they bounced and split, reflected and interfaced. It was the silent chaos in the holography lab where they were desperately searching for order. She reached in the side of her bag for her key card and swiped it through the long slit to open the steel door. She saw Ned, Jeff and Jonas huddled around a computer absorbed in what was on the screen. Just as she stepped into the test lab Ned hit Enter to activate an experimental equation and a mix of colored beams scattered and instantly cast their glow directly in Cheryl's path. She screamed and her body, so easily, withered in a black-hole like spiral and hit the floor. In that instant the guys were paralyzed, their minds numb, then reality hit.

"Oh Cheryl!" Ned cried out.

"Get her!" Jeff shouted. "The beams crossed at the wrong place or something!"

"God yes, and she got caught in them! No! — No!" realizing what probably happened.

All three voices shouting at once, they ran and knelt at her side.

"Oh lord, she's out!" Jeff said in a nervous squeak. "Ambulance," he yelled, as he grabbed his cell from his pocket and punched 911.

They unrolled her and Jonas held her head. "Her pulse is too slow," he said, as his fingers lightly touched her neck. "Breathing, too shallow. And god, mine too."

Ned, his face bleached white and hands trembling, yelled, "The beams were supposed to intersect that thing," and he points to a statue in the middle of the lab, "and send an image of it to the back room, but they hit her!"

"Go check, see if her image is there!"

Ned ran and at the door, cried out. "It's not here! God, where did we send it?"

"Go check the computer and see if the equation is still there!"

"I saw it leave when I hit Enter," Ned said, his face contorted and voice quivering.

"Is it written down?"

"Yeah, it's scribbled, — but in the computer, after I hit Enter-Register, another part of an equation intercepts. You saw it happen."

"Can we reverse it?"

"Yes! I don't know! If a reverse doesn't work there's the hard drive info. Oh god, I can't think straight!" They were all in a panic but Ned was worse.

Amid the chaos and turmoil Jonas shouted, "Somebody go down stairs and wait for the ambulance. They'll never find us up here."

What seemed like hours, were only minutes, the paramedics rushed in and were told what happened. They were not sure what to do under the circumstances but they stabilized her. They placed her rag-doll like body on the stretcher and were on the way to the hospital.

"I'll go with her and call Zach," Jeff yelled, as they started to leave.

The lab was as silent as dark. Ned and Jonas stared at each other both pale and frightened, knowing they had transmitted her image, but they did not know to where or when. Their digital time equation had deviated from its course.

With the call to the ambulance the police had also responded. An accident in a scientific lab warranted a call to the U.S. Accident Prevention Board for investigation. The police had placed the call to the agency upon their arrival at the lab. They asked Ned and Jonas to remain until someone from the agency arrived.

After they closed the lab door and yellow tape was posted, the two police officers and Ned and Jonas waited. They explained briefly what had happened, knowing the police did not understand, but trying to accommodate their questions.

Within the hour, two middle-aged gentlemen arrived from the agency and asked coherent questions about the lab, their purpose and the accident. Ned and Jonas explained that its director Dr. Seigbahn had left for the day, but had been called and was on his way back.

After discussing and questioning, the men from the agency explained they had to take all of the computers in the lab to examine the hard drive contents, which they proceeded to do. All loaded they drove away. Ned and Jonas were extremely concerned that their lifeline to Cheryl had just been confiscated and they did not know when the computers would be returned. The agency representatives had also requested a meeting with the entire team and Dr. Seigbahn tomorrow at eight here at the lab.

Saturday morning the team and Dr. Seigbahn gathered with the men from the agency and the police.

Everyone was anxious about Cheryl and Dr. Seigbahn explained she was in a deep coma. He did not have to explain further. They all knew what had happened to her and until they got their computers back and the hard drive information they could do nothing. That could be several days and then they would have to find the right equations to reverse her image and that could take another several days.

The group was all day answering questions. They were tired and hungry. When released they all went to Daisy's for dinner and to further discuss the current problem among themselves.

ꕥ

CHAPTER TWO

ꕥ

Patches of slate gray smoke floated in the pale sky. Rubble of wood and stone that had been a market and a home lay on the cobbles, its neighbor untouched. Emaciated horses slumbered along with their carriages in tow. Trees in the parks and along the streets were hacked to the earth. Women in dark peasant dress huddled in front of buildings, where shops appeared to be open. Distant shouts and the sound of gunfire rolled at intervals, piercing the silence. Sad and depressed was this injured city.

Coiled and almost invisible, Cheryl lay under a large clump of evergreen bushes that had escaped the terror. She appeared dead. Although in a semi-conscious state, she groaned softly.

Time passed and she could feel parts of her body, but her brain seemed frozen. Sinking into a blackness, fear and cold went with it.

The smell of smoke jolted her from the inert

state and she tried to move, but only her eyelids fluttered. Gunfire caused her body to jerk. Her muscles tightened. I don't want to see what's out there. Her hand trembled as she pulled her hood over her face. Waves of cold chills traveled through her body, but she could feel sweat oozing from dark places. Slowly piecing her thoughts together, I think I'm alive. I seem to have a whole body. She felt her purse. She felt the roughness of the gym bag. Oh god, where am I? Did something hit me? A car? I don't hurt. Have I been kidnapped and dumped alongside a road? Nothing made sense, but she knew she was very cold. Zach, where are you!

As her muddled brain cleared, she suddenly remembered the intense light… the beams and what they were working on in the lab. Oh n…!

The terrifying thought was broken when something hit her knee. "Ouch!"

A deep voice responded expressing concern. Slowly she peeked from under the hood to see a much worn pair of black boots at the tip of her nose.

Jacques spoke again, not English, but French. He said, "You look like a heap of garbage all in black, but it moved." He offered his hand. Her long damp hair fell covering her face. It's a woman! "Let me help you!" She managed to sit up but fell back. She tried again, then was able to stand and take a few steps.

"Hurry. There's a lot of danger out here. That bush is no protection. The mobs are crazy these days."

Her French classes had been long ago. Although, she understood from his gestures and facial expressions that something in the surrounding area was seriously wrong. Run. She looked around, destruction.

In a flash running did not seem like the best choice, neither did going with a stranger.

He took her bag and hand, "Let's go, quickly." He pulled her through the sad looking park, across the cobbles, and up a side street that was less crowded.

"In here. Upstairs." She held back, and he could see the fear in her eyes. He spoke in a gentle tone, and she understood the word safe. She drew her lips in as a hesitation. It's a deep chance. My only chance. Her face sank and her body turned. Reaching the top, he flung open the first door he came to.

Cheryl was gasping and breath failing, not from running but from fear. Her heart the hammer, her body the anvil and trembling beyond control. Eyes so blurred the forms in front of her were not clear. Her bladder was pushing. Oh god I'm going to pee. Her head filling with dark shadows, realizing the last bit of awareness was slipping away. Her legs gave way and she slumped toward the floor. Jacques caught her and carried her to a cot in the corner of the large room.

ꕥ

Cheryl's breath caught at the sudden reality as she lay facing a wall. She shivered. Her short loss of consciousness had not exhausted her fear. The cool cloth on her head felt soothing. I could feel that I was going to pass out, but I remember the large room. Her thoughts quieted as she listened to the mixed voices speaking in French and their exchanges were of excitement and laughter. She lay quietly trying to understand a few words. Guard, food, Henri, Edouard. She inhaled, burning wax, a solvent, food. Wax provided light, solvent an artist used. The food did not smell as if it came from a chef's kitchen. Are they having dinner? Rubbing her feet together, no boots and no coat either. A few thin blankets covered her.

Cheryl moved and Janine was at her side. Helping her sit up, she asked quietly, "Would you like to go to the water closet?"

Cheryl understood, "*Oui.*" Located across the hall, Cheryl went in and Janine waited for her. Fortunately, the building had a water closet on three of its four floors.

Back in the large room and to the big, round table, Janine motioned for her to sit. She pointed to each person and gave a name, then pointed to Cheryl.

"Cheryl," she said, with a blank stare and straight voice.

Renée's gesture told Cheryl she was offering food. She shook her head no, and said, "*Merci.*"

"*Vin.*" Jean-Pierre smiled, and held up a carafe. She declined that too.

Everyone started directing questions to Cheryl. Facial expressions and body language paired their words. "Are you hurt? — Are you lost? — Were you attacked? — Do you live here? — Where did you come from? — Were you looking for someone?"

Confused, fingers splayed against her blank face, mouth slightly open, they all knew she did not understand.

Janine, with concern told the group. "Leave her alone. Maybe she was attacked by a mob. She is traumatized. Answers later." She paused, "We know how devastating it can be out there, don't we, Henri."

"Yes dear wife. The soldiers were so close you

could feel their breath. We cried in each other's arms when we arrived here at Jacques' building."

"We cried when we saw you," Renée said. She pushed her long, light brown hair back and took Jean-Pierre's hand. Her eyes a little full, remembering those first bad days.

"The war was over in January, but it's now March and we still don't have peace. Every day French troops and the mobs clash," Edouard said. "It's a civil war among the citizens."

"What bothered me the most was when they killed Pollux and Castor. An elephant provides a lot of food, but I was so saddened," Elise said, with a somber voice and blinking back tears.

"When this is over the zoo will just have to get two more." Jacques added to her sad statement.

"Not much better than what the local butcher had toward the end, rats, cats, dogs," Lucie said. "When I saw that I refused to buy anything. I would be sick at the first bite."

"I'm glad to know you never served any of that secretly," Edouard said.

Janine, who worked in a makeshift hospital, said, "It's awful when you have to tell a mother that her son was taken to the morgue. And hearing someone scream as the last utterance of their life." Her tearful voice faded away and she glanced at Henri.

"Dear one, I know how you hold these things close to your heart. Maybe you should take a rest from the hospital for a while," he said, as he put his arm around her and pulled her close.

"That's the easy way. These wounded are suffering more than I am. My scars will heal. Their scars are no arms or legs. I would feel selfish if I didn't help."

Adding their body language and voice inflections, Cheryl understood enough to know they were discussing a sad and stressful time. She felt their sincerity, but fear still held her body taut.

Nicole didn't want to hear all this sad talk and changed the subject. "Where's Ben tonight?"

"Guard." Edouard replied rather harshly. "Nikki you'd better look the other way. He's going to London as soon as he can get out of here. He's thirty, too old for you." He wanted to add other words but did not.

Eyes squinting and mouth elongated, her nasty expression translated, mind your own business.

As Cheryl listened to their discussion, her breath flowed more easily. Her facial expression relaxed into a faint smile. Her mind poised, she tried to decipher more French words and put them into a relevant meaning. Reviewing their names was like on the job training.

This group of young friends had decided to live together during the war for safety and share survival necessities such as food and news. Jacques' building was large and he had insisted they stay there. In the evenings they gathered for suppers that the girls prepared. Jacques had a root cellar in his building and it was full when the city was first surrounded, but they did not know how long it was going to last so the girls were frugal with their meals. Jean-Pierre almost always brought a newspaper. Henri and Ben offered information they had obtained during the day at guard duty. They all gathered extra food from any available source. Being together gave them support during these disruptive times.

"Time for bed everyone. Our time pieces are getting low," Jean-Pierre said, as he pointed to the candles and gave Renée a knowing smile. They all agreed in some manner, nodding, a sigh, standing. Conversations faded as everyone said goodnight and left the big room.

Janine said to Henri, "I'll be up in a few moments after I get Cheryl settled."

Janine took Cheryl's hand and led her back to the cot. "You don't understand French?"

Cheryl indicated with her thumb and first finger, a little, and then said, "English."

"Oh, Ben's English. Nice man." Cheryl realized Janine knew a few words and that was the start of their communications.

Janine suddenly gestured, turned and exited the big room. Cheryl assumed she would not be back. She took a deep breath of relief. For the first time all evening her body and mind came together in a relaxed state. I haven't been ravished. I was spoken to kindly. Maybe I made the right choice not to run. The door opened and Cheryl jumped what seemed like a foot. Janine returned with a gown that was once white for Cheryl to sleep in. She placed it on the cot and put her hands together and to the side of her face, indicating sleep.

"I'll see you in the morning, early."

Cheryl understood, and said, *"Oui."*

Janine took her hand, and smiled, *"Bonsoir."*

"Bonsoir," Cheryl echoed. Janine turned and left the room. Cheryl heard the click of the lock. It was so loud in the silent room that it sounded like the clang of an iron bell.

I'm a prisoner and all alone brought diverse thoughts. What do I do? At least I've been taken in and safe. They all seem nice, about my age. I'm not sure where I am. Can't ask. France probably. The guys in the lab don't know where I am either.

Nothing she had seen or heard had given a definite indication of time or place. She just knew she had been accidentally transmitted to somewhere. I'm in a terrible mess. My lab sent me here, and they have to get me back. I can only wait. I have absolutely no control, helpless as a newborn. As a twenty-first century woman, she had never experienced this feeling so completely.

Reluctantly, she undressed and slipped into the gown. Better than sleeping in my clothes. She stuffed them into her gym bag and pushed it under the cot. Checking her cell phone — nothing. With her purse strap around her arm, she blew out the candle. Sinking into the cot she pulled the thin blankets to her chin. As she stared into the black… oh god, it's only part of a day, already seems like a year. Our developing the hologram is in the early stages. They may never get me back. How bizarre. Oh God, help me through this!

She was not prone to crying over problems. Saving her tears for a good book or when Lassie came over the hill after being thought lost forever, now she wanted to bawl like a baby. She turned on her side, tears rolled fast and she slipped into the true black of sleep.

ꕥ

CHAPTER THREE

ൾ

*T*he sun was bright and high on this warm day. She tripped lightly under the heavy foliage, along the calm and narrow path. Thick, dark green moss covered the broken rocks and weathered logs. Ferns sprayed the cool dank earth. "Glück, das mir verblieb" swirled among the trunks of the trees. I'm dead. But the forest opened up to that brilliant day. Water gently slapped against the rocky ledge. He was sitting on a large rock gazing at the distant shore. As she walked to him, she called, "Zach."

"No, it's Janine," she said, as she tapped Cheryl lightly on her shoulder. Her body stiffened and her heart beat fast. Where am I? She turned, slowly sat up and looked around bewildered. She felt the dried tears on her cheeks. Her dream flashed through her mind, I'm not dead. She wiped her face and hoped her eyes were not swollen. Candles flickered in the kitchen area. She glanced at the long upper window. It was still dark, but light enough to know dawn was near.

Janine spoke softly, "It's morning and I made you tea and toasted bread with cheese. Did you sleep well?"

Cheryl understood enough, took a deep breath, smiled lightly and nodded, yes. The steaming tea gave her the waking effect even before the first sip, but the tasty bread clogged in her throat. The tea loosened the bread but not her fear and uncertainty.

In the kitchen area Janine busied herself, stoking the fire in the iron cook stove, filling the tea pot, slicing bread, and giving a stir to the grain cereal. She was also preparing a table setting for two, bowls, cups and utensils. In her plain white blouse and faded blue, ankle-length skirt, she appeared energetic and youthful, but her beauty had been tinted by stress.

Cheryl thought of the talk last evening. Not understanding everything, but knowing it was a disturbing time and wondering how long it had been going on. Their boots worn, skirts frayed, and jackets weathered, yet these individuals did not seem to fit into this shabby existence.

Janine had their breakfast ready when Henri arrived. They sat together speaking softly in French. Cheryl could not hear, but she could see the loving way Henri looked at her and Janine often touched his hand. He soon left and Janine gave her attention to Cheryl.

She went to the water closet to refresh herself and dress. Not much from yesterday was still with her. More alert today she looked around. There's water and a bluish copper tub for bathing. The sides are so high I would need a step stool to get in. Opening her gym bag, I am so glad I have my tooth brush. Dressed in sweat pants and matching fleece jacket, she went back to the big room. Janine smiled and made an accepting gesture of her attire.

Janine said, "I have to go to work at the hospital now." She mimed that Cheryl should stay here in the room. Cheryl nodded yes, but her fear questioned why. Janine pointed to the easels at the other end of the room and Cheryl assumed someone would be coming to paint. After their rudimentary communication Janine left, but did not lock the door. Cheryl still felt like a prisoner, safe from the outside world, but unsure of those around her.

She thought, being alone was almost as frightening as having someone around. She realized she was clutching her tea mug with force that could crack it.

Cheryl refilled her mug and sat down at the big table. Alone, but not for long. Jacques came for his breakfast. He chattered happily to her as he warmed his bread. He inquired how she was feeling. She knew, but had she not, his expression was unmistakable.

She replied, "*Bon.*"

He continued to talk and she continued to nod, hoping her expressions were compatible with his words.

Jean-Pierre opened the door and waved to Cheryl. He motioned to Jacques, "Ready to go."

Jacques got up and before he joined Jean-Pierre he went to Cheryl. He laid his hand lightly on her shoulder and spoke softly. She pulled back as if to listen, but actually so he would not be too close. His voice was warm and reassuring yet he frightened her. The light touch and words she did not completely understand, but they did relax her. After he was gone she hoped he had not felt her flinch as he touched her. She thought his intentions were probably trustworthy. I'm the one with the uncertainty.

My goal today, to find out where I am and what year it is. She noticed the sun touched the edge of the long upper window in the kitchen area of the big room. That's east. Her mind went to the easels at the big windows. That's west and my cot is at the north end.

She strolled casually to the windows to see what she could identify. Mars had definitely been here. Many building were in shambles, others not touched. She gazed from side to side, across the staggered roof-tops. Her eyes stopped abruptly. Oh yeah. Notre Dame. I'm not surprised. Now the Eiffel Tower. This must be near 1943. No, Paris wasn't destroyed, just occupied. Notre Dame was not much help. She remembered it was finished sometime in the 1200's.

Her eyes dropped. A light-colored stone wall enclosed the spacious courtyard. The grass was in winter mode. The large patch of bare earth had been the garden. Too early for flowers. The stone arrangements were the only decorations, but one large, brown rock stood out. Looks like a big hunk of lignite and carvings on it. Could be a natural formation. Six small trees lined one side of the wall. Cherry. She wasn't familiar with the others.

Her eyes traveled to the dark-red carriage house at the back of the courtyard. A little, round window in the peak and two below were framed in white. A small door at the side and big doors opened into the alley way, but they were not in her line of vision. What's in there? Nice setting, I wish I had my camera, definitely a camera, otherwise no one will believe me. Maybe I won't even remember, but the camera would.

She walked back, sat down at the table and looked around. This was the first chance she had to observe this large communal room without fright dominating her mind. The pendulum on the vintage wall clock ticked away time. Each tick will bring me closer to home. Above the round table was a gas lamp with four tinted globes. But there was a candelabrum in the middle of the table and other candles spaced around the room. She learned later they used candles when the gas had been turned off last November because of the war and not fully restored.

The brown stone hearth was open on both sides, sending heat to the kitchen and to where Edouard painted. Near the cook stove was a breadboard bread box and bits of coarse flour that had missed the cleaning rag.

The mixture of furniture was eclectic. Chairs, large and small, wood and plush. An old style, chaise longue and a red, tufted sofa. A sideboard under the long window held a mix of colorful vases and bowls. Underneath were baskets of lace. Several chests standing, against the wall, where they appeared to have been dropped without thought. At the other end, her cot. This room was crying for an identity.

However, there was vitality. It was the colors that sprang from Edouard's paintings. They ran like a lifeline on the wall, to the shelves, and on to the floor. Landscapes with greens of Kelly, lime and emeralds with sky blue covers. Flaxen hair waving with the breeze. The calm, still life of apple red, lemons and a bottle of crimson wine. On a board, yellow and white cheeses that you could taste. The sweet, red rose in the indigo vase. Water's reflection of the orange sunset.

She found it hard to leave one and go to the next, to see a new color and feel a new emotion. Edouard and a tiny date in each corner. These paintings were the one thread of beauty in this otherwise drab room.

Cheryl's thoughts perked her senses. Edouard. Could it be? She glanced quickly through the collection, but did not recognize any as a Manet. She did not know what he looked like that only he was an Impressionist painter. Her nerves made her giddy. This little side trip in my life might be worthwhile. Although to relax and possibly enjoy did not seem an option.

Her eyes traveled around the room to all of the books. Every nook and every corner was overflowing. This is so wonderful. I can review my French. *Birdsong* is in my bag. It's Kim's.

Several rifles hung on pegs by the door, their message clear. What was not clear to her, how this hodge-podge of things and people fit together? I'll be patient and it will unfold. For the moment her fears were concentrated elsewhere.

Cheryl selected a book, found a French dictionary and started to read. Elise came in carrying her basket of bobbins and white thread. She spread her craft on the table and made another pot of tea. Cheryl pointed to the baskets of lace under the sideboard.

"*Oui,*" Elise said

"*Tres belle, tres belle,*" Cheryl replied.

"*Merci.*"

"*Vous vendez?*" Cheryl asked, did she sell her craft work?

"*Oui.*"

Cheryl moved closer and looked on with interest as Elise made her fingers fly. Cheryl had never had time to develop a craft. Science was her craft and career, but Elise making bobbin lace fascinated her.

Edouard came to paint. He did not say much, just a wave and words of good day. Cheryl observed him closely. I'll casually ask his last name.

Near mid-day Elise gathered her work into her basket and said she too worked at a hospital a few days a week when needed.

Edouard left, but soon returned with dried apples, peaches and two small blocks of cheese. He spread them on the table for himself and Cheryl to have a midday lunch. Edouard was generally quiet, but they talked and stumbled over words. She tried hard not to show her anxiety. Her smiles and nods were the masks she was hiding behind.

Cheryl gestured to the paintings. "These are yours?"

He nodded yes.

She thought hard for the right words, in French, to express how beautiful she thought they were. "Your colors create so much feeling and emotion. They're absolutely beautiful." She wished, if only I could take one home.

"Thank you my dear."

When Cheryl was about to gather enough courage to ask him if his name was Edouard Manet, piano music was heard coming from downstairs. Cheryl pointed in the direction of the music.

Edouard said, "Chopin."

Her thoughts grabbed her, oh my god, I'm going to faint! If that's Chopin, he can't be Manet. It has to be the 1830's. She became flushed. Is George Sand around too? I can't handle this living history. She smiled meekly at Edouard hoping to hide her wind-whipped thoughts.

After tea, Edouard excused himself and went to his easel and Cheryl to her reading.

She knew she was an outsider in this close-knit group. When they were together there was an air of warmth toward each other and they extended it to her. I'm like a mistake in a play. The play goes on and the mistake is seamlessly woven in. My fear of these people seemed to be unfounded, but that I am in a world other than my own is terrifying.

Totally enthralled knowing Chopin was downstairs, she found it hard to concentrate. I want to run right down there, now. What if I get transmitted back before I get to meet him? A distressing thought interrupted the Chopin excitement. I will have to explain why I'm here. That means a good story. Oh, where do I start!

Later in the afternoon Janine, Lucie and Cheryl went down into the cool dank, root cellar. "This is where we keep our food," Janine explained to Cheryl.

Lucie added, "Most of the vegetables," pointing to the remainder of the beets, potatoes, and carrots, "came from Jacques' garden. We were almost out of meat, but now that the war is over, Jacques and Henri can take the horses and go out into the countryside and buy meat from the farmers. They also get fresh milk."

Cheryl's thoughts perked, a war, Paris, there had been so many European wars.

"All the fruit came from the little trees in the courtyard. Apples, peaches, cherries, the trees were loaded last fall. It was like they knew we would have a bad winter," Janine offered. Two oak wine barrels lay in the corner.

Back upstairs the women prepared supper and placed it on the back of the iron stove. Renée and Elise arrived and they chatted and helped Cheryl with her French. She was grateful for their kindness and they quelled her fears. Knowing she would be gone soon helped her relax her body and mind but a fraction.

Cheryl mentioned Chopin to Lucie. "Yes, he plays. And he eats with us." It was a confirmation she was going to meet one of the greatest composers of piano literature. She was afraid to speak because her voice would quiver and squeak and she could not control it. The thought of meeting Chopin overrode her tension.

Dusk was settling when the men arrived. Jacques and Jean-Pierre each had a carafe of wine.

Nicole quipped, "Where's Ben?"

"He'll be up. I saw him earlier," Jacques said. "You know how he is when he gets started working on his music, he loses track of time."

Cheryl was puzzled. Is this Ben the English guy Janine mentioned? I can talk to him more easily. I hope he's nice. Where's Chopin? Did I misunderstand Lucie?

As everyone was slowly arriving for supper, the door opened and a tall, solid, beautiful man entered. His short, dark brown beard matched his big eyes. He wore Hessian boots like the other men, but he had on a funny shirt.

"Hello everyone," Ben said in French, exposing his happy energy. "I thought I was going to be late. I am working on my Chopin recital, got tired and fell asleep. Guard was late last night."

Cheryl knew that was not Chopin. Not only disappointed, but she was back to being confused about what year it was.

Ben's big, brown eyes immediately fell heavily on Cheryl. Janine took his hand and said, "Meet Cheryl. She's English. Jacques saw her and knew she needed help."

"Hello to Cheryl, I'm Ben Rutherford," and he took her hand. "From England. Where?"

"No. America," she said passively.

"What bring you here? Not the best of times."

Oh god, what do I say. "I'm not ready to talk about it yet," she said, in a most dejected tone putting her hands over her face hoping to convince him.

"I am so sorry. I didn't mean to upset you. Come let's have a glass of Jacques' wonderful wine." He took her hand, guided her to the table and sat down beside her. He poured a glass of wine and handed it to her.

"Thank you," she said, with a faint smile.

Nicole bristled. Everyone else relaxed and shared the food. Nicole sulked.

Ben spoke to his friends in French and to Cheryl in English. She told him she had studied French, but a while ago. "I'll be happy to translate."

The long evening was coming to a close and they all began to say good night. At last Ben and Cheryl were alone. They bonded quickly. She wondered, is it the circumstances or something else. Suddenly she realized she needed someone in this strange place and Ben, being English, could serve the purpose.

"You're English and live here in Paris?"

"I grew up and went to school in Paris and London. Studied piano with Holstein in London and Koenig in Paris. Now I go back and forth giving recitals. I did before the war."

"That is why your accent is not so decidedly English. Do you have family in England?"

"My sister, Beth, and her husband, Reggie, live in our home in London. My parents are there. My dad is an import-export merchant of foods, textiles, raw products like wool. He travels all over Europe and my mother goes with him. We also have a small estate near Cambrai, east of here. We were there and planning to go to London, because there had been several battles along the French and Prussian border. It was too dangerous to stay. I thought I had time to get down here and pay Jacques for my rooms I rent downstairs and do some other stuff, get back to Cambrai and we would go on to London. I was a little late. The Prussian troops surrounded Paris while I was here and I couldn't get out."

Cheryl asked, "That sounds so awful. How long has that been?" She smiled inside. Finally I am getting somewhere.

"Since last September. It was a bad winter. Food was running out. People were starving. Jacques and his father own this building. Jacques and I were here and we had our friends move in with us. We thought we would be better off together."

"I believe I understood the war is over, but the Prussian soldiers are still here?"

"Yes, the war was over at the end of January. The armistice signed February seven. The soldiers are to stay here until France pays war indemnity. I have no idea when and they probably don't either." He paused. "You haven't been in Paris long?"

"No," she answered softly, and knew it was time to get upset again to avoid answering questions. She put her head in her hands.

"I'm sorry I won't mention it again." He paused. "The people didn't like the terms of the armistice so they formed mobs and named themselves the Commune. They are constantly clashing with French troops. That and the Prussian soldiers being here, although they are supposed to leave the people alone, doesn't make for a safe surrounding."

"It still sounds so dangerous and are you still going to London?"

"I am when the weather is better. Hopefully that will be soon."

"The war was right here. What did you do?" Her facial expression and voice exhibited concern.

"Not much — just trying to stay alive. The object of the surrounding was to starve the city out. When that didn't work, they started a bombardment the beginning of January, every day for several hours. You can see the destruction outside. Fortunately Jacques' building wasn't hit. We huddled in the cellar lots of hours, not knowing what we would find when we came up. After the armistice, everyone was elated, but then the mobs and troops started fighting."

"That's awful. I feel so bad for all of you. You don't know where your parents are and they don't know if you're okay."

"I sent messages out by balloon. I don't know if they got them."

"Hot air balloon?"

"Yeah. That was the only way messages and things got out. They could get aloft before gunfire could reach them. They set up factories here to make them. The tailors and seamstresses went to work. We all had guard duty somewhere or joined the troops. There was a ring of French forts around the city, then there was empty space, then further out a ring of Prussian forts. And there were always confrontations in that empty space."

"So no supplies came in and life in the city was totally disrupted."

"Very. There was a lot of food at the beginning, cattle, grains and stuff, but that slowly was depleted and people starved. Our supplies were running low. We hoarded what we could get at first. We didn't know how long this was going to last. That was our salvation and Jacques' garden and the fruit trees. The enclosed courtyard kept the trees safe from becoming fire wood."

"I just can't imagine." She paused. "You gave recitals here before the war."

"I did, here and in London and hope to again. I want to expand to other parts of Europe too."

"It's unfortunate you got caught here, your life was literally on hold. Everyone's."

"Soon I'll be on my way. First I am going to Cambrai to check on our estate and see about my parents. They were not in the direct path of any of the battles, but too near for comfort."

The candles were low, and Ben asked, "Where are you sleeping?"

"Behind that screen," and she pointed. "Jacques brought it today."

"Oh gosh. There are rooms upstairs but they

have stuff stored in them. Lucie, Nicole and Elise are together in one of the larger rooms. Jean-Pierre and Renée have one and Janine and Henri another. Edouard has a small one in front. Jacques has a room, but sleeps mostly in the carriage house with his horses. He made his loft quite cozy."

"How sweet."

"He had to. They were taking horses for food. Jacques would go before he let his horses go. We needed them to get around. Hopefully they are somewhat safe now. The Prussians are sending train loads of food, but their soldiers are not to be trusted. We have heard about several bad incidents." He hesitated a moment and stared at her, "Oh Cheryl, it's so nice to meet you and the day is gone. Would you like to go to the water closet before I lock the door?"

"Yes, but why do I have to be locked in?"

"We're not locking you in, but locking the burglars out. Does it make you uncomfortable?"

"Yes! What if there's a fire?"

"This building is all stone. Not about to burn, but I'll leave you my key and will be up early in the morning for it. I have guard all day tomorrow."

"Thank you. That makes me feel better."

"Next day we'll go for a walk, if everything is quiet. But please don't go out alone. You can't trust the Prussians or the mobs." He kissed her lightly on the cheek and said good night.

She realized he relaxed her by just being near, but he had introduced a new situation for her concern, remnants of war. If he is willing I need him until I understand my surroundings.

She lay on her cot and again stared into the

black night. I know where I am and it has to be the end of the Franco-Prussian War. 1871. I don't remember much about it, looks like I'm headed for a living history lesson.

She pulled the thin blankets to her chin as if they would protect her from the fear and uncertainty she felt. Zach, oh Zach, do you know where I am. Did we do the right thing? Will I ever know? Will I get out of this ungodly place? If this is what holography can do I don't want any part of it. What happened that this happened? Cheryl mused for a while then her thoughts stretched and she gently drifted to sleep.

ꟹ

CHAPTER FOUR

Coming from a scattered dream, Cheryl listened. A deep gong. A lighter clang. One far away, faint and slow. Another closer, loud and deep. One that paused between each lighter tone. A steady beat flowed from another with its mélange of quick and mellow. A cacophony of tones reverberated from these huge, iron beasts. The call to worship floated across the city as an unseen cloud.

Sunday was not always a day of rest at home. It was the catch-up day. Cleaning. Laundry. Visiting parents. Sunday evening's Cheryl and Zach always had a candlelight dinner and afterward made love in a special way before going to sleep.

That schedule had changed before she was thrust into Paris, but she missed him. She missed her lab and her colleagues. She missed everything, but fear was slowly leaving her body, especially after meeting Ben. He could not help her get home, but somehow she knew he was going to be her protection while she was here.

As she sipped her tea the door opening slowly and Ben entered with his rifle slung over his shoulder. He hung it on a peg, and said, "Good morning. I see you're up and ready for the day." He walked over and kissed her on her cheek and sat down. "Too bad I have guard all day."

"Good morning. What are you guarding today?"

"I work at the fort near the Louvre. None of us guys belong to the National Guard, but we work with them."

"You guard the artwork?"

"In a way. Most of the paintings and sculptures have been placed in vaults and in the basement at the Louvre. Other pieces of art from museums and Versailles have been brought there for protection. Bags of dirt are protecting the windows. It wasn't hit during the bombardments in January. The main gallery is now an armament shop. Lately a couple galleries have been turned into make-shift hospitals, although there has been some rehanging. The Prussian soldiers still strut around like they own the place. God help them if they touch anything. Another war would start."

Cheryl immediately thought of her and Zach's visit to Paris last year. Those gold ornate ceilings, cherubs and angels now looking down on guns and explosives. And they are going to have to do it all over again when World War II starts. Love the Parisians for protecting this precious art. She remembered what she had read about the German occupation of Paris during World War II. It sounds like it was a replay of this time. German soldiers came in and tried to belong.

"Would you like a cup of tea before you go?"

"No, thank you. I have only a few moments. I'm a little late now. I slept hard. I just came for my key." She reached in her pocket and handed it to him. "I don't know what time I will be back tonight, but please save me some supper. Tell Janine."

"We'll do that."

"I'm free tomorrow and we'll spend the day together. See you tonight." He kissed her on the cheek and was on his way.

Later Cheryl felt claustrophobic and decided to explore the courtyard. Ben told her it was safe. The big room had been her world since she arrived and even a small change would be welcome.

Downstairs, through the hall, she opened the back door. Directly in her vision was the colorful carriage house. "Ah, that's where Jacques keeps his horses," she said, out loud but quietly. She lifted her face to take in the sun, took a deep breath and walked slowly to observe the stone formations in the courtyard. The buds on the fruit trees were itching to pop. As she got closer to the carriage house she heard movement. She knocked lightly on the small side door.

"Cheryl, good morning." Jacques said, as he open the door. "Come in and see my horses."

"Good morning. I'd love to." As she stepped inside she saw two beautiful animals. The stalls for the horses and a small carriage on the other side with a loft above was their home.

"Honor, my boy," and he got excited when Jacques called his name. He was big and sleek and his coat shined as if it had just been polished. His mane matched his black, swishing tail. "Good boy." Jacques gave him a pat as he walked to introduce his companion. “La Belle, my girl.” She pranced around in her stall loving the attention. She was much like Honor, but had four white knee-sox. Cheryl patted La Belle’s face and she responded with a nuzzle on her neck.

“They are absolutely beautiful. Ben says you sleep out here with them. I can see why.”

He flashed a beautiful, wide smile. “Do you ride?”

“No. My family never had horses.”

“Would you like to try?”

“Maybe some time.”

They were doing well communicating. He and Ben had been friends for a long time. They went back and forth between the English and French languages.

Cheryl said, “You need a dog.” His face softened and he closed his eyes. She knew.

“Jacquie. I named him after me.” Cheryl wanted to laugh, but it was so sweet it brought tears to her eyes. “He was like me. Happy. Expressive. Loving.”

“What kind was he?”

“A fawn colored briard. I loved him so much. He died last August. He ran alongside when we rode. His long hair flowing behind him. He got jealous when I kissed Elise. He’s close by.”

Cheryl remembered losing her dog when she was in high school. “I am so sorry. It’s hard to give them up and you never really do.”

Jacques walked to the small window and gazed into the courtyard. “He’s under the brown stone. Ben helped me lay him to rest. He was fourteen. I had him from a puppy. They call briards, ‘heart of gold wrapped in fur.’ And he was.”

Cheryl felt this man was not only handsome but a compassionate individual. He saved me, flashed through her mind. She gave him a light touch on his arm as an expression of understanding his love and his loss.

"Ben likes you." He abruptly changed the subject. Perhaps he's trying to avoid his emotions, she thought. But his statement left her a little surprised.

"He's very nice too. Thank you for showing me your beautiful horses. I'll let you get back to your work."

As she was going back upstairs, she thought, what a nice visit. Each day she seemed to get to know another of the group personally. Janine in her faded clothes, so sweet. Elise with her bobbin lace. Edouard wanting her to sit for him. That will be special. Now Jacques and his horses. And — Ben.

I'll start *Birdsong.* She took her pen and carefully inked out the copyright date.

As the sun was sinking, Janine, Lucie and Renée came with food. She joined them in preparing their evening meal. She told Janine that Ben wanted her to save his dinner that he might be late.

And late he was. Everyone was finishing their custard when he arrived. He sat down next to Cheryl and kissed her on the cheek. She poured him a glass of wine and went for his plate.

"Thank you, this is wonderful," he said, as he took in the aroma of ham, carrots and warm fruit compote. "I haven't eaten all day."

Nikki's observation was daring. No one noticed.

Ben told about a scuffle with members of the mob. "I believe too much wine started it rather than their cause. Thankfully it was settled peacefully. Everyone went their own way when we threatened them." He told the story in French and then in English for Cheryl.

Nikki left the table in a hustle before he finished his English version. Everyone said good night to her, but she did not respond. Again no one seemed to notice.

Soon it was only the four. Janine and Cheryl were washing the dishes. Henri and Ben discussed the problems of the day. Everything put away, Janine took Henri's hand, and said, "You promised." He raised his eyebrows and after saying goodnight they went upstairs.

Ben said to Cheryl, "I'm very tired, but I have to practice some. Would you like to go downstairs with me and listen to the rough stuff? Then I'll bring you back."

They went to Ben's rooms. "I'll show you around tomorrow when it's lighter."

He went to his piano and touched the candle he was carrying to his candelabrum. It slowly became hauntingly beautiful as each candle came alive to send its flickering shadows around the room. Cheryl curled up on the sofa and closed her eyes and listened. Even his practice session is wonderful. She could hear the beauty in each tone before it was lost in the silent room.

A half-hour passed and Ben said, "That's enough. It's hard to concentrate when you're tired." He reached for her hand and they walked upstairs. Just inside the door he handed her the key. "Tomorrow we'll go for a walk."

"I'd like that. I need to exercise a little."

"Good night," and he kissed her on her cheek.

He went back downstairs and stripped and slid his naked body into the bed. Just enough time for a few thoughts and they were about Cheryl.

Cheryl went behind her screen, undressed, and put on the gown. Her thoughts hurt. How could I fall for someone so fast in my mistaken state? This is a punishment rather than a reward.

ଓ

CHAPTER FIVE

ശ

In the last throes of sleep, Cheryl heard the tiny tick of the pendulum. Slowly *The Mission* joined the tick with its steady beat. The music whirled and whirled then settled into a softness of peace. With her sleep on the edge, she tried to grasp time, day or anything. Then she heard the click of the key turn the lock. Her senses sharpened. Janine I hope.

She had managed to get in a sitting position when Janine called.

"I'm awake," Cheryl answered.

After Cheryl came back from across the hall she sliced the bread, while Janine made a large pot of tea for their breakfast. Janine reached into the cabinet for the last jar of jam. "Peach. Henri brought it in our pack of food, when we came."

"Wonderful, warm bread and homemade jam."

Henri arrived for breakfast and to accompany Janine to the hospital.

This morning was going as the other two. Elise came with her basket of lace. Edouard had finished his still life and was ready for Elise to become his *Lace Maker*. Others were in and out.

Another cup of tea and Cheryl settled with her book. Ben — she laughed to herself thinking he was Chopin. He said he would be here early. Maybe mid-morning is early for him, or not come at all. But true to his word he soon arrived. Their smiles met and grew closer. Before he spoke he kissed her on the cheek.

"Good morning. How did you sleep?" He went to make his breakfast. He lifted the lid on the oatmeal pan. "Some left."

"Good morning to you and I slept rather well," adding softly, "considering that cot isn't the most comfortable. But I'm not complaining. I'm very grateful to you all for taking me in. I'll find my way eventually."

With his toast, tea and oatmeal in hand, he sat down next to Cheryl. "Are you going back to America?"

"I don't have identification papers. I escaped, although I shouldn't have left without them. But I was frightened for my life." Back to America — ridiculous. She decided to wait a few days and maybe by then her lab would get her home.

"We'll work it out. You may stay as long as you need to. There's a mess outside and until it's settled, we're all displaced. This civil war type of fighting could go on. God help us. We are already hungry and the city needs attention. Now, let's think of today."

"I'm glad you remembered. It will be nice to get out in the fresh air. Although I went into the courtyard yesterday and Jacques was in the carriage house and I met Honor and La Belle. He told me about Jacquie. He still misses him."

"He named him right. They were alike. He loves his horses too. Jacques and I have been friends for a long time. I have rented the rooms from him since I first came to Paris."

"What about him and Elise?" Cheryl asked softly. Elise was at the far end of the room sitting for Edouard.

Ben continued softly. "They are kind of waiting for this mess to get over. She and Lucie are from a small town near Toulouse. Their family is well off but the girls wanted to come to Paris. Elise and Jacques met and were getting serious when this upheaval started. The family she was working for was going to leave and Jacques didn't want her to go, so he brought her here and Lucie came too. He hasn't said much lately. They still go off together a lot." He paused. "How about today? I scouted around before I came up here and things seem rather quiet. We can walk up the street to a little park or it was a park. They felled the trees to keep warm last winter."

He finished his breakfast and sipped his tea. "So glad Lucie is here. She bakes wonderful bread. Don't you think? Do you make bread or bake other stuff?"

"Not much. I seem to have spent most of my life studying. Now I'm not using any of my education."

He looked her up and down and then asked, "I don't mean to get personal, but I see you have the same clothes on. Did you have to leave your clothes behind when you escaped?"

"I did. These," and she touched her sleeve

lightly, "I put in my bag and wore my heavy pants and sweater under my coat. Boots and the shoes I have on are all the clothes I have." She covered her face with her hands faking distress. He put his arm around her to comfort her. It was comforting for Cheryl although for the wrong reason.

"Would you like to buy some things? There are a few stores open nearby."

"I have no money. They kept all of my identification papers and the little money I earned. They said I could have them later. When I asked for them they refused. Oh! I can't talk about it," she finished quickly.

"That's okay." And he rubbed the back of her neck, which had an effect on Cheryl other than comfort. "Maybe there are some things in the old store downstairs." He called to Elise, "Are there any ladies clothes left downstairs in Gezot's store?"

"I don't know. Ask Nikki. She worked there."

"Is she here?"

"In our room. Go ask her."

Ben went upstairs and knocked on their bedroom door. Nikki answered.

"Oh! Hi Ben," she said sweetly. "Come in."

"No thanks. I just wanted to know if there are any clothes in the store downstairs."

"There might be. What are you looking for? Shirts, trousers?" she continued her sweet voice.

"Not for me but Cheryl. She escaped with only a few things and she would like to have different things to wear."

"Cheryl!" Her tone changed drastically. "What do you care?"

"Well, she needs a few pieces of clothing and I thought we could start here. She needs help like all of us. I think she's a nice person. Can we go look?"

"Yeah, I guess," she answered abruptly.

Ben noticed her surly responses, but did not know why and just ignored them. Maybe she doesn't feel well. What he did not realize, Nikki wanted his attention, but he only thought of her as a young girl, part of the group.

They entered the back of the store. Counters pushed together, boxes stacked, hardly enough room to move around.

"This is a mess. At least the boxes are labeled," Ben said.

They rummaged around and Nikki found a box of clothes. "Here are some skirts," and she held one up. Seeing it was very large, Ben shook his head no. She found another that would fit and threw it at him.

Ben looked at it. "Perfect. Anymore?"

"No!" Loud and nasty. There were, but she wasn't about to accommodate Ben's request.

Ben opened another box labeled Shawls. "Great. I know she'll like these." He held up several and looked at them closely.

"You seem to know a lot about her." Another sharp remark from Nikki.

"Not really. All girls like shawls." He chose a soft beige, knitted in a delicate lace pattern. "I'll take this red one too. Are you sure there are no more skirts? What about blouses?"

"You're looking, what do you see?" she snapped again.

Her remarks settled on Ben. "Okay. Let's go."

On the way back upstairs, "Thank you, kid. See you at supper."

Kid, you fool. She thought, try me.

He did not realize she had not answered, because he was anxious to get back to Cheryl.

"Found you a skirt and two shawls. We'll tell Jacques we took them and I'll pay him." He held up the blue linen skirt and the shawls.

"They are beautiful, but I have no money," she emphasized again.

"I heard you my dear. I will settle with him. Now let's go to the store down the street and see what else we can find."

"No, I can't let you do that. I'll manage."

"I have extra money left. I brought enough when I came back. I helped all my friends financially during the war. I can help you. I want to. — I insist."

"Oh Ben…" He put his finger to her lips to stop her words.

"Where's your cloak? The sun is out but it's cool."

"I have a coat. We have different styles in America." She gave in and they were on their way.

He took her hand as they walked to a busier area. "That store over there has a lot of stuff. I was in there last week looking for some shirts. Nobody bought clothes during the war. We thought mostly about food and staying alive."

"Is that why your rifles are by the door?"

"Yes. There were some bad times. I think the bombardments were the worst. Usually in one area at a time and about the same time every day. You had some bad times too. Someday we can sit down and open our hearts so all the bad and ugly can pour out."

They passed several sad looking shops. Façades damaged and boarded up. Signs hanging by one hook. Some buildings' upper floor lay on the cobbles. They went a little further and he said, "In here. Pick out what you want and I'll pay. Some day you can pay me back. Fair enough?"

She smiled and nodded yes. That she would soon be gone was foremost in her mind.

The store was filled with textiles of every kind, clothing, rugs, parasols, towels, coverlets. If it was made, it was here.

"I don't usually need clothes. My mother buys all of us lots of stuff when she travels with my father." They dug around in boxes and looked on the racks and she found two more skirts and two white blouses. Quietly he held up a pair of split drawers and with a mischievous grin, "Need any of these?" She gave him an uncertain look. What would he think of my pink bikini underwear? He'll never see them. I'm glad I have a change, but how am I going to wash and dry them. Not over the cook stove. On second thought she said softly, "Maybe I'd better. Also could I look for boots?"

"Absolutely."

They added a light weight riding jacket to their other selections and Ben paid.

"Thank you. I truly appreciate your help. I will pay you back as soon as I can."

He smiled at her, wanting to say so much more. He just took her hand and they started back.

In the big room Ben said, "Let's have some lunch and then I want to practice. Do you want to come down or do you want to stay here?"

"I'll get my book. If you're sure I won't be a bother?"

After their bohemian lunch they went down to Ben's rooms. "I promised to show you around. So here it is." Beams stretched all the way across the rectangular room, connecting living, dining and cooking area. A large dark-brown rug defined the living room space. Chairs and a sofa were organized around the rug. His grand piano sat at the far end in front of a large window. Near the middle on the outside wall was a large hearth for keeping the entire area warm. His bedroom was a nice size for his big bed and other necessary pieces for clothing. A smaller brick hearth was in the corner.

"That door goes to the downstairs water closet and no one else uses it but me. Come, you can relax."

"I'll read." She kicked off her boots and curled up on the sofa. Ben at his piano, they were each in their own world.

The afternoon went by as Ben went over and over his passages of Chopin, Beethoven, and Schumann. Cheryl noticed how hard he worked. His long fingers had wonderful control of the keys, making each note ring in just the perfection he was striving for.

Much later he stopped his practice and went to the sofa with her. He stretched out, laid his head in her lap and closed his eyes.

"You don't mind do you?"

"No. You definitely need to rest. I didn't realize how hard you needed to concentrate. Listening to a recital, it looks and sounds so easy."

"That's what people don't understand. I don't believe Edouard has to concentrate, but he certainly doesn't have to go over and over his paint." He laughed and closed his eyes.

She gently massaged his temples and to the edge of his thick brown hair. She picked up his hand, rubbed each finger softly and ran her thumb around his palm. He gave a contented hum and slid into a deep relaxation.

What am I doing? She put her head back and closed her eyes.

Enough time passed and she said softly, "Ben."

"Yeah. They're probably waiting supper for us."

"I should have gone up and helped Janine."

"Later, I wanted you here. But let's go."

They all gathered once again to share their companionship and feast. Edouard brought the only news. There would be a dance at Manghan Hall next Saturday. That was exciting after a long cold winter.

Ben and Cheryl were once again alone after the supper hour. "I'll go too," he said after they talked a while. She walked with him to the door. He reached in his pocket and gave her his key. One hand on the latch, with the other he tipped her head and kissed her lips ever so gently. And long enough for her to respond, ever so gently. "Tomorrow."

As she lay staring into the black — on the cheek, now on the lips. Next a passionate kiss, then his warm body next to mine. She closed her eyes and let the wonderful thoughts flow. It only lasted a few seconds when reality split like a dagger, oh god, I can't. I can't.

ෆ

CHAPTER SIX

ᔕ

The last two days the clouds emptied relentlessly over the city. The rain barrels overflowed, and the gutters ran full washing away the filth in the streets. It was extra water for the horses and washing clothes. These friends took the precipitation in stride. The women went to their work. The men guarded and Edouard brought beauty into their lives.

Spirits rose when the armistice had been signed. Their city could be rebuilt, but unrest grew and the days had fallen again into uncertainty. French troops and the mobs were clashing more often. The cold rainy days kept the outside calm, but boil they did in the closed rooms and the bistros. It was day to day with no rainbow in sight.

A tiny ray in these harsh times was the dance this weekend. They were looking forward to seeing other friends who also had their activities limited. Manghan Dance Hall was a few streets up the hill from their building. It was far enough off the main streets to not expect spontaneous or planned violence. Walking as a group offered more safety.

This day as others, Cheryl read while Ben practiced. It was late afternoon, although it looked like the shadows of dusk on any other day. Like always when he finished his practice, he lay down on the sofa with his head in her lap. She started to put her head back when his hand pulled her down and he kissed her passionately. The kiss on the cheek was history.

"I've wanted to do this from the first moment I saw your beautiful face. I knew I had found my love at last. I always thought it would be in some salon giving a recital. Maybe at a tea, a ball or introduced by a friend. But there you were sitting at our big table, looking bewildered. I knew I had to rescue you from what I did not know, but something."

Following his steps to express his love made her smile. "Oh Ben, these are lost times for you and for me," she said, as she caressed his face. I have to stall his desires and mine.

He sat up and pulled her into his arms. "You are but a wisp." Cradling her he kissed her long and with desire. Her arms slowly embraced him. He knew. "I want more of you, dear one. I want all of you," he whispered. He reached under her blouse and caressed her silky warm body slowly easing to her small firm breast. "I want to kiss you there." He paused and captured her eyes. "I love your face, laughing, sad," as he ran his fingertips across her cheek. "I love your hair," as he carefully tucked a strand behind her ear. "I love your mind," as he gently touched her forehead, "and how you listen. Now let me take you to my bed and love your body." She nestled closer in his arms as consent.

Just as Ben rose from the sofa there was a loud knock on his door.

"Ben," Jacques called. "Supper."

"Thanks Jacques," Ben said softly, but perturbed. "We'll be up in a few minutes," he called louder.

Supper, but everyone was not there. "Jean-Pierre went for Renée and Lucie and they should be back by now," Henri told Ben. "Renée said they are not making or repairing balloons, but changing back to making wearable's, so their days are even shorter for a while."

"Maybe we should go look for them. Take the horses," Jacques offered.

"Let's give them a little more time."

It was not long until a disturbance was heard in the distance. The shrieks and screams grew louder in seconds. It was unusual this far from the main street that a commotion of this magnitude would occur. It grabbed everyone's attention. Cheryl noticed Jacques' eyes getting bigger as the sounds neared. She looked at Ben, his were wide and angry. Screams were heard at the downstairs front door. Without a word, the men were up and grabbed their rifles from the pegs.

In the hall, they saw Jean-Pierre lying half inside the door. Renée was desperately pulling his body as tears flooded her face. Lucie was gripping his boot with one hand, turning every second and with her other hand trying to keep an angry fist from coming down on her head "Pull Renée!" Lucie yelled hysterical.

"I am — he's heavy! He's out and can't help!"

Bright-red blood seeped from the ragged hole in his trousers, in the thigh area.

Instantly seeing the women and Jean-Pierre in trouble and the crazed mob at their door, Henri, Jacques and Ben flew down the stairs, cocking their rifles as they went. Jumping over Jean-Pierre into the mob, Ben yelled in French, "BACK, BACK," and in English, "You rotten rebels!" They continued their ear-splitting shouts. Henri fired a warning shot and that got their attention. Slowly they backed away and into the street, Henri guiding them with his rifle in their faces. The rag-tag crowd was not large, just loud and threatening.

"What happened to Jean-Pierre?" Henri yelled.

Ben and Henri rushed back into the hall. Jacques had stopped to get Jean-Pierre completely inside. Renée was sobbing frantically and trembling as if she had been shot. Lucie yelled to Cheryl, who was on the stairs, to get rags. "He's bleeding badly." Janine was already on her way with them. "His thigh!" Lucie cried, pointing to the hole in his blood-soaked trousers. Henri ripped his trousers to expose the wound. Janine and Cheryl started sopping up the warm, sticky mess and trying to compress the area.

"We have to get him upstairs," Jacques said. The rifles were handed to the girls and the guys carefully carried Jean-Pierre upstairs. They laid him on the floor. Cheryl ran for her cot and brought it to the middle of the room. They placed him on it. Henri ripped his trousers further back and exposed the bloody flesh that lay open.

Janine said forcefully, "We have to stop the bleeding!"

"He was shot?" Ben asked Renée quickly.

Tears still streaming down her face, her breath in gasps, unable to speak, she shook her head yes.

"Then we have to get the bullet out first," Janine called, knowing from experience. She started giving orders just like at the hospital. "More rags and tear them into wide strips. Hot water. Henri please get my bag from upstairs, I'll have to sew this up." Everyone worked in unison.

Janine dipped her hands in the hot water and carefully laid back the loose skin, working her fingers into the slimy tissue. She said, "I feel it! It's not deep, but it has to come out!" With care she inched the ugly slug from the bloody flesh and threw it on the floor. Cheryl was compressing and cleaning the fresh bright-red blood as Janine worked. Holding rags in place for some time the blood began to ease enough, so she could clean and suture the wound. The men lifted him so the bandage could go around his thigh. This part was over. Through it all Jean-Pierre only moaned.

Cheryl lifted his eye lids and saw his pupils were dilated. She felt his neck and his pulse was rapid, but his breathing was not forced.

"I believe he's in shock, although mild. He could vomit."

"What's shock?" asked Renée, her voice tight.

"It's a reaction when your body has been traumatized, like what has happened to Jean-Pierre. Tell her Ben. We have to get the rest of his clothes off or loosen them. You guys lift him carefully and we can get his coat off and anything else that is restricting." Ben translating, they managed and Cheryl drew the blanket to his shoulders. "Can we move the cot nearer the stove? And we should elevate his legs."

Jean-Pierre was stabilized to the best of their abilities. Everyone took a deep breath.

Janine said to Ben, “Have Cheryl tell me about shock and will you translate so I can identify it at the hospital?”

Ben told Cheryl and she said, *“Oui.”*

Jacques asked, “What happened?” Renée still in a hysterical state, Lucie began to fill in. “About half way home we noticed a small mob trying to get people’s attention. We didn’t want any trouble and started to run. I don’t know where the bullet came from but it hit Jean-Pierre. He managed to run for a while, but slowed down and the mob caught up with us and just kept harassing. He kept reaching for his leg and there was a lot of blood. We didn’t know how bad it was. Just as we got to the door he passed out. I was thankful he got this far. We couldn’t carry him and nobody would help us.”

“You don’t know who fired the shot?” Henri asked.

“No, there was too much confusion. We were just trying to get away.”

Frantically Renée asked, “Will he be okay?”

Cheryl said to Ben, “Translate for me.” She turned to Renée. “I think he will. The bullet was small and didn’t go too deep. Janine cleaned the wound and bandaged it well. We will have to watch for fever and make sure he doesn’t vomit and choke.” She looked at Ben. “Please get a cool rag for her head. She is terribly upset too.” Cheryl took her hand and led her to the chaise longue and motioned for her to lie down. She applied the cool rag to her head and sat beside her and held her hand.

Lucie was still trembling and pacing even as everything appeared to be under control. Jacques went to her and said, "We have done all we can for now. Why don't you try to get some sleep? Through these months we have all experienced some very unpleasant situations, but this was entirely too close."

"I can't stop shaking," she told him.

"If you lie down it will help eventually."

She nodded in agreement. "Call me if anything changes and I'll do what I can." Reluctantly she went upstairs to her bedroom, knowing Jacques was probably right.

Cheryl asked Ben, "Does this happen often?"

"I've heard of several incidents where they attacked innocent people, but this is the first time I've known that someone was shot. It sounds like drunken rabble-rousers looking for trouble, nothing to do with a cause. A third element in this chaos we have to contend with — the troops, the mobs and those out just for trouble. Most of the gunfire is between the troops and the mobs, not innocent people."

Henri added, "That mess at our door didn't seem to be brandishing firearms."

"The only gunfire I heard was the one that hit Jean-Pierre and it sounded far away," Renée added.

"A shot can travel a long way. Maybe it wasn't even from that mob. It still did its damage." Ben said as he glanced at Jean-Pierre. "We're going to have to arm you girls and the war is over." The irony was not missed in his voice.

"Someone has to stay with him tonight and watch for fever," Cheryl said.

"I can stay with him," Jacques offered.

"Why don't we work in shifts? That way we would be less apt to fall asleep," Elise mentioned.

"Good idea. We can plan that."

Everyone was in deep thought trying to make sense of what had happened and plans to be with Jean-Pierre for the night.

Ben took Cheryl's hand and they walked to the back of the room. With his hand on her waist he pulled her close. She put her arms around his neck and felt every part of him all the way down. "You all right?" he questioned.

"Yeah," she said slowly. "I've done a lot of dissecting, but this is the first real live incident I have encountered. It's upsetting when it's so close."

He kissed her lips and then gazed into her eyes. "Looks like you have lost your cot. Stay with me tonight and I'll relax you from this terrible scene. I'll take your mind on a trip far from here. I'll take your body to another world. As morning approaches we can sleep in each other's arms."

She did not respond, although her thoughts were rapid. It wasn't that sleeping with him would be unpleasant, but my situation and I can't tell him. I know I am going to fall madly in love with him and something could happen at any moment. What if I never get back, should I deny myself his love?

He waited and finally her eyes spoke. He smiled and nestled her head on his shoulder. "I've fallen in love with you, Cheryl." Moments later, hand in hand, they rejoined the group.

Jean-Pierre was resting so they decided to nibble on the food as they watched over him. The night was planned. Renée wanted to stay with him, so the longue was moved near the cot. Ben and Cheryl would take the first night watch. Jacques and Elise next, and toward morning Janine and Henri would come down. Someone would be awake all night in the event he needed help.

Everyone gone, Renée had fallen into a much needed sleep. Ben and Cheryl cuddled on the sofa. Their bodies hot with anticipation of an hour or so from how. There wasn't much more to say, they both realized they had fallen in love with each other. "I'm so sorry about this tragedy, but it did bring us together quickly. I knew it would have happened anyway. This way it was sooner. Probably the only good thing," Ben offered.

They talked softly about the incident and Jean-Pierre's condition. Cheryl was reassuring.

Ben asked, "You seem to know a lot about this. You were right there with Janine, helping her."

I'm going out on a limb. "I am a scientist and educated in physics, biology, chemistry."

"Oh! My gosh. That is unbelievable. I knew you were highly schooled. I like that. Do you know a lot about music?"

"Some and you can teach me everything else."

"I'll be so willing."

The hours passed and Jacques arrived, hair disheveled, eyes drooping, he said, "Elise will be down soon. I knocked on her door."

Before leaving Cheryl felt Jean-Pierre's head. "No fever yet," she said to Jacques. "He probably won't vomit, but watch and feel his head often. If he feels warm apply cold rags to his body and head. If he gets real hot call me and Janine. If we have to cool his body it will take all of us. We'll change the bandage in the morning."

Cheryl got her things from behind the screen and went downstairs with Ben.

"Want a cup of tea or something?"

"No, just some rest."

"Rest after something very important."

His words were so heartfelt and his voice so sensual she walked into his arms.

The left-over rain clouds played in the moonlight as they undressed each other. After the last piece of clothing puddled on the floor, he pulled her naked body next to his. Cheryl smiled to herself. When I was close upstairs I thought he was hard, but now.... She ran her hands down his side and fondled him gently. She could feel his grip tighten and he pulled her body, with a gentle force, even closer into his. Releasing her he picked her up and laid her on his bed and moved his naked body next to hers. He embraced her tightly in his arms. "Say you'll marry me darling. We'll go to London where I can get you identification papers and then we can be married and we will belong to each other, forever. I love you dear heart. I'm going to touch you and caress you until you're weak. You have already made me weak, but I need you to fondle me and your hands on my body. I need to be inside you and to feel what I can give you. Then we will know each other completely. This will be our first love that will go with us for our lifetime. I love you darling Cheryl. Be my wife."

She did not hesitate. "I love you Ben and want to be your wife." She surrendered to him body and soul.

He kissed her long and passionately and they

made love until the moon, once high in the midnight sky, reached the tree tops on its way to seek another night.

ᔓᔕ

CHAPTER SEVEN

ɞ

*T*he sunrise was glowing. The rain clouds were on the other side. Cheryl's sleep was on the fringe of the waning night. She lay quietly as her senses came alive and her thoughts took over. Ben. She knew she loved him, but last night and all that it was, internally and externally, left no doubt in her mind. I will love him always, but always could be profoundly short. I want to make every night like last night. But no birth control pills. I can't deny him that would be denying myself. Getting pregnant now, my god what would happen. It would vanish with my image as if it had never been. This is scary. Suddenly she did not want to go back to the far off tomorrow. But she knew it was out of her control and she would have to accept the consequences. Knowing she could not reason with fate she was not going to try.

Ben stirred ever so slightly.

She whispered faintly, "Ben."

"I'm here Cheryl love." He rolled over and gathered her in his arms. "I feel your body and hear your voice. I was so afraid I was dreaming. I love you darling. I never thought I could love someone so completely. And it's so easy."

"I am real." Her words startled her. It was the most ironic statement she could make. "I love your whole self. I feel like a rag doll with a beating heart."

"May I make love to you again?"

"Oh Ben, you don't have to ask. Just a smile, or a look and I'll know." She moved closer. "I feel your desire, please touch me and feel mine."

Their love was passionate and then slowed to a tenderness then they nestled together without words.

Ben finally said, "We'll go to London as soon as possible. I can get you identification papers and we can be married. You can't get much of anything in Paris now. The government moved out to Versailles and left the mobs and French troops to fight it out. It leaves the citizens who are trying to hold things together vulnerable and that's not right."

"You certainly have a strong feeling for the Parisians, yet you're English."

"I do. Paris has been a second home since I went to school here in my early life. Paris was a home base for my father's business in those years, and we had a house here for many years when I was young. After my sister Beth and I became adults, they went back to London but my mother travels with him."

"How is the travel situation now?"

"Rails have been damaged, so that leaves horse and carriage. We'll have to go on horseback to the estate at Cambrai. I'll have Jacques teach you to ride. I have guard from noon until nine today." He pulled her close and she could feel his body was ready for her again. "One more time before we begin our day."

Their loving was not long but as intimate and romantic as before.

Cheryl slumbered in a haze of unbelievable ecstasy while Ben dressed. She still felt warm between her legs. She could still feel his powerful release that sent her into another world. He kissed her lightly and broke the spell. "I'm going to go up and see how Jean-Pierre is doing and get us some tea."

She rolled over, sat up and smiled. He knew he had contented her soul. "You should, because the first hours are the most crucial. If he got through the night without fever, then we can rest a little easier."

Cheryl dressed while he was gone. In these moments alone she wrestled with both sides of her being. Ben made her feel safe and content in her existence. She loved him deeply. But uncertainty of knowing any moment could be their last together shadowed the good, the wonderful and the future. A cruel fate for both and worse he would never know what happened. It was a black cloud she was living under not knowing if there would be silver lining.

Ben returned with tea and two pieces of Lucie's bread covered with peach jam.

"How is Jean-Pierre?" she quickly asked.

"He's talking and said his wound hurts, but not too much. He seems okay. Renée said she thinks he had a good night. She said she did and felt guilty. Janine had been there and changed the bandage and apparently no fever."

"That is the best sign of all. I can stay with him

while you're at guard and change his bandage. Janine did a beautiful job of suturing the opening. Thankfully the bullet was shallow and not too large."

"And thank God for Janine, she has held us together in this mess." He paused. "They weren't causing any trouble and this happened. That bullet in any other place, he could have lost his life. A horrible thought. It shows how dangerous it's out there."

"It really is scary and they were so innocent. He should move around some by tonight. Henri and Jacques can help him."

They finished their small breakfast and Ben suggested they go upstairs and refill their tea mugs.

Cheryl's language barrier was getting shorter. She and Ben spoke to each other in French so she could practice. She mostly spoke to the group with a minimum of translation, as she did this morning.

"Good morning Renée," Cheryl said as she touched her lightly on her shoulder. "Ben delivered the good news. You look wonderful Jean-Pierre. May I feel your head?"

He smiled faintly and nodded lightly.

"Cool. Maybe tonight you might sit up. Are you warm enough?"

"I'm always warm when Renée is near."

Cheryl didn't expect that answer, but accepted it with a smile.

Edouard arrived shortly, offered a good morning and inquired about the patient. He then addressed Cheryl. "I have finished painting Elise making lace and if you have no plans today maybe you could sit for me. Wear that red shawl I saw the other day. We'll also be close to Jean-Pierre if Renée would like a break."

"Yes, the timing is perfect. Ben is going to guard at noon."

"I want to do a small one for him and it won't take long. Later, I would like to do one of you reading. Right now I have a few things to do, but will be back soon."

Ben said, "Since everything is okay here, I want to practice before I go to guard. Please, Cheryl love, save me some supper. I'll be hungry for everything by nine o'clock. I'll be up before I go."

Ben came in later with his rifle dangling over his arm. He also had been to the root cellar for food. He placed the cheese, dried fruit and ham slices on the table. Cheryl and Renée joined him for a quick lunch. Jean-Pierre declined in favor of sleep. Eating quickly, Ben gave Cheryl a quick kiss on the cheek and he was off.

The afternoon was quiet and peaceful. Renée napped while Cheryl read to Jean-Pierre. It helped him to relax and for Cheryl to practice her French. He too closed his eyes and she softened her voice and then stopped altogether. She quietly moved to the sofa, curled up and read silently. Without Jean-Pierre listening, it was hard for her to concentrate on the words. She kept thinking of Ben and how he suddenly came into her existence, and the possible consequences of their relationship.

Edouard returned, seeing the others asleep motioned to Cheryl. She followed him to the far end of the room where he painted. "Sit here sweetheart and look straight at this pin on my easel."

She draped the red shawl over her shoulders. "Is this okay?"

"Perfect my dear. I'll just work for about an hour."

"Do you talk while you paint?"

"No, I don't. My strokes are hugs and the color kisses. I give them the attention as I do my girl. I'll make your little portrait full of love for Ben. He needs something he can tuck in his pocket close to his heart."

Ben — his name gave her a warm feeling and it must be obvious.

Undecided, the sun and clouds exchanged places in the wide afternoon sky. Later the women came with vegetables and meat. Edouard released her to help prepare their supper. Janine fixed a plate for Ben and placed it in the warming closet. The guys helped Jean-Pierre sit up long enough to eat. Henri announced that he had seen Edgar and had invited him to dinner soon. And that he wanted to go to New Orleans, to visit family, as soon as he was released from the National Guard.

Cheryl asked Lucie, "Who is Edgar?"

"Edgar Degas. He's our friend. He joined the troops to fight the Prussians. He comes to dinner once in a while. He brings news that we don't get in the newspaper."

Cheryl was elated. Finally I'm going to meet someone famous. I hope Ben is here and he can fill me in.

After supper and conversation, Cheryl took Ben's plate and went downstairs. She built a fire in the kitchen stove to keep his food warm and to send the chill outside. She curled up on the sofa with her book. The waning light outside made it difficult to read. She closed her book and rested her head on the back of the sofa. Quiet moments always brought precarious thoughts. The eerie shadows from the candles that played around the room were not comforting. She pushed her thoughts out, closed her eyes and knew Ben would soon be here. Nine ticked by on the mantle clock. Nine-thirty, any moment. Ten, and now she was disturbed. She was worried not only for Ben's safety, but for herself. What if something happens to him? A real possibility. What would I do? She felt guilty and selfish, but these were the facts. I can't control my thoughts, like wanting to be perfect, it doesn't happen.

She was now extremely nervous and she could feel her heart thumping, her throat was harsh, and she felt warm, not the warmth of a hearth or a featherbed. She peeked out the drapes knowing it was too dark to see anything, but it was something to do. She paced. She listened. She stoked the fire. I don't want to think she told herself. Two hours late is a long time and no way to get in touch. To relieve her anxiety, maybe it wasn't nine but later.

Near eleven she was ready to go upstairs and inform Jacques or Henri that Ben was not home. She went to stoke the fire one more time when she heard the big front door open and close heavily. Her better judgment said wait, it might not be him. A light knock and "Cheryl love," allowed her to breathe. She opened the door and put her fingers to her eye lids to hold back the tears, but they were seeping through.

"Oh Ben, I was so worried. After what happened to Jean-Pierre. — I'm sorry." She closed the door and his arms opened for her.

He wiped her tears. "Oh sweetheart, the person that was to relieve me was late. Then just as I left there was a disturbance, but didn't last long. I decided to take the long way home since it's usually quieter, but I ran into another bunch. I slipped into an alley until they passed."

"Maybe they were going home from a meeting."

"Could be. I'm sorry I upset you."

"It's okay. I was so afraid for you." He touched her face and with his fingertips tucked her long hair behind her ear and he kissed her tenderly.

"I built a little fire. The room was cool and I wanted you to have warm food after the long day."

"You're sweet darling and I will make it up to you."

She took his coat and hung it by the stove as he pulled off his boots. "I'll get your plate and a glass of wine." She joined him with her wine at the little table in front of the hearth, knowing it would relax her shaky body. They filled each other in on the day's happenings. "Jean-Pierre is doing well. What happened at your fort today?"

"Not much, but there was a problem across the river and they brought a couple stretchers into the Louvre. This is such a horrible existence. Killing, fighting when there are so many other wonderful things to do."

After he finished eating he took her hand. "It's been a long day. I am going to the water closet and freshen up. I thought maybe you would be in bed without anything on your beautiful body so I can touch your back."

"My back," and they both smiled. Hidden behind their smiles was the need for comfort.

He slipped in bed and moved close to her. "All

day I couldn't think of anything else but this moment. Now that I'm here I'll show you what I thought about.... Oh — I have to relax a moment.... When I am near you I get crazy. I want to work on this and bring you along."

It began with a few kisses and ended so much later with her nestled closely and his arm resting across her warm body.

ᘓ

CHAPTER EIGHT

ᔓᔕ

The soft, blue sky was the background for the bright rays of the morning sun. A welcome change after the gloomy days and chilly rain.

It was Saturday, the day of the dance, and everyone was looking forward to the event. There had not been a dance since late January. It had been a celebration of the signing of the armistice that proved a little too early for the joy to last.

War creates many unnatural problems and boredom had been one for the Parisians. Gas for lighting had been shut off in late November. Candlelight was not conducive for reading. Oil too had its downfall. It gave off a yellowish glow and left an odor. Prussian troops had surrounded the city, so everyone stayed home most of the day and definitely at night.

Now, conditions were somewhat better and a dance was scheduled. Everyone was excited. But their spirits were dampened. Jean-Pierre and Renée would not be able to go.

At breakfast they discussed whether to spend another evening at home or to go. Jean-Pierre immediately halted the conversation. "There is no reason why you all need to stay with us. You need the outing. Renée and I will be fine. No more talk, you guys go."

Edouard added, "I don't have a girlfriend right now, so I will stay here and challenge you two to a game of chess. I'll take on both of you." That brought a few chuckles for they all knew Edouard would win if he took all of them on. So it was decided. They would have their large meal at twelve o'clock, meet here at seven and walk to the dance together. After the dance they would gather and have a big snack before going to bed.

Manghan Hall was about five, long blocks that zigzagged up the gentle incline from their building. Fortunately they lived on the Right Bank where there had been less damage from the bombardments in January. The Left Bank had not been so lucky.

They all walked fast to leave the evening chill in their wake. Nikki with Jacques and Elise, then Janine, Henri and Lucie followed by Ben and Cheryl.

"You look beautiful in your new, black silk skirt and white blouse." Ben complimented his girl. "Does that shawl keep you warm enough?"

"I was saving them for a special occasion. And yes the shawl is heavy. Your choice was great."

"This is about as special as the events get in these times. I never asked you, do you dance?"

"I love to dance."

"That's good. Alain's band is brass. No strings. They get some nice tones. Although they're heavy on some instruments, but they all love to play."

As they got closer the music gradually filled the air. "Sounds wonderful," Ben said as he squeezed her hand.

Men and women were coming from all direction. Happy talk started as they approached. Inside Ben did not wait, but swept Cheryl in his arms and they fell in step with the music and did not stop until the band took a break.

Pink, yellow, green paper flowers hung just above the dancer's heads. The decorations were old and faded, but their meaning was not lost. Gas lights sconces flickered on the side and back walls. A large red, white and blue French flag was a backdrop for the band. The blanched decorations and the happy music cheered the spirits of the dancers.

"Ah sweetheart, this is wonderful. How about a little rest?" he asked her.

"You don't know what you've missed until you experience it. It does the soul good."

They had cool sweet cider as refreshment after the long dance. They mingled with others. There was much to say and much to hear. Everyone trying to talk at the same time was evident they were suffering from the same isolation and starved for conversation.

The band had left the polkas and waltzes as a trail and begun their sentimental and romantic selections. "This is for us," Ben said softly. They joined others and let the music soften their hearts. They held each other close, her head on his shoulder and his leaning into her. "To be like this forever," he said softly. "So close and our heart full of love and passion for each other." It was about to be the best moments of the dance, but was suddenly cut short.

Two Prussian soldiers stepped inside the door of the hall, stance brittle, egos bloated, arrogance seeping. Instantly a hush fell over the crowd. As the soldiers proceeded around the perimeter of the dance floor, the tones from the instruments ceased one by one. The musicians stared in defiance, but one lone baritone player puffed a quick note in time and tone with the click of the heels as the soldiers strutted around the floor several time and then out the door. Insolence at its best, Ben thought, with his hand against the cold steel piece, ready.

Ben felt Cheryl's tense body. "It's okay darling. They knew they were outnumbered. They wanted to show their haughtiness and superiority. I am well armed and so is everyone else. You thought it was something else, but just my pistol," smiling.

She hid her face on Ben's shoulder and laughed. "I'm not used to carrying a gun to a dance or to the grocery store." The soldiers gone the crowd slowly gained back their festive air.

After dancing a while longer, Ben said, "It is probably getting late. Maybe we should go home and see about the others." They found Henri and told him they were going to start down the hill.

Henri said, "We'll follow shortly."

Ben and Cheryl started their trek into the shadowy night. They walked in the middle of the street, if anyone approached there would be time to reach for protection. A few minutes into their walk, Ben whispered, "I believe we are being followed."

"Could it be the others?" A twang of fear went through her body, hoping to hear yes.

"No, it sounds like the tap of a boot on the cobbles. Let's go faster and if the tap gets faster, we'll know we are being followed."

Ben listened as they quickened their pace. "I don't believe it's a problem, but around this next corner let's slip between the buildings." As they did, he pushed her and wedged himself in tightly. He put his hand on his pistol and they waited silently. The click of the boots got louder. It was in their presence, but it moved on and gradually faded. It was a Prussian soldier and he was not alone.

When they were out of hearing distance Ben whispered, "It was a girl with him. Definitely not two men. Maybe it was one of the two in the hall, looking for their girl." They waited a few more minutes before they started on. They heard and saw nothing for the remainder of their walk home.

Renée had started preparing the food and Cheryl helped her finish. Ben and Edouard helped Jean-Pierre walk. Soon they heard the heavy door open. Laughter and loud talk floated up the stairs and it came with them into the big room. They all gathered around the big table when someone said, "Where's Nikki?"

"She was there when we left," Ben added.

"I thought she left with you," Henri said.

"I saw her leave immediately after you did. I thought she was with you," Lucie confirmed.

"No, she didn't leave with us. Did we leave her there alone?" Ben said with concern.

"Oh no! We'd better go look for her," Jacques said, as he got up.

Just then they heard the big door downstairs. Jacques walked over and opened the door to the hall and it was Nikki.

"Oh Nikki, we were worried about you."

Curtly she replied, "That's nice," and went straight to her room.

"I'll try to ease things over when I go up to bed," Lucie said, her expression doubtful.

"She has been upset lately and I don't know why," Elise added.

"She is by herself and it hasn't been easy for her. She should have gone back to Baden with Mr. Gezot and his wife when they closed the store downstairs. We all have someone and she doesn't," Jacques said, as he gazed lovingly at Elise.

They chatted about the dance and their friends they had not seen in a while. The evening grew late. Everyone was tired and needed rest after the walk, to and from, and the vigorous dancing.

Ben and Cheryl made their day a little longer, but shorter than the previous times they had made love.

ᔓᔕ

CHAPTER NINE

ᔕ

Sunday worship service was brief or only in the heart.

Cheryl was beginning to feel the monotony as the days trickled by. These empty spaces in time opened to fear, anxiety, about her future or what her lab was doing for her. There was extra time for reading, but often hard to concentrate. Elise taught her to knit, and she embroidered a few towels for Renée. Spending time with Ben was wonderful, but he had guard duty and he needed practice time.

She missed not exercising her scientific mind that she had worked so hard to attain. At this time, going to the hospital to help Janine was the only possibility available. She assured Ben and Janine the sight of blood did not bother her, although she thought of the diseases that could be transmitted. I'll just have to be careful, if only I had some gloves.

She explained, in America she had studied life

sciences, dissected animals and even cadavers. Blood was nothing compared to going out in the midst of mobs, troops, or gunfire that was absolutely terrifying to her.

Ben thought, women are treated so much different in America than in Europe and England. If it makes her happy to work there, I approve.

Jacques walked with the girls to the hospital, and then returned to clean the stalls, walk Honor and La Belle, and put his cozy loft in order. He checked the garden space. Elise had carefully packaged and labeled the seed last fall before the upheaval. Jacques remembered he wanted to make the garden smaller last spring. It would be less work for Elise since she planted and tended it. He thought at the time it would only be for them, although she didn't live there she spent her extra time there with Jacques. She had insisted and he was glad he listened to her. It had been their major food source during the winter. Soon they would spade and plant again.

Ben would practice. He hoped for a good session. Like Edouard and his painting or any other art form, complete concentration was needed.

So quickly he missed Cheryl without her curled up on his sofa with her book. He had not realized the effect she had on him at practice until this day. He consoled himself knowing she was not far and his fingers hit the keyboard running.

Well into his practice session he saw two Prussian soldiers pass his big window going to the back of the building. That's unusual. They never come up here. They are to leave the citizens alone, but not always. In those few seconds of thoughts, he knew he should take action. He grabbed his rifle, cocked it and made his way through the back hall. Carefully opening the door, he listened. Although the carriage house was some distance, he heard loud voices. He quietly walked across the courtyard and silently stepped inside the small open door with his rifle drawn. The two soldiers had their backs to him and they were arguing with Jacques. Just then one of the soldiers pulled a knife, held it at Jacques throat and started to untie Honor. Terror seized Ben's body and he knew he had to act.

Jacques saw him but did not look at him, to give his presence away, shouted in French, "No! You can't take them!"

"*Nein!* You will not take them!" Ben shouted loud and firm.

The soldier turned and seeing the rifle pointed at him was startled and reached for his pistol. Ben pulled the trigger and the Prussian slumped with one shot exploding his chest. Instantly the other soldier turned and started toward Ben with his knife poised ready for the thrust. Jacques pulled his blade and plunged it into the soldier's back, hitting his heart. It was over in seconds.

Blood spurting and gushing from the bodies stained the golden straw. Honor and La Belle were frantic at the gunshot and pranced wildly and kicked their stalls with such force a board fell off and the back doors flew open.

"Oh god, Ben what have we done?" Jacques said, as he quickly rushed to close the large doors that opened into the alley and to calm his horses.

"It's there on the floor and we have to face it." Ben was visibly upset and almost frozen, his voice wobbly and his gun shaking uncontrollably.

They paced, rubbing their faces and running their hands through their hair, trying to gain some composure.

"One of them said in French, someone told them they were here."

"The horses and they wanted them." Ben repeated but used different words.

"Yeah. Oh god, we have to get rid of these bodies. We can't go to the authorities. They probably wouldn't do anything, but if the Prussian command finds out, they would come after us."

"I hope no one heard my shot. Everyone is gone except Jean-Pierre and Renée. Hope they're napping."

"Let's hope. The fewer that know, the better."

With two dead bodies at their feet, not just bodies, but Prussian soldiers, they discussed what to do.

"Bury them and fast — but where."

"After dark dump them at some Prussian command door."

"No, too dangerous, we'd get caught."

"I don't want them in my courtyard."

"Yeah, they would pollute the ground."

"They have to go far away." And Ben saw an idea flash through Jacques mind.

"The caves. They're all around and I know where. Elise and I went berry picking last summer and found one."

"Best idea yet."

"Tonight after dark we'll throw the bodies over a horse, ride out. Settled."

"Lock up and we'll tell Janine we'll be late for supper and that we have to get feed."

Ben went back to practice, but quickly found he was too shaken-up and angry. It was a little hard for him to concentrate after killing someone, even in self-defense or even a Prussian soldier.

Cheryl came home and later they went upstairs for the supper hour. Ben said to Jacques, "Do you want to get the feed before we eat?"

"Oh, Janine," Jacques said, "Ben has offered to help get the horses' feed and we should do it before we eat. If you guys don't want to wait that's okay. I'm not sure how long we'll be."

"No, we'll wait," she responded, "the evening is long and supper is not quite ready."

Henri and Edouard offered to help. Ben and Jacques finally convinced them that only two would be needed for the job and there were only two horses. They thanked them and proceeded to the carriage house.

Cheryl thought their actions a little strange. Ben had stared at her. She didn't get the message, but she knew there was one in his eyes.

In the carriage house, "We'll each take a horse and a body and we'll go to the cave I remembered. It's far out." Horses saddled and bodies slung over their backs and covered, they started. Cautiously galloping the horses, they took all the back roads and paths they knew. It was supper hour and dark so likely everyone would be inside enjoying their first glass of wine and not worrying about what was outside their window.

Traveling about fifteen minutes they came to one of the last group of caves. Jacques cut the brush from in front of the opening. They carried the bodies in, and rolled them until they fell into a deeper crevice.

They replaced the brush, scuffed their footprints with their boots and raced home.

In the carriage house relieving Honor and La Belle of their saddles and wiping blood, they discussed who would have told the Prussian soldiers about the horses. They couldn't believe any of their group would betray them. If they did, why? They decided to relate only part of what happened and test the group when they were at supper.

"Never tell we killed two soldiers, because the fewer that know the better."

"I agree."

They washed up in Ben's water closet, checked for blood on their clothes, and went to join the others in the big room. They had waited supper and then gathered around the table as Janine and Renée served.

Edouard asked, "Did you get the feed?"

"Yeah, it was heavy," Jacques responded.

Ben found his words so ironic, but showed no emotions.

Cheryl sensed that Ben was uneasy, but did not ask him why.

The conversation went forth. They talked about the dance. The soldiers strutting through. Seeing friends.

"Lucie, you found your friend. You should invite him over sometime," Ben said.

"Oh, he's nice but..."

Jacques changed the conversation. "I had two visitors today."

"Who?" Elise quickly asked.

"Two Prussian soldiers," he said softly, slowly gazing across the faces at the table.

Heads turned, eyes popped. As he spoke Ben and Jacques watched each one of the group carefully.

Janine quizzing, “Where were you?”

“In the carriage house, cleaning.”

“What did they want?” Henri followed, his voice forward and his expression set.

“They wanted my horses!” and he noticed Nikki turning pink.

“What happened? Were you alone?” Jean-Pierre questioned, even more concerned.

Anxiety increased as Jacques released snippets of his encounter with the soldiers.

Ben interrupted, “I saw them pass my window and went out. We talked them away. I don’t believe they were too happy and might come back.”

“Did anyone see anything? Cheryl? Elise?” They both shook their heads no.

“We weren’t even home,” Elise said.

“Renée, did you hear anything?”

“No, we both slept a long time this afternoon.”

Realizing she was about to be questioned, Nikki jumped up and headed for the door.

Being from Baden and the only one who spoke German, Jacques knew. He was up so fast his chair smashed against the floor. He grabbed her by her arm, jerked her around and shouted, “Why?” She struggled to get away. He grabbed her hair and yanked her head back. She screamed as he threw her to the floor. “You traitor! We took you in when you had nowhere to go and this is what you do to us. Ben and I could have been killed and the horses taken. You little bitch.” He started to kick her but Ben was on his feet and held him back. Jacques kept yelling, “Why! Why!”

Shocked, astonished, everyone was out of their chairs. Renée, near tears, held tight to Jean-Pierre. Cheryl had her arms around herself trying to make sense out of what was happening. Lucie frozen. Elise, startled at Jacques action, grabbed his arm, "Jacques, what are you doing?" she screamed.

It was so sudden in the midst of a peaceful supper and only a few knew why.

Elise pulled Nikki to the chair. "What have you done?"

"You heard what I said Elise, she told the Prussian soldiers about my horses and they came for them," he said almost shouting. Then he went to her and took her in his arms, "I'm sorry. I didn't mean to shout at you. But sweetheart it was so bad. I just lost it for a moment — thinking…"

Nikki got up and tried to run. Ben grabbed her. "No, you don't go anywhere!"

She screeched at him, "Take your hands off me!"

He eased her back into the chair. "Now tell me why?"

She looked at him with venom oozing red. "Don't you know you fool?"

"I do not, but you had better tell me!"

Half yelling, she revealed. "Jacques brought Cheryl in and you like her."

Everyone was as astonished over what she said as much as the scuffle. They all knew, except Ben that she liked him, but had no idea that she would take her emotions to this extreme.

"Was that you last night with the Prussian soldier? We saw you. You left just after we did. Right."

Shaking his head in disbelief, he went to Cheryl and took her hand. "I never gave her a second glance other than she was a good kid. But I guess she isn't."

"Oh Ben. I know. I'm sorry all this happened," her voice strained.

Jacques came over to Ben, "Hey buddy, we're in this together. What do we do with her?"

"It's your place, but I think she should be out of here."

"Definitely out. Since what we had to do, I think we should take her to the authorities and they can decide. Keep quiet about everything else."

"I agree, completely. Lock her in her room by herself. Lucie can have the cot and Elise can sleep with you. Tomorrow we'll take her and I will go with you."

He said softly, "Elise and I have never slept together."

Ben pushed his hair back, and looked at Jacques puzzled and surprised. "You love her don't you? I know she loves you. What are you waiting for? You are adults and know your mind."

"I do, but we were going to wait until this war and stuff is over."

"You need her now. You need the comfort she can give you."

"She may not want to sleep in the loft. My room upstairs is all junked up with stuff and I can't clean it out tonight."

"The only way to know is to ask her."

"Wait here. I'll be back." As Jacques went to get his coat from the peg by the door he motioned for Elise to join him. In the hall he almost barked, "Get your shawl."

She came back and he led her down the stairs into the courtyard. He turned and reached for her and pulled her close, his arms surrounding her. Neither moved. Neither spoke.

Finally she asked slowly, "What is this all about? You really scared me. I never saw this side of you before in the two years that I have known you. What did she do?"

"It was a close encounter that set me off. Even all winter nothing like this has happened. For a moment I couldn't help myself. I can't talk about it right now, but it was bad. Trust me."

"You know I will." She rubbed his head and the back of his neck.

The air was cool and still. The sky was dark and distant.

"We have to lock her up tonight in your room. I love you Elise — will you sleep with me in the loft."

She was surprised. His request was so direct, it confused her, and not that he said I love you, but the reason. "Jacques I want to sleep with you, but not because of some situation. I want to sleep with you because you want me near and we love each other."

Jacques realized, being so upset, what he said had not sounded proper and it was fair for her to question his intentions.

"I'm sorry. You're right. I know we talked about waiting because I knew if I started making love to you I couldn't stop. Conditions outside so unsettled, people around us starving, and if I got you with a baby. I want this but under better circumstances." He paused and took a very deep breath. "Believe me darling that loft is cold. I had to be out there this winter to keep watch over our horses. I don't know what else to say, except will you sleep with me tonight in the loft because I love you." His voice was tense, strained and wavering.

Elise was glad it was dark because she felt he was near tears. She knew she was.

"I will," she whispered, as she held him tighter.

"Tomorrow I'll clean out my bedroom upstairs for us. There are some curtains around and you can make it cozy."

"I love you Jacques and have for a long time."

"I've loved you Elise, for just as long."

"I'll get some blankets and a pillow for tonight."

"I'll go tell Ben."

Jacques went back upstairs to the big room, and walked to Ben. "She consented and is going to get more blankets and a pillow. Will you and Henri lock Nikki up?"

"We'll get her up there," Ben answered.

"Loving her shouldn't have happened this way. See you in the morning."

Nikki was on the floor with her arms folded on the chair seat and her head buried.

"Well girl, this is going to be a sad end for you when we tell the authorities that you are a traitor. You should have thought. It's out of our hands whatever happens to you. Don't blame us, it's your doing. Henri and I are going to lock you up till morning. Let's go."

Jean-Pierre was able to go to their bedroom, so Lucie claimed the cot. Everyone settled for the night Ben and Cheryl went downstairs.

"This has been an awful day," Cheryl said.

"Darling, you don't know how awful."

"Why, did something else happen?"

"Yes." His stare into her eyes was frightening, "Jacques and I killed the two Prussian soldiers in the carriage house. It was not feed we went for but to dispose of their bodies."

She gasped. "Oh Ben, how awful — how awful." Her hands covering her twisted expression.

"I saw the soldiers pass as I was practicing and went out and they were arguing and one pulled a knife to Jacques throat. I yelled, *nein.* He turned and lunged at me as he reached for his pistol, and I shot him. The other started for me and Jacques put a knife in his back."

"Oh Ben, you poor man. Poor Jacques." She took his hand and pulled him close.

"These are horrible things you have to do in war. I was not about to let Jacques take a knife."

"I've only read about things like this. I've never been so close. I'll be at your side. Sleep tonight and tomorrow will be better."

"Let's give it a try."

They nestled close, but Ben too upset to make love and apologized.

"I understanding darling. Tomorrow will be new and you can start to heal."

ഗ

Tomorrow had not left things behind. Ben, Jacques and Elise took Nikki and turned her over to the local authorities, such as they were. They were not happy to hear she had betrayed Jacques.

On the way home, Elise was morose and she

said to Jacques, “Perhaps we were a little hard on her.”

“My dear Elise, the blade against my neck was cold and about to make me cold all over. I was alone and helpless, but I was going to fight. Then Ben appeared at the door. Pardon me Ben, but you were never so beautiful. I didn’t tell her the whole story. Perhaps you can fill her in. I was too upset to say much.”

As Ben added a few details, Elise’s expression became more distressed and she stopped sharply and grabbed Jacques, her arms circling him. She looked at him, and her eyes were full of tears. “I didn’t know how close I came to losing you. You didn’t tell me.”

“I was too upset. That’s why I couldn’t make love to you. But holding you meant so much. Your nearness kept me alive. Tonight I’ll love you long and not in the loft.”

She wept in his arms.

ও

CHAPTER TEN

A few warm days and spring leaped into place. Snowdrops waved in the breeze as crocuses cracked the dark brown earth. Tiny buds peeked on the apple, peach and pear trees in the courtyard. The men had been spading the garden and the women would soon plant. With spring comes the fresh, the new, happiness, but not this time. A personal tragedy had struck the close-knit friends.

The Nicole incident had dampened their spirits. Jacques, Ben or both could have lost their lives. That would have been unimaginable. They held the life-blood, strength and heart of the group in their hands. Their devotion to everyone throughout the long hard winter had been unquestionable. Now they had been betrayed personally and by a traitor to their country.

Ben felt bad for her. She was young and had made an extremely bad decision. He had made no advances toward her so he harbored no guilt. He saw her as a friend, the same as the other girls.

They did not tell her or the authorities that two Prussian soldiers had been killed and rolled into a cave. Even though the French would consider this a casualty of war, if released Nicole could take revenge or Prussian command could come for Jacques and Ben. It had to be kept a secret.

Depression hovered over the city as French troops and mobs continued to clash. Even the back streets were not as safe as they had been. More people were being brought to the hospitals. Cheryl went every day with Janine to help. Ben, Jacques or both, with rifles slung over their shoulders, accompanied the women to and from their voluntary work.

Lucie, being a seamstress as well as a wonderful baker, had joined Renée at the textile factory to help make and repair balloons. They had not been to the factory recently, because of the distance, the constant trouble and no more need for balloons. Their city seemed to be reverting to the previous months of turmoil. Was there going to be an all-out civil war?

To lend comfort in their sad times, Ben was going to play a recital for his friends one last time before going to London. They invited Edgar to join them for supper and the musical evening.

The women chose food from their root cellar because the food stalls and butcher shops did not have much, if anything, on a daily basis. Janine placed new candles in the candelabrum, a fresh tablecloth and place settings, all different, were arranged.

Ben was downstairs playing over a few passages when Edgar arrived and knocked on his door. He welcomed him in and they talked about the political situation for a few moments. Edgar expressed concern about the organized movement that was spreading over the city. "They are radical. They are fighting the government. People are getting killed. We just went through a winter of war with the Prussians and now this." He was getting excited but paused. "This group has made themselves heard. Now to achieve their cause they have to stop fighting and do some talking. I suspect this is the beginning of something bigger."

"I certainly am tired of carrying a gun and looking over my shoulder. Many others are too and I know you are," Ben added.

"My paint brushes are calling and I want to answer."

"Your brushes and my piano keys."

"Knowing he was getting heated Edgar changed the subject. "I hear you have a girl."

"She is not just my girl. She is going to be my wife as soon as we can get to London."

"Congratulations. Why wait until London?"

"She's American and well, it's not totally clear to me because it upsets her to talk about it. But seems she escaped from a school or convent in southern France. She was a teacher there and wanted to leave and go back to America. She felt threatened. They told her no she couldn't leave and kept her identification papers and money she had earned. So she escaped and ended up here in Paris. I can get her identification papers in London, but not here."

"If you want I'll check, maybe I can help. I know a few people here."

"If that's not too much trouble. I'd certainly appreciate that."

"When do you plan on leaving?"

"Before the disturbances get worse and we get trapped again. The weather too. I don't want to get stuck in a mud hole somewhere. I know the rails are damaged so that means horse and carriage. I want to go to Cambrai first and see about my parents. I left them at our estate before the war and haven't heard from them since. Then we'll go on to Calais."

"I suggest you go to Amiens first, then east. There aren't as many problems up that way. The rails to Amiens are out, but I believe carriages leave every day. It's a temporary thing."

"That sounds reasonable. But I believe the girls have supper ready for us, then I'll play one of my recitals."

Upstairs Edgar greeted everyone, the girls with a kiss on both cheeks and the guys a pat on the arm and half-a-hug.

"Edgar, this is Cheryl, my wife to be and soon." Cheryl was pink and excited to meet someone she only knew from art books.

"My dear, it is a great pleasure to meet you. Trusting Ben's choice, I'm in love with you too." He took her hands and kissed each one. She thought, I'm never going to wash my hands again.

Her emotions so disrupted she was speechless. After a moment she managed control. "It's a pleasure also." Then she could only smile.

Jacques poured the wine and the women placed roasted carrots, parsnips and thick slices of ham in the center of the table. Everyone had their eyes on Lucie's bread just out of the oven.

The conversation varied from politics to art. Edgar didn't have much new to offer other than what he and Ben had talked about earlier.

"When I saw you a few weeks ago you said you were going to New Orleans," Henri asked.

"Soon as I'm released from guard, I'm going to start planning. My brother is there and other family."

Cheryl was mesmerized and wanted to ask questions, but could not think of one that made sense, so she just smiled. She wanted to compliment him on his blue dancers, but she knew they might not yet be a thought and he would gaze at her with distance in his eyes.

"I heard about that girl that stayed here. I think they deported her, or plan to, and she isn't ever to come into France again."

"We can only hope," Jacques added.

They continued to discuss other topics that pushed the supper hour to recital time.

Gentle flames shimmered in Ben's large open hearth. It advanced the atmosphere and softened the chill. Everyone found a place on the floor, sofa or chairs and Ben's music flowed into every heart. Among his selections were Bach partitas, Chopin études and Beethoven sonatas. As the natural light waned Ben stopped for a brief respite. He turned on the gaslight for this special occasion. He relaxed and everyone moved around before he played his last few pieces. He closed with a special étude.

He turned to his friends, "This is Chopin Étude No.1, A-flat Major, and I play it for Cheryl. It is one of her favorites." When he finished he got up and went to Cheryl, took her in his arms and kissed her lovingly. That received a gentle applause as did his offering of music.

Everyone expressed their gratitude to Ben for the beautiful evening filled with music. Cheryl served little *patisseries* that she and Lucie had put together. The evening was so long they enticed Edgar to spend the night. The cot in the big room was at last available.

ꕥ

On sunny and warmer days Jacques was teaching Cheryl to ride. He first showed her how to mount, then sit and how to move her body with the horse. La Belle was a willing participant. Jacques alongside on Honor, first they walked, next they trotted, and then galloped and later they ran. Cheryl was enjoying the lessons, but the thought of riding to the English Channel did not excite her.

For their trip from Paris to Calais, Ben was not certain what transportation would be available in the aftermath of the war. Horseback would be their last choice, but he wanted her to be prepared. From Cambrai to the family estate and the cottage it was definitely horseback or walk.

He acquired a Lefaucheux revolver for himself. It wasn't his first choice, but not much was available. He gave Cheryl his pistol and taught her how to use it. A knife to carry in her riding boot was added to her weaponry. She was not comfortable with all of these things that kill, but she knew it was for both of their safety during these times.

ꕥ

A few days after the recital, Cheryl asked Ben if

they could walk around the city before going to London. Along the Seine, down to Notre Dame. Today.

The day was bright with soft feathery clouds overhead and most of all it was quiet. Mornings were almost always free of mob violence. Most disturbances occurred in the late afternoon and on until midnight.

Hand in hand they walked from their arrondissement on the Right Bank, across the Seine at Pont Neuf to the Left Bank. "There was more damage over here from the bombardments in January. Looks like they have already started cleaning up. Some of these mobs should get busy rather than causing trouble. We can walk along the river to Notre Dame," Ben suggested.

As they walked, Cheryl compared the city now to last year when she and Zach had visited. Not yet the Eiffel Tower, the Louvre full of weapons and surrounded by bags of dirt. The signature sidewalk cafes were inside or not at all. It was a sad resemblance. Her thoughts were a mix of years.

Inside the church Cheryl remembered it as beautiful as last year. "Casting your eyes upon it for the first time leaves one humble." Ben said noting her ill-at-ease expression. She simply answered yes. They sat for a few moments in this house of God that had a long past and Cheryl knew a long future.

Outside Ben said, "Perhaps we'd better start back. We don't want to push our luck, but let's relax on that bench over there and enjoy the peace for a moment."

Sitting close on the iron bench, he put his arm around her. They watched the small boats glide along and waterfowl play and swoop. Others strolled by. In the distance horses clopped, creating a rhythm.

"There is someone painting over there at the edge of the water," she said.

"That's Renoir. Throughout the bombardments and turmoil nothing seemed to faze him. We have many of his painting in our home in London."

Cheryl was astonished and wanted to go over and see what was on his canvas, but she held back. Maybe I can kind of guide Ben that way. But now for the real reason for the walk.

"Ben darling, someone is going to London with us." She gazed lovingly at him with a guarded smile.

He responded with a frown. "What? Who?"

"Our baby."

Astounded, then excited, he gathered her in his arms and stammered, "Oh — Cheryl love, nothing could make me happier, except you to be my wife. I didn't expect such wonderful news, but I shouldn't be surprised. Darling I love you and baby. Making love to you every night and every morning. You so willing and receptive to me, till I am satisfied. Our passion could do nothing but make a baby. A baby made of love. Oh, Cheryl darling, I love you more than you can know."

"But Ben, I love you more." They gazed into each other's eyes with a power that not even the strongest force could break.

He managed to get himself under control and told her what Edgar had said about getting her identification papers. "If he can would you like to be married here instead of waiting until London."

"That would be so much better. Along the way we could be asked where and why we are going. Without identification I could be in trouble."

"We'll make our announcement at supper tonight and start plans. I'll get word to Edgar that we would like to be married here. Then we can leave as soon as conditions permit."

A day or so later Edgar informed Ben that the registrar was one of the government agencies that had moved to Versailles, because of the mobs. But he would go out with them to get papers to make her legal.

The next day Edgar, Jacques, Ben and Cheryl rode out to the nearby village. Coming from a war zone, it was easy to get all forms of new papers. The officials registered her as an American citizen and issued her legal papers that would allow her to enter any country. While they were there they obtained their marriage papers and they could be married before leaving for London.

At supper that evening they told of their plans, baby, getting married and leaving soon.

"Cheryl has expressed she would like to be married in church and I would like that too."

Janine immediately spoke up. "Where Henri and I go, across the park to St. Céciles. It is small and a beautiful, wood carved altar. Father is warm and kind. I'll go first tomorrow and see if you want me to."

Ben and Cheryl looked at each other with agreeing smiles.

Events moved fast and all plans were made for Ben and Cheryl to be married next week-end. Janine loaned Cheryl her wedding dress. Jacques and Elise found, after much searching, a flower shop that had a few white flowers.

The women dressed in white, long gowns and the men in gray trousers, white waistcoats and black jackets, crossed the park to the old stone church. The organist played Bach as they walked down the aisle. Jacques and Janine were their main attendants, but everyone gathered around and witnessed as one.

Handel's "Largo" whispered as Ben and Cheryl gazed into each other's eyes and spoke their words of love and devotion. He kissed her lightly and they led their friends out of the church into reality. Edouard had made arrangements at a near-by café for a reception. Happiness was flowing like the spring breeze and after the long day they made their way back across the park to their home.

A beautiful day, beautiful friends, and I have a beautiful husband. This has been the most precious day of my life while here, maybe always. It was made of pure happiness. This is where I want to be forever. But her heart wept.

ᔓ

CHAPTER ELEVEN

ᔕ

*T*he last several days had been warm and dry. Today was different. A light rain fell and it felt like the sea was just over the hill.

Ben decided they would leave regardless of the rain because it would take a few days before the roads, trails or paths would affect travel.

The evening before, they had their farewell supper. Each of his friends had words of *adieu,* but as something special, Edouard gave Ben the small portrait that he had painted of Cheryl.

"It's a treasure, Edouard. It's so special and a perfect likeness. Thank you my friend." Ben placed the portrait in a pocket over his heart. "We'll be back next spring for sure. Our baby is coming," and he looked at Cheryl fondly, "in January, so by spring they will be able to travel. I'll get some recitals scheduled here in Paris again, hoping everything is back to normal."

"Your rooms will be waiting," Jacques assured Ben.

"We'll keep them for a stopover when going to other parts of Europe. Also we'll get to see everybody." Bens last words to his friends, "Remember, you all have a home in London. If things turn bad here again, you have the address and someone is always there. Just show up."

On their day of departure, a light rain fell. Jacques hitched Honor and La Belle to the carriage. Jacques, with Elise, was going to take Ben and Cheryl to the station. It was across the wide city. They had a minimum of baggage, but it was still too far to walk.

Now that they were definitely leaving, Ben sent a telegram to his London home informing them that he was on his way with his wife. He decided to wait with the baby news.

Ben and Jacques reminisced as Honor and La Belle slowly pulled them over the cobbles. Ben had left many times before, but this time was different. They had been through a horrible winter at war, and shared personal experiences they both wanted to forget. Ben married with a baby on the way. Jacques and Elise promised to each other.

"Remember if you have problems stemming from the carriage house event, I'll be back at your side." Ben made it clear.

"Hopefully that's behind us. And I see you both have your riding clothes on."

"Probably from Cambrai to the cottage, then back. I'm hoping that will be all the horseback we have to do."

"Jacques, your riding lessons were wonderful and I feel comfortable if I have to ride any distance. But mostly I thank you for saving me. You don't know how frightened I was. I don't know what I would have done. I get chills all over again just thinking about it."

"Yes Jacques, thank you for finding Cheryl for me." A happy smile spread across Ben's face as he glanced her way.

"I could feel you were desperate and I could help. It was fun showing you how to ride. Now that spring is here, Elise and I will have to go riding. Okay sweetheart?"

She smiled and nodded with a reply of yes.

Ben knowing both well asked, "When are you two going to get married?"

Jacques smiled at Elise, "We talked about it and as soon as things quiet down a little more but soon. We've talked about opening old Gezot's store, when we're sure we won't get bombed out or taken over by Prussian soldiers. Lucie has already committed to baking bread for us."

"That would be a good neighborhood store. The ladies wouldn't have to walk so far every day," Cheryl added.

"I could be in the store while Jacques did all of the other things."

As they approached the station a sad silence hovered over the four friends. Just the clop of the horses and the sounds of the city rang through the air. Jacques already missed his best friend. Cheryl was apprehensive about the unknown. Edgar had assured them that further north there were fewer disturbances, but in times like these only the moment is the moment of truth. Ben knowing they would probably have at least one bit of trouble did not share his thoughts with Cheryl.

They waited on the platform as the big Shires leading the carriage rattled to a stop. Cobwebs still under the wheels were the lesser problem of this old conveyance. One last hug and all eyes full, Ben said, "Love you my friends."

They boarded along with another couple. Ben had mentioned to Cheryl earlier they should speak English and pretend not to know French. That would relieve them of unwanted conversation. One of them should stay awake at all times and watch everyone closely. They waved as the carriage pulled away and headed to their destination of Amiens.

ഗ

Ben and Cheryl occupied the last two spaces in the carriage. Already on board, two couples, a man alone and a younger man slumped in the corner with arms crossed with an expression ready for battle. Ben settled in a corner and pulled Cheryl close to him. She put her head on his shoulder, hoping she wouldn't disappear in his arms. It was the thought she lived with every moment. Her prayer today and every day, they never find the equation to get her back or that she would be alone when and if it happened.

As the carriage moved so did the conversation. The younger man did not participate or seem to understand. Ben stammered out in French, "We don't speak French only English." All the while shaking his head no and pointing to Cheryl. She smiled and nodded.

The English couple became the subject of conversation. Were they spies? Was she his wife? Were they here during the war? As they talked about Ben and

Cheryl they would give a quick glance their way. Not too coy, Cheryl thought as she looked out the window and listened. To hear herself and Ben discussed was strange and humorous, but she did not release any emotions or facial expressions to disclose their identity.

Time brought unpleasant body odors, irritable expressions, and heavy breathing, all a cacophony of untouchables that added to the deep ruts and swaying of the carriage.

Ben said softly to her, “Close your eyes if you want. I feel alert.” She did and the rhythm of the carriage lulled her into a diluted sleep.

About an hour later the carriage pulled into the village of Beauvais and stopped. Cheryl was alert instantly, “What’s happening?” she whispered.

“It looks like we’re going to change horses. That won’t take long.”

The new horses were hitched and the carriage started to move when two Prussian soldiers rode alongside and yelled at the driver to halt.

Ben thought, why would they be here and what would they want. The carriage house incident. Are they looking for me? What would Cheryl do if they took me? Oh god and our baby! It can’t be. I just left, maybe, that’s why they’re acting now. Before I left the country. If it’s me they want I will fight. I will not go easy. Ben watched as they talked to the driver. He heard a few words and they were French. His body tight he began to move around unnecessarily, but tried not to let Cheryl know he was concerned. In his mind he started preparing for what he would do. I should prepare her too. That is why I armed her. What do I say? Let me try.

"Darling, are you prepared for the baby?"

She knew immediately what he was asking. "I am darling."

Oh god what a wife I have chosen. He looked at her with his eyes bigger than usual and tried a smile that didn't work.

The driver and one of the soldiers went into a little shack disguised as a station. Ten minutes or so passed. Ben became more concerned as the moments crawled by. They came out and the two soldiers talked, almost seeming to argue. Then one of them approached the carriage and with force yanked the carriage door open.

In French he yelled, "Out! Papers!"

Ben thought, this is it. "We won't start anything, but…" Ben whispered to Cheryl. She responded with her eyes.

The other women finding it hard to move finally stepped onto the wooden platform. The men followed and last were Ben and Cheryl. Ben noticed the young man in the corner still asleep and made no motion to him. The soldier slammed the door so hastily he did not notice someone remained in the carriage.

"Papers!" he yelled again. Everyone searched their pockets and bags and found their identification. At that moment Cheryl was so glad she had something to present.

One soldier yanked the papers, without respect of their importance, from the hands of the people and pretended to read. The other obviously could not read French. They looked at Ben and Cheryl's last.

"English."

Ben replied in English, "Yes, I am English and

she is American. We are married and on our way to London, where we live."

"Coming from Paris?" He surprised Ben by speaking English. "Why are you here?"

Ben knew he had no right to be questioned, but did not want to cause trouble, so he answered. "I was in Paris to pay for rooms I rent. I'm a pianist and travel back and forth from London to Paris for recitals." Ben did not want to be totally dishonest, yet he did not want to say that he had spent the war in Paris. The soldier looked up from his papers and tried to smile, but his face did not know how. He handed their papers back without further expression or words, and motioned for them to get back into the carriage. He even stepped to open the door, and after a quick glance noticed the young man slumped in the corner. He immediately yelled in German, "Out! Why didn't you get out before?"

The young man appeared to be just waking up, but Ben saw the fear and panic in his eyes. He hesitated and the soldier reached in the carriage, grabbed his arm and jerked him onto the platform.

"Papers!"

He fumbled and searched his inside jacket pocket and finally found documents that were a little tattered.

Cheryl could see Ben was about ready to intervene for civility. She grabbed his arm and looked at him with frightened eyes. He relaxed, acknowledging her request. Everyone on the platform huddled together in fright. As Ben held Cheryl tightly, she could feel his hand trembling.

Ben watched the soldier as he carefully looked

at the print and then at the man. His expression told Ben that something was wrong. It made him tense. Should I intervene? Maybe he's a criminal and they found him.

The soldiers started throwing him around. They were shouting at him in a long string of German with expressions that were not gentle. As one of the soldiers was taking out a rope from his side pack, the other looking to help, the young man delivered a blow to the side of one soldier's head, turned and ran. The Prussian staggered. The other soldier pulled his gun and with lightning speed pumped a bullet straight into the man's back, puncturing his heart or near enough. Without another step his body contorted and rolled to the ground with such apparent ease. His mouth gaping and his eyes staring into space. Blood slowly trickled from underneath his lifeless body.

In the next instant there was an unbelievable silence and no one moved. It was a frozen frame after the action. The women screamed, and their hands went to their tortured faces. Then one of the male passengers started shouting at the soldiers. Ben turned Cheryl's head into his jacket. "Oh god! Oh god! Why did they do that," she said.

Ben and Cheryl were in shock with disbelief at what had just happened before their eyes. Ben quickly assessed the situation and decided it was not worth the risk getting involved. It was over. They would probably shoot me just as quickly. He whispered, "Darling, let's stay out of this. Good or bad the poor kid is dead." He turned his body away from the tragic scene pulling Cheryl along.

One of the men was still shaking his fist and loudly railing at the soldiers. He turned and gave him a daring look and indicated they all get into the carriage, now! Frightened, they quickly obeyed. The driver got in his seat and slapped the strap against the Shires' large rumps and they were moving, at last.

Immediately the five started a loud conversation about the tragedy that just happened. Ben whispered to Cheryl, "It was awful, but we don't know why and never will. We have to put it behind us." Although still in shock, she laid her head on his shoulder and closed her eyes, but the scene kept rolling like a film over and over.

The others did not stop their heated exchange, cursing the soldiers and asking why, until the next stop when they all exited the carriage. Ben and Cheryl got out giving their tense bodies some freedom. No one got on, so they were alone the last few kilometers to the Amiens carriage station.

At last they could talk freely. "It's so upsetting to witness. You must have seen too much during the last few months," Cheryl said.

"I have, too much. It appeared they were looking for him. That's why he ran."

"It did. I'm so glad I have identification papers. Thanks to Edgar."

"When we get into Amiens, I'll inquire about the next carriage to Cambrai."

"You don't look so well. Are you sick?"

"I think. Maybe what just happened or maybe morning sickness is kicking in."

"We'll stay here tonight. Carriages usually leave early in the morning. I am anxious to get to our estate and see if everything is all right. Especially to find out about my parents. They must have heard about the battles nearby and left. Our caretakers will know if they did. We'll go to the cottage first. Then I'll go to the manor house by myself. It could be occupied by Prussian soldiers and I'll deal with that. You will be safe in the cottage till I get back. We'll get food for a few days. You can rest there. It's quiet and isolated. Just us and the birds."

"I hope it works out as easily as you are saying."

"I do too, Cheryl love. Darling wife, in London you can rest all you need to until baby comes. Our house is big, and we have our own suite and I'll try to get my career and life back on track."

The carriage advanced in spite of the ruts and furrows. Ben saw it was becoming more populated. A sign for Amiens was around the next bend. They eventually stopped. The driver climbed from his high seat, and Ben and Cheryl got out. They talked a few moments, speculating about the tragedy. Ben asked if he could suggest a nice place where they could stay for the night.

"The Corner House," and he pointed up the road. "It has clean rooms and good food. I stay there when I lay over."

They exchanged farewells and Ben went to inquire about transportation to Cambrai. No rails, only carriage and it would leave in the morning. He reserved space. He hoisted their bags over his shoulder and they walked to the inn. Ben checked the room. He pulled back the blanket, checked the wash bowl and found everything clean and paid for the night. Upstairs Cheryl sank into a chair and her tears came fast and heavy. He pulled her up into his arms and held her as she released the tension that had built the last few hours.

"I'm sorry darling. I just couldn't hold it back. I never saw anyone killed before and so quickly. We don't even know why. No one deserves to die like that and without a trial."

He tilted her head and kissed her lips. "It's all right. You don't have to apologize for crying at such a tragedy. I cry too" He rocked her in his arms. "It's too early to eat. Maybe we should take a nap and I can hold you close." She nodded yes.

He helped her with her riding clothes and as he undressed she slipped into the freshly made bed. He eased in next to her. He curved his naked body around her and gently stroked her breast and her belly. Slowly easing his motion they fell into a much needed sleep, lowering the black curtain between them and the last few ugly hours.

As evening was just arriving, Ben felt her move. He rolled on top of her and she spread her legs so she could feel his desire. "I love you darling."

Awake, she knew she felt better. "Then love me wildly."

"My plan."

It was a love they made their own. It was a love from their hearts. It also released the stress in their bodies the day's events had thrust into their innocent lives.

Later she said, "I'm hungry."

"Good. Who affected your appetite more, me or baby?"

Their supper was delightful, just as the driver had said. After their meal their walk took them to a garden filled with pink, salmon and red tulips. The sun had set, but the evening light held for one last glimpse of beauty. "What a beautiful way to end this otherwise sad day, an omen — a good omen — of what's to come," Cheryl said, as she gazed at the garden and the sky.

"Beauty is all around us and we have to let it in. But nothing is as beautiful as loving you."

They walked back to the room as dusk was upon them. They washed and found the bed as comfortable as in the afternoon. Their desires were strong and sleep had to wait.

ꟹ

CHAPTER TWELVE

*M*orning broke with a thick haze that signaled rain. Ben knew before he opened his eyes. He could smell it. He could feel it. He peeked from under his eyelids and saw there was enough light that it was time to meet the day.

He whispered, “Cheryl love.”

She groaned a little and he chuckled. Is she a morning person he wondered? There is so much I don’t know about this woman that I have embraced with love and who carries my child. To be fair, she doesn’t know me. We started with love and our lives about each other will unfold together.

He rolled over and put his arm around her. “Are you ready for another ride?”

“Do I have a choice? I don’t want it to be like yesterday. Let’s not talk about it anymore.”

“Fair enough. There isn’t anything more to be said. Do you want me to go down for tea or do you want to dress and then go down?”

As she was deciding there was a light knock on the door and it alerted their senses. It was a heavy knock that meant trouble. Ben lived with the incident that he and Jacques had with the Prussian soldiers, but he worried more about Cheryl and their baby than himself. With identification papers she would have a better chance returning to America, than without. That was a consolation to him.

"I'll peek out," he whispered. He got out of bed, took the pistol and slightly opened the door. A bucket of warm water. He chuckled deeply again. He brought it in and they washed before it cooled. As she swept the warm cloth across her arms and around her neck, it seemed to have an emotional cleansing effect. Ever so slight, after yesterday, it was welcome.

"By the time we get to London these clothes will have to be thrown away. Your family's first sight of me won't be pretty. I hope they see through the grime I've collected along the way."

"Don't worry. My parents are forgiving. Ready for breakfast." He held her head close and stroked her hair. "I'm sorry you had to witness yesterday. It puts a stake in the memory."

"It does, but I am strong. We'll be strong together."

"I know. Let's get some breakfast. We'll pretend it will nourish our minds as well as our bodies."

They walked to the *Patisserie* near the station. While they were eating the haze turned to a light rain. From under the awning they watched the big Shires being harnessed and hitched to the sad looking carriage.

Their first stop would be the village of Albert where they would change horses. Ben inquired about the condition of the road. He was told the carriage trail was not the best. It was temporary until the rails could be repaired. Consequently they have received no attention.

The carriage ready everyone boarded. Ben and Cheryl, a young couple, a middle-aged couple and two men traveling alone. Eight people and baggage was a good load. As they traveled the rain became heavier and steadier.

"Is this too much rain for these already horrible roads?" Cheryl whispered.

"They seem pretty rutted."

"It makes my stomach lurch."

"Sweetheart, are you sick?"

"Not yet." She closed her eyes and molded herself into Ben's warm body.

He stared out the window. Wooded areas, the forest floor covered with decaying logs. Meadows greening. Trees with new buds waiting for a cue from the sun. But this was all a blur. He was running the music of Chopin, Schubert, through his mind. It was his silent practice session.

The rain rolled into a storm. Lightning streaked, thunder cracked and the horses became spooked. They hesitated, prance idly and then would go forward. The driver coaxed and slapped the strap to keep them moving as best he could although he understood their fear. In a few kilometers the storm moved faster than the carriage. Everyone relaxed, even the horses were moving easier along the unkempt trail.

Suddenly the animals stopped. Ben looked out. The creek through the woods was running full. The driver got down from his high seat. Ben and another man got out of the carriage, and they discussed, was it safe to cross?

The biggest problem was that the other side of the road was not directly across. The entire team and carriage would be in the creek bed before they reached the other side. The water was strong but not too deep. It would not reach the carriage step. The driver assured the men that the creek bed was relatively smooth. He had been this way many times since the rails were out.

They decided to cross. The driver approached the creek bed slowly. The horses did not hesitate. Heads bobbing, they pulled ahead and cautiously stepped into the water. Everyone was holding their breath as they watched the water bubbling and foaming below their feet. Inching, then a thud and one side of the carriage went down slightly. Horses, carriage and hearts stopped with the jolt. The horses pulled but nothing happened.

"Oh no, sounds like something broke," Ben whispered. "Right in the middle of the water?"

"Not a good place to be stuck." Cheryl's voice tense and anxious. Ben had no reply.

The driver got down into the water to survey the damage. He saw the problem and opened the carriage door. "A wheel is caught in a long crevice between the flat stones. It doesn't look deep and I don't think anything broke. I believe us guys can lift it out. But you all will have to get out and the baggage will have to come off."

Ben mumbled under his breath, "We'll all get wet. We have no choice. Cheryl love, I'll carry you out. No need for both of us to get soaked. You are but a wisp."

"Not for long."

He trudged carefully through the water with her in his arms. Reaching the other side he eased her down and went to help the others. The other ladies would have to face the consequences of wet boots, skirts and petticoats, because they were too padded to be carried.

Relieved of baggage and people, the men went to free the wheel as the driver encouraged the horses. The driver gave the call and the men lifted as one. Clanging and clattering of metal and urging of horses the carriage moved enough to free the wheel. Ben's hand was a little too close to a spring that relaxed a second too soon and caught it. Before he could even voice a call for help, the man next to him quickly lifted and Ben's hand was free, but the palm had a deep cut, the skin ripped and was starting to ooze. He tried to make a fist but his fingers wouldn't move and it hurt like hell. He thanked the man, put his hand in his pocket and walked out of the water. The horses with their carriage had also made it to the other side.

Ben walked to Cheryl and she knew something was wrong. His hand in his pocket was not his way.

"What happened?" she immediately asked, her eyes wide.

"My hand got caught and it's bleeding."

"Oh, let me see."

He pulled his hand out of his pocket. Blood was all over his hand and clothes. She looked at it carefully. "It's a deep cut and we have to clean it. Does it hurt?"

"It does. My whole hand hurts."

"Let's go to the creek and wash the blood off."

Ben held his hand under the fast running water.

"Do you have a handkerchief?"

Ben gave her the white square and she pressed it

into his palm and wrapped her scarf tightly around his entire hand. "This will help stop the bleeding until we can get something better. We could use some ice."

"At the next stop," Ben replied hopefully.

Baggage and people loaded, it was forward once again. No one spoke for a long while. The ladies sat still but were shivering. The cold on their feet went up through their whole bodies.

"Are you cold?" she asked Ben.

"Not too much, my Hessian boots kept me pretty dry. My mother brought them from Germany."

"How is your hand?" she asked later.

"It hurts like you know what."

"Really." She was concerned. A cut should not hurt as bad as he said. Was there a broken bone? She decided not to mention that unpleasant thought until she could examine it better.

Not soon enough the village of Albert came into view. As they were changing horses, Ben inquired about an ice house. One was around the corner and the man who freed Ben's hand volunteered to run and get a chunk.

They both expressed their gratitude and Cheryl unwrapped the make-shift bandage. It was swollen and starting to turn blue, but the bleeding was much less. "Ice just in time. Before we wrap it up, let me examine it. She touched the major bones where he had the most pain. She ran her fingers along the back of his hand carefully feeling the metacarpals. He only grimaced. Then she pressed the area between the bones along the connective tissue and got a definite reaction.

She looked into his big eyes and smiled, "Ben darling, I can't be sure but I don't feel a break, but you did react when I pushed the connective tissues. There are a lot between the bones. And I suspect you have a bad bruise and a cut. Both will heal and leave no trouble."

"Are you sure?"

"From what I know, that seems to be the problem. The injured connective tissue between the bones are causing the pain."

Trusting her judgment, he felt better. He thought, my hands are my life. My hands are my soul. If I can't play what will I do? Go into business with my father. Horrible. I love my father, but not interested in being part of his business. I know it would make me miserable. I hear him talk.

The baggage loaded and everyone aboard they moved forward. A few more hours of doldrums lay ahead.

Ben tried to run compositions through his head but pain and thought interfered. He was getting anxious about getting to their estate. Was it still standing? Were Prussian soldiers there? Had they taken over with my parents still there? They seem to take what they want. If no one was there they could trash it. He also knew Cheryl did not feel well. Now my hand needs attention.

Nestled close to him she laid her head on his shoulder. She tried to sleep, but instead fell into the chasm of boredom. Ben's hand worried her, but she felt sure it was just a bad bruise. What haunted her more was her existence. Could I be transmitted back pregnant? Definitely one for the science journals. There must be an image of me at home. Am I dead there. Oh please don't bury me. They will have to come up with a return equation. Maybe no one knows that I exist in another time and will never look for me here or anywhere. That's not so bad, I have Ben. The trail was smoother now and her thoughts waning she fell into a light sleep.

The giant carriage and its load arrived in Cambrai later than expected. Everyone was anxious to get into dry clothes and said their goodbyes quickly. The man who relieved Ben's hand from the carriage spring offered them a room in his home for the night. Ben thanked him generously but did ask about stables and inns.

"Stables have horses for rent that way." And pointing in the other direction, "Collette's. She is nice and her food is great." Ben thanked him and bid *au revoir*.

As they started for the inn Ben spoke. "It is a little late so we'll start for the cottage tomorrow morning. We'll lodge here for the night."

They found Collette's to their liking, quaint and clean, and in the dining room ladies and men were enjoying their evening meal.

In the room Ben changed into dry clothes and Cheryl cleaned his hand. It looked awful. She knew what was going through his mind. "Darling, I believe it looks worse than it really is. Serious bruises are often colorful. Let's find an apothecary and get some bandages and a salve for the cut."

"Food too and I'll see about horses for tomorrow."

After finding the apothecary and stables they went back to their room to bandage his hand properly. Then they went downstairs for their supper. They made it long with small talk and enjoying the food. The sun was low but they decided on a short walk. Ben questioned about the baby. "Will you tell me all about how it grows and when we can expect him?"

"Him," she smiled. "It starts out as a tiny dot and then all of the parts are added slowly until it's perfect and then it comes out. First part of January. I studied biology but my specialty is quantum physics."

"I never heard of that. You'll tell me all about it? But it's getting dark and we have a ride before us tomorrow. And you and Baby need your rest."

ഗ

CHAPTER THIRTEEN

ꕤ

A small divide in the drapes told Ben morning was outside the window.

He was moving around when Cheryl asked, "Is it time to get up?"

"If you want."

"I don't feel too well."

"Baby, not feel too well?"

"Yes. It will pass."

"If you don't feel like riding, we can stay here another day."

"I'd rather go, but give me an hour or so."

Ben went for warm bread, hot grain cereal and tea, and brought it back to their room. He looked over his music as he ate. Cheryl slept.

She woke later and sat up. "I seem to feel better. Now I will take you up on tea and bread."

Ben went for her breakfast adding a bowl of oatmeal.

After eating she felt better as she expected. "How long will it take to get to the cottage and how does your hand feel?"

"My hand feels good and about an hour to the cottage on horseback."

"After we change your bandage, I would like to start. I can't stop doing things. It's going to be like this for a while. I'm anxious to get to London. I know you are too."

After selecting two gentle horses, apothecary supplies and food stuff they started for the cottage.

Ben warned her. "The path off the main trail will probably be in bad shape. Winter can wipe out a path as if it had never been there. It's pretty isolated. Just follow me."

"Darling man, I'd follow you to the ends of the earth."

His acknowledging smile was pleasing.

They rode from open ways to a densely forested area and new bushy undergrowth. Dead branches were down and fall leaves were packed. They had to guide the horses around puddles of water. Rocks had heaved from the winter frost. Cheryl noticed the white trilliums, spotted trout lilies and tiny fronds starting their way up. Horse and rider trudged cautiously on.

Suddenly, a small building appeared through the new growth.

"We're here." Ben said happily and rather loud, as if telling the forest.

In her mind she was looking for a white picket fence, surrounded with red and yellow flowers, a dainty light in the window. Hardly a cottage, this is a shack.

"Oh, it's really isolated. You could get lost

rather quickly in this dense forest.

"Coming from the direction we did, I wasn't completely sure. I'm glad the sun was out. It helped guide me."

My amazing husband. Every time she thought how much she loved him, her thoughts quickly turned to being torn from him. The reflections were attached like mind and body.

Ben pulled a large bolt and with a rusty key, opened the door. A rush of hot stale air met them.

Inside she looked around. One big room, a bed, table, chairs and an upright piano. A small cook stove and a lower cabinet completed the necessities.

"Do we have water?"

"We do. There is a pump outside in the back yard."

She looked and laughed because all she could see were solid branches just beginning to leaf.

"There is also a hole out there to keep food cool. But no water closet, just a chamber pot."

Cheryl was speechless but her expression spoke loudly. Ben read her face. Her arms reached for him. "Love, my love Ben, as long as I have you it's a palace."

"This is about as bad as our life will get. And we'll soon be out of here. Now let's get some fresh air in here and it will be better."

As they dusted, shook curtains and pillows, he told her about the estate. It had been large, but was divided into two sections. His father bought the house and a small amount of land, and the cottage was part of it. The other was sold for harvest. The outer part of Cambrai was nearer to the house. The house was about a kilometer from the cottage. His father frequently had business guests and Ben could not practice so he moved his piano to the cottage.

"You are the only girl that I have had here, my wife. Sometimes I would stay here a couple days at a time. Read and practice. — Read and practice. The weather is hard on the piano, but it served its purpose."

In an hour it was amazing how much better three hands made the inside look and feel. She checked his hand again to make sure he had not opened the cut.

"Does it still hurt?" she asked, as she gently pressed the connective tissues.

"A little, better than yesterday. It even looks better."

"I feel that it's going to be okay," as she wrapped and bandaged it again.

"I'd like to ride up to the house. Since I don't know what's there, I'd better go alone."

"I'll nap or try."

"You will be safe here and you have your horse and pistol."

"That's confidence," she said, trying not to be sarcastic.

She relaxed on the bed as he rode off. I have to go to sleep quickly because I don't want to think.

Still in a light sleep, she heard her name. "Cheryl love," he whispered.

"Gosh, I thought I was dreaming. I went right to sleep. How is your house? Are your parents there?" She sat up.

"No one is there. Not even a caretaker. Nothing seems to be damaged, but there are a lot of track made by horses."

"Does the caretaker live there?"

"No, but not too far. I thought I would come back and get you and then go find him. We can take everything up there. There are a few more comforts at the manor house such as water closets. It's closer to Cambrai and civilization, if we need anything." Water closet alone had a comforting ring to her ear.

They rode to the house and did some more dusting and airing out. They gathered wood from the forest, and Ben built a fire in the cook stove. He ushered her through the house. Large everything, parlor, library, bedrooms. Upstairs and at the end of a long hall, Ben said, "This is my bedroom and we'll sleep in here. I'll build a fire in the hearth if we need it. Rooms on the third floor are for servants when we're here." He did not take her up.

After they had eaten supper they relaxed in the parlor and she asked, "How long have you been here?"

"Around nine years. My father bought it after Beth and I finished school. At that time his base was Paris. They were remaking the city, widening streets, tearing down houses. Some of his business associates did not like meeting there, so he decided to base in London, where a larger company office was located. He sold our Paris home and bought this estate as a stopover for other parts of the continent. Also it was nice in the summer away from the noise of the city. And it was good for meetings that lasted several days. I spent a lot of time with them between recitals and that's when I had my piano moved to the cottage."

"Did you have a home in London too?"

"A small one when we were growing up, but then my father bought the house where we all live now.

It's a house for adults. We each have our own suite."

"Which do you like best Paris or London?"

"Paris before the war, I trust. I like them both for different reasons. Equally, I guess."

"You were fortunate to be schooled in both English and French."

"I was and I should learn German, because I want to expand my programs to Germany, Vienna."

"What did you do in America before you came here? I don't believe you even mentioned anything but school."

"That was it and working in a science lab."

"Then you came here." He stated hoping he could find out more about her past life.

"Oh Ben, I'm not ready to go there yet. I promise someday."

Dark, although they had candles, they decided to talk in his bed.

They were naked and warm under the featherbed. As he rubbed her soft body, he asked, "When do we have to stop making love?"

"We don't ever have to stop entirely."

"I have been wondering ever since you told me about Baby. We both need the closeness of physical love." He curled her in his arched body and caressed her breasts and belly as they talked softly. "He will be the first grandchild. He'll be born in London."

"Ben, I know it's not usually done, but will you be with me when I give birth?"

"If that's what you want, no door will be strong enough to keep me out."

"Nor do I want to be confined as the baby grows. I want to be out and about. I don't want to be isolated in a dark room or away from you. The body needs activity. I know this is best."

Their voices became a whisper as they desired each other and then they slept in entwined arms.

The thrush had sung his evening song. The new leaves ceased their twitter. The woodlands were at peace. Only the night critters stalked silently.

ço

CHAPTER FOURTEEN

ᔓᔕ

The French countryside awakened to the warbler's sweet, morning song, and the leaves rustling in time with the breeze. The sun's rays crept in the window where Ben and Cheryl slept. Ben heard seven chimes from the French clock in the hall. He slipped quietly out of bed taking care not wake Cheryl.

In the kitchen, the cook stove had remnants of last evening's fire. Ben teased it with dry sticks and brought it to life. He plundered the cabinets for different flavors of tea leaves. He hoped to find peppermint and his search was successful. He made himself a large mug and went to the back portico to enjoy the fresh air and new sunshine. The beginning of the day was promising.

Not long he heard her pattering through the kitchen and jumped up and went to greet her.

"Good morning, my Cheryl love."

"Ben, you're such a darling, good morning," and she gave him a quick kiss.

"How do you feel today?"

"Okay, so far."

"Look what I found," he said, as he held up a cloth bag of peppermint leaves. They were not labeled but the aroma floated easily through the fabric. "This will help your stomach."

Inhaling the fragrance, "Oh, I love mint." He made her a mug and they went to the portico to enjoy the new morning air together.

"It's very nice here, but when can we move on? I'd like to get settled before the baby gets further along. Engage a doctor." Her thought traveled through time. I probably know more about birth than these doctors, but I need someone to help me.

"It will probably take us another week, considering the slow travel and layovers, to get to London. I don't know how long we will have to wait for a boat crossing at Calais." He knew there could still be Prussian Navy boats in the area near the Channel. Edgar had informed him. They could be a problem, but he did not want to alarm her unnecessarily. "We'll leave soon." He took her hand as a gesture of comfort. "Today I am going to ride over to Monsieur Bonnard's, our caretaker, and see how he is and see if there are any problems. Also, when did my parents leave?"

"How far is it?"

"Not far through the forest, but I have to go around the trails, almost into Cambrai. About a half-hour. If you want, you can ride with me or stay. You'll be okay."

"I'll stay and check out the library and don't put too much pressure on your hand. I'll rest up for the last part of our trip."

After a mid-morning lunch Ben rode off. As she watched him turn out of sight she rubbed the back of her neck and a light shiver went through her body. Everything will be okay. I feel this way because I'm alone in a strange place.

She walked out to the stables to check on her horse. "Nice girl," as she patted her face. "We'll ride soon." She was as gentle as La Belle and Cheryl appreciated her disposition.

Back in the house she went into the library. She chose several art books and sat down at the library table. Engrossed in landscapes of Turner and Constable and trying to read the captions, which were in French, when she heard a horse whinny. He's back, he forgot something. She looked out the window and her heart nearly stopped mid-beat. Two Prussian soldiers were leisurely ambling along the wide road to the house. Two! Up here! Why? Oh god they're everywhere and trouble. A thousand what should I dos ran through her mind. I can't confront them. If they aren't decent I don't have a chance. Her mind and body went into panic mode. Her adrenalin spiked. Fear was in her eyes and her face lost its glow, although no one was there to witness.

Hide! She quickly closed the books, not to give another clue that someone was here. The warm kitchen stove and unmade bed would be enough. She ran upstairs into a bedroom and jerked open a door that was a walk-in closet. It was piled high with boxes, coverlets and clothing. Good hiding stuff. She stepped inside, closed the door and crawled behind the boxes and pulled things over herself. She tightened into a fetal curl and shuddered as ripples of cold crackled through her body like fire through dry brush. She lay cramped hoping all of her was out of sight should they open the door. Oh, my pistol — Oh Ben! Come home soon. But she knew it just wasn't time and was on her own.

She listened — in the dark and packed she could feel sweat popping from her body — she trembled — her breath was short and staggered — she waited — muffled, she heard a deep voice calling in German — distant noises like the impact of closing doors. Faintly at first, then closer she heard the slamming of boots against the oak stairs and hall floor.

Oh god they're up here! It will be worse if they find me. My baby. The voice got louder and boots smacked heavier and closer. Doors were opening swiftly and slamming shut all too close. They're in this room! The closet door was yanked open. Pain stabbed her chest. They found me! The last thing Cheryl heard was a cacophony of the German language spewing forth.

ᔕ

Ben, on his chestnut gelding, plodded along at a relaxed pace to their caretaker's home. He found him working in his garden. They greeted each other warmly and exchanged pleasantries. "My parents, when did they leave and have they been back? I haven't heard from them since I was here last September and we were going to London." Ben was anxious for information.

"Don't remember the day, but when they heard Paris had been surrounded and you didn't return they left for London. They said if you came back, send you on."

"Well, I tried to get out a couple times, but got shot at, so I decided to go back to Jacques and stay there." Ben paused. "Hot air balloons were going out, but they didn't like to have casual passengers. Paris is still in turmoil. It's all internal now, so we decided to try to get to London before it turned tragic again and that seems a possibility. We arrived yesterday and we'll go on soon."

"Is everything all right at your house? I was there a couple days ago."

"Nothing has been bothered that I could see."

"You said we, who is with you?"

"My wife."

"You are married, congratulations, my boy. I'll ride back with you and show you some of the repairs I made in the stable. I want to meet your wife. We can go through the forest. I made a path and it's a much shorter ride."

"How is Madame?"

Just then she appeared at their back door and came to greet Ben with a big hug and welcome words. "What happened to your hand?"

"A little too much weight as we lifted the carriage out of a crevice in a creek bed. Cheryl thinks it's okay and just bruised."

"Who's Cheryl?" Madame asked.

"My wife, as I was just telling Monsieur."

"Congratulations my dear," she said, as she brought her folded hands together under her chin.

"Thank you both. Was there any fighting up here or soldiers?"

"No, but we could hear the big cannons. Is there much damage in Paris?"

"The Left Bank was damaged pretty badly. Other parts here and there. People ran out of food. We fared well. Jacques had a garden and our friends moved in with us and we all scavenged for food and survived," Ben explained.

"There are still soldiers around on horseback. They don't bother us. If they did it would be the last thing they did." Monsieur paused. "Mother, I'm going to ride back with Ben. I won't be long."

"Do you need lunch first?" she asked them.

Ben expressed that he had eaten before riding over. Monsieur said he would eat when he returned.

They trotted along the trail through the forest, reaching Ben's house in about fifteen minutes. Ben noticed hoof prints that he didn't believe were there before. He pointed them out to Monsieur. "Better see if she had a visitor," Ben said, with concern in his voice.

He rushed in the back door and through the kitchen calling, "Cheryl — Cheryl!" All was quiet and no answer. He went to the bottom of the stairs and called again. No response.

"She must be napping," his voice a little shaky. "I'll just make a quick check." His heart thumping as he took the stairs two at a time. He slowly eased their bedroom door open so not to wake her. The bed covers were still crumpled from the night. He went over and felt around to make sure his senses were not deceiving him. "Oh my god, where is she?" he said out loud. He ran to the other bedrooms slamming doors in haste. Not finding her he ran back downstairs. "She's not up there." Monsieur could see the fright in his eyes and hear it in his voice.

"The stables. Let's go out there. Maybe she

went for a ride." Knowing that was not likely, but he had to give himself a reason. Ben ran in the direction of the barn with Monsieur following as fast as his short legs would carry him. Finding her horse content and munching on grasses, he ran the expanse of the stables. Even up the ladder to the loft. "Where are you Cheryl?" his voice trembling.

They started back to the house, "We'll find her my boy." Monsieur trying to relieve Ben's anxiety.

Ben looked at the hoof prints again. "I do believe they are new. Did someone come and take her?" He was near tears and felt so helpless. "What do I do? Ride into Cambrai and look around. Oh god what do I do?" He paused. "The third floor. I didn't go up there." He ran into the house and up the stairs, again two at a time. He found just cobwebs and undisturbed dust. Obviously no one had been there for a while.

Outside they searched the edge of the wooded area. As they walked, they pushed the brush to the side and they called. Ben frantic did not know what more to do but to ride into Cambrai. "Monsieur, would you stay here while I ride into a more populated area and see if I can find out anything?"

"Oh yes, go my boy, go. Maybe when you get back she'll be here. I'll keep searching."

Ben rode hard to the edge of the city. He galloped through some of the near streets. He stopped several times and asked people if they had seen anything unusual — a woman by herself or with someone. After searching and questioning he decided to return home and check one last time. On the way he stopped at a few houses and inquired. The last house he stopped at said they had not seen a woman, but two

Prussian soldiers had ridden out that way. They came back later, but no one was with them.

Ben was frantic. They found her and took her into the woods and ravished her. I have to find her. Why did I bring her here? Why didn't we go straight to London? I have to get back!

He raced, but as he got nearer to his house, he leaped off his horse to check the growth at the sides of the road. He called her name again and again. Why doesn't she answer? She could be dead. No! — No!

Observing the undergrowth for disturbance, he quickly moved on. She didn't shoot anyone. There's no body. Oh, Cheryl love and our baby. Oh god, they both could be gone. I can't live without her.

He arrived back at the house and Cheryl was still missing. He related to Monsieur what he had been told about the soldiers. They decided to check every inch of the surrounding woodlands. Ben just knew they had taken her out there and didn't want to think what could have happened. His heart exploded over and over.

ꟹ

Cheryl in the dark and suffocating closet realized she had passed out. She remembered that loud German language. Her thoughts wavering and full of fear, I guess they didn't see me. How long have I been here? She moved some of the coverlets to get a whiff of the stale air. She lay quietly for a while longer. Silence. Time went on but she had no idea how much. They have to be gone by now. She tried to uncurl her body and found that stiffness had set in, which indicated she had been there for some time. She moved from under the clothes and boxes. She quietly opened the closet door. Silence. Slowly she moved out into the bedroom. Carefully, she opened the door into the hall and waited. Only the ticking of the clock. She eased into the hall, stopped and waited to see or hear something. She went across the hall into another bedroom and gazed out the window. No horses there. But she noticed movement in the underbrush at the edge of the road. She watched. A fat little man came out of the thicket. Who's he? I'd better get back in the closet. Just then he yelled to someone on the other side of the house. She waited to see who else was here. She looked again. It was Ben. "Oh Ben!" she screamed.

Ben heard her but could not detect the origin of the scream. It was too far away. She ran down the stairs and out the door frantically calling his name and sobbing. "Ben! Oh Ben!" He didn't wait for her to reach him. He ran to her and grabbed her into his arms.

"You're here! Darling, you're here! Did they hurt you? Did the soldiers hurt you?" He was so choked up he could barely speak. "Please don't let me be dreaming." He held her close. "It's okay. I've been crazy. Were soldiers here? Did they hurt you?"

Through her sobs he felt her shake her head no. They stood wrapped into each other, releasing their hearts and souls into one embrace.

Her face blotched with pink and on her cheeks ran rivulets of tears. Her eyes were barely slits. He took out his handkerchief and blotted her eyes and then his. He gazed at her unsightly face, but saw only beauty and love that she expressed in those moments.

Monsieur stepped closer and rubbed Ben's back. "My boy, it's okay now. Come let's rest. I want to meet your lovely bride. Come, let's go to the portico."

They stepped apart and smiled tenderly at each other. He took her hand and all three made their way to the house.

"Sit here darling. I'll fix us tea," Ben said.

"No, you stay here with your love and let me fix the tea," Monsieur offered.

Ben continued to console her and with his warm words and gentle touch, she managed to get her emotions packaged. Monsieur brought tea and its healing properties took effect with the first sip. They knew each other well, but Ben introduced his bride properly.

In a while they both related what had happened in the last few hours. They finally relaxed and were able to enjoy the soft afternoon breeze when there was a rustle in the path through the woods. It was Madame. Monsieur rushed to her and brought her on the portico.

"You said you would be gone only a short while. I got concerned and thought something might be wrong."

"Very wrong, but now right," and he told her briefly about their troubled afternoon.

"So awful and Ben, you not knowing where she was." Madame took Cheryl's hand in comfort.

"I was afraid twice, for Cheryl and our baby." Ben smiled as he related the information.

"Oh, my boy. God bless you and her."

"My dear and you had to go through all this today. Are you all right?" Madame was understanding.

"I believe so." She lied, as she felt moisture between her legs.

As they talked the tension settled and Monsieur

asked, "Mother we should be going and let Ben and Cheryl rest. They both had a bad afternoon."

"Maybe I could fix your supper before we go." She looked at Ben for permission.

"I do believe Cheryl should rest and I will take you up on your offer only if you stay and eat with us."

"No, I'll just fix."

"I insist," Ben answered firmly.

She smiled, giving in. She found enough in the kitchen to make a supper. Monsieur helped with the extras, preparing the table, keeping the fire going, while checking to see if Ben or Cheryl needed anything.

After their supper Madame and Monsieur saw the light was waning and decided they should be on their way before night darkened the forest completely.

"We're going to leave tomorrow. We need to get to London," Ben said. "Does my father owe you for watching over our house?"

"No, he paid me well."

"I'm sure someone of us will be back this summer. I wish our visit could have been better, but it turned out okay."

"Godspeed my boy and to your beautiful wife."

"Yes, Godspeed to all three of you."

ᔓ

CHAPTER FIFTEEN

ೞ

*T*he days of June were often filled with the sun playing in and out of the willowy clouds. Evening with a soft coolness ushered in the chilly nights. Ben and Cheryl waved from the back portico as the forest, green and lush, enclosed Monsieur, Madame and their horse.

Cheryl excused herself and went to the water closet. As she suspected, blood. She had no pain and that consoled her. It's stress. I'll tell Ben in the morning if I'm still bleeding. She went back to the kitchen holding her feelings within.

Sitting with Ben at the long trestle table, a mug of mint tea and candlelight dancing romantically, she reflected, this is the only moment I wanted to log into my memory about today.

As they chatted, she noticed Ben pulling his hand to his chest, and even grimacing.

"Your hand is bothering you, isn't it?"

"Yeah, gripping the reins and scrubbing the

bushes irritated it. I forgot all about my hand."

"Let's put a clean bandage on."

Removing the torn and dirty gauze she saw the cut was puffy and redder. Shades of purple and yellow rolled together. "Your hand looks like a piece of batik fabric."

"What's batik?"

"It's fabric that has been painted with blue, red, yellow, lots of colors all running together. Quilters use it."

"Do you make quilts?" he asked, excitedly.

"No, my grandmother does. I would go with her to buy fabric." She pressed the connective tissue. "Does that still hurt?"

"Not much."

"That's good. It's the bruise that colors it and will go away. Should I make you a little sling as a reminder not to use it?"

"No, I'll just tuck it in my jacket when I ride."

"I'm sorry you had to go through all this today."

"Oh my, you are the one who needs consoling."

"Well, I will accept," she paused. "I don't think I have ever been so frightened." Her facial expression was tense as she thought of doors opening and thundering words she did not understand.

"Fear is a terrible emotional response and it affects the body too." He put his arm around her and pulled her close, a tangible move to accompany his words. "I so want to go to America and meet your family and have recitals there."

She smiled sadly. "Someday." There was a lull in their conversation while contrasting thoughts of the future occupied their minds.

"It's late, everything is telling us. The birds are asleep. Dusk slipped away when we were not watching. I'll go see to the horses and meet you in our bedroom." She was thankful he gave her space to check the bleeding.

She went to the water closet and found there was still a showing, but less or was she factoring hope into her mind. Morning will hold the decision, stay another day or go.

She was in bed when Ben returned. Naked, he nestled close to her, lifted her hair and kissed the back of her neck. His nearness enclosing her was more than comforting. It made her wild.

"Are the horses okay?" she asked, quietly as if almost asleep.

"They are."

She had to deny him just this time. "Oh darling, I am exhausted and your hand. We both need to rest."

"I know, it's been a hard day and a few more ahead. I'll just hold you. We have to think of our baby. He has to feel the stress, too."

Softly and slowly she said yes. Her breath was a little heavier. He knew she was falling asleep and he edged to his side of the bed. He didn't realize she was feigning sleep.

As she lay rolled in a ball she forgot her fears from earlier in the day and thought only of their baby. A new day would bring a refreshed body and mind. Even a small amount will help. Her fear of a miscarriage followed her to the fringe of sleep.

ᔕ

Ben woke and lay motionless not to wake Cheryl. He slowly raised his eyelids. It seemed a little dark to be morning. It wasn't long until the hall clock sent the message. He listened and counted six chimes. Then he realized it was the dark clouds deceiving his perception. He eased out of bed and stepped silently into the hall. On the other side of the window it looked like the middle of the night, but he trusted the faithful old time piece.

In the kitchen he laid dry slivers of wood on the quivering orange coals to heat water for their tea. As he waited he gazed out the window hoping the rain would hold off. It was early but the dark, rolling clouds looked rather ominous. He thought of thunder and spooked horses.

Cheryl was awake, but she had pretended to be sleeping when Ben slipped out. She wanted to wash and see what had happened over night. She went to the hall water closet and was relieved to find no blood. She did not feel the need to mention this to Ben. I'll take my chances and ride. I want to get to London.

She padded into the kitchen with a smile on her face.

"I can tell you feel better this morning," he said, as he kissed her lovingly.

"I do. A new day always brings something different and right now it's better. A new incident helps you get over the last one. But I don't think I will ever get over seeing that boy killed. That was so terrible."

He made her tea and they sat at the long, trestle table. "I've seen a string of things like that living through the war. I'm not sure what it did to me. I don't have nightmares. My music kept me grounded. It goes deep in the soul and it was a safe place to hide from the bombing, killing, starving." He paused and gazed intensely into her hazel eyes. "Cheryl love, you don't know how glad I'm to be on my way out and with you. Being able to help Jacques and my friends helped me. We had each other. If I had made it out I would never have found you."

Cheryl thought how sadly this could end and then maybe not. A part of her heart cried. She put her hand lightly on his bandaged one. "How does it feel today?"

"Still sore."

"That is to be expected after yesterday. I'll put a clean bandage on and are you sure you don't want a little sling."

"No. The ride into Cambrai isn't far and I'll be careful."

Cheryl rose from the table and went to the back window. "Is it going to rain?"

"If it does we have rain capes. Then it's rail all the way to Calais. Do you want to eat before we go?"

"Not now, but when we get to Cambrai."

"We should get ready. It is beginning to look better and brighter."

They packed their clothes with the odor and grime squeezed, tightly in their bags. Windows down, shutters bolted, and doors locked they went to the stables. Cheryl led the horses out as Ben latched all the doors inside and out. Their bags over the horses, they mounted and rode taking one more step toward their destination.

When they reached Cambrai their rain capes were still packed. They returned the horses and walked toward the rail station a few streets away.

"I'm sure you are hungry after that hard ride in," he said teasing her, but knowing she was probably ready to eat.

She smiled ready with an answer. "I saw a *Boulangerie* just over there."

"I saw you doing a double-take as we passed. Let's go back."

In the bakery they bought meat wrapped in crepes, petite fours and a Napoleon each. Outside, under the red-striped awning, they spread their food on a cozy, little table, so cozy their knees touched.

"This is so much nicer than in Paris now," she sighed. "No mobs, no gunfire around the corner. Poor Paris."

"There were beautiful parks and trees and gaslights. We watched as it all was slowly desecrated. It is hard to forgive the Prussians, but Napoleon has to take some of the blame. It was beautiful before and will be again. The ladies in their fancy gowns and parasols strolling on the arms of their men. It will be that way again and we'll be back and be a part of it."

Ben went back in for tea to pair with their pastry. The creamy custard seeped from the thin flaky layers as they bit into their Napoleons "This is the best I have had lately," and he grinned like a little boy. "Although Lucie made wonderful custard when we could get milk. She made everything good."

"Are there pastry shops like this in London?" she asked, eyes wide.

"There are, but our cook, Mrs. Johnson, who lives with us, bakes wonderful things."

"On the way you can tell me about London."

"It will take less than a week, depending on how long we have to wait for a boat at Calais. Someday we'll take the boat to America." She knew it would never happen. Her heart beat fast. She felt like she had to hold on to the table. Every time the thought of being taken away entered her psychic, it seemed to be worse than the last.

"Sweetheart, are you okay? You had a horrible expression. Are you having pains?"

"No." she said quietly. "No! Just anticipation." He wasn't sure which anticipation she was referring to, there were so many. I'll talk to her later when we get on the rails.

"It is getting close to twelve o'clock, so we had better walk on over to the station house." Bags in hand they strode past shops, turned the corner and on a little further to where the steam engine would stop.

Not long the wind brought wafts of the tar-colored smoke rising above the distant tree line. The little, black beast chugged into view. Cheryl thought and smiled, Little Toot. As it advanced laboriously closer to the platform the engineer pulled the chain that released the ear splitting whistle announcing its arrival. Four passenger cars trailed and bringing up the rear, a tiny caboose. Toy or not, it looked wonderful to her after horse and carriage bouncing along rutted tracks through the dense forest and running creeks.

They boarded, found a seat and placed their bags in the seat facing them, hoping it would not be needed for passengers. She sighed and Ben put his arm around her and kissed her cheek. "We're on our way to Lille."

His little poetic phrase was funny and ordinary,

but she had to laugh at him. Sometimes he was such a boy — the boy she loved so passionately. "Will we have to get on another train at Lille?"

"This will go all the way. With a stop there we'll be in Calais by evening. Tomorrow I will inquire about a boat to good old England."

It was a short stop at Lille, long enough for Ben to get off and get crepes at the *Boulangerie* he saw from the carriage window. They enjoyed the treats as soon as he returned. Shortly the train was chugging through the countryside, children waving, tiny huts in the distance and fields being prepared for planting. The engineer would give a long or short toot to each as he passed. Cheryl laid her head on Ben's shoulder and closed her eyes. The repetitive motion of the carriage was calming and she fell into a light slumber. Ben studied his music.

The sun was far from overhead, but had not touched the horizon when they arrived in Calais. Out of the rail carriage they gazed around and saw many shops, taverns, and people scurrying about. Ben inquired at the station house about lodging for the night. The man gave him names of several inns in close proximity. Walking around and checking the outward appearance of each, they chose *La Maison de Jardin* and they asked to see the room. It was large, clean and more than adequate for the night.

After refreshing her body, Cheryl put on a skirt to be more presentable. She traded her riding jacket that smelled like horse for her heavy shawl.

There were many choices for supper. They chose one where ladies were eating with a companion. Roast beef, turnips and greens were a tasty mix. After a tart they strolled along the cobbles with others. It was nice to be moving around after the long ride with Little Toot.

The sun had fallen completely out of sight, and the Channel waters chilled the evening air. Back in their room, they realized their day had been without tragedy or harm.

"Tomorrow I will go to the docks and see what and when a boat leaves for Dover. We're so close darling, but I want tonight to be without end. I want to love you all night." He grinned, "Since you have rested all day."

"Well, that's why I did," she said with purpose.

∽

CHAPTER SIXTEEN

ꕥ

The following morning they slept late. After breakfast Ben was ready to go to the wharf.

"You stay sweet, and rest," he suggested. "You had to be tired after all of the traveling."

"All I do is rest, sleep and eat just like a dog." Ben frowned at her simile. "I'm not used to being so quiet, bodily or my mind. I haven't read much and I realize my exercise has to be limited. I hope when I get to London I can be more productive, although I'm not sure how." She was thinking about her career in science and all the time she had devoted to study was totally useless in this year. Will I ever be able to touch the computer keys or read a science journal? A distressing thought. Even more distressing, I may never see my parents again or Zach or electricity. But I'll support Ben and his music and be the best mother that I can be. Mother and wife will be my new career. The one consolation was that she loved Ben dearly.

He kissed her lightly and was off. Cheryl went to the courtyard and the fragrance followed her as she strolled around naming the flowers in her mind. Pansies, violets, lily-of-the-valley, primrose. She went back upstairs to their room and waited. The activity out the window was the same over and over. Horses trotting, people walking fast and slow, a few children playing. She caught a glimpse of Ben returning. Regardless of her distressing thoughts, her heart throbbed at the sight of him.

Upstairs he delivered the not so good news. "Boats are not crossing to Dover too often because the Prussian Navy is still floating around in the North Sea and harassing those crossing the Straits. Apparently some boats go down further where the Channel is wider to cross and then back up to Dover. The navy hasn't attacked, but has caused a couple bad accidents. No lives have been lost. So sail boats and others are reluctant to cross unnecessarily. The good news there are paddle steamers that come down the coast from Amsterdam and Belgium and from Calais some go over to Dover. They carry mail, some products and take a few passengers. There is no schedule. You just have to be there. I rented a room closer to the docks so we will know when one comes in and ready to leave."

He read the expression on her face and took her in his arms. "I'm sorry darling. I realize we shouldn't have come this way."

"It's okay. Everything will work out. I don't expect you, and I know I can't, always make perfect decisions. I'm bored, I want to be home, I want a hot bath, and you want your piano and we will. Please just know that I'm with you, love you and all will be well."

She wanted to be positive. She felt bad for him knowing how hard he was trying to make the right decisions.

They gathered their bags and walked to their new room. Not the best, but the best in the surrounding area that was available. It was an old inn trying to be presentable, but suffered from the indifferent weather from the North Sea, and disrespect of individuals who had lodged there before. The furniture scratched and broken. The rug was thread bare in places. No wood for the hearth, although June was extremely cool at night, it was deemed summer by the inn's owner. However, the bed coverlets were worn but clean. The wash bowl and pitcher was clean and no dust in the corners of the small room. These were the little things that made the inn go for another day.

"At least I can air out our clothes. I walk around leaving a trail of horse smells," she said, as she gave a little laugh but did not think it funny. She unpacked and hung their clothes around the room.

Ben stretched out on the bed and the springs squeaked as if they were in pain. "This is going to be fun. Every time one of us moves we'll wake the other and…" They settled in.

Sailboats, steamers and fishing boats bobbed in the harbor. Some were going down the coast of France, others headed back to Belgium. A few were waiting to cross the Channel.

"When was the last mail boat through here?"

"I did ask. Three days ago."

"So it could be a while."

"It could." He hated to say.

She crossed the small room and he opened his

arms for her. They snuggled into each other, and then relaxed on the squeaky bed and waited for the time to pass.

Each day Cheryl watched the wharf through the bubbly glass for new arrivals. Ben went several times a day for information. In the afternoon they would stroll away from the wharf to another part of Calais leaving the sounds and smells behind. The change of atmosphere was not inviting just different. Small houses, buckets and brooms by the doors. A dead cat in the street. Places to eat with week old smells rolling out the front door. She hated this existence. Tiring without exercising. Mind-numbing. Nothing to read. We hardly talk. It gives me a headache. London has to be better.

On the fifth day Ben went out early. The air was fresh and the sky was clear, but near the ground lay heavy fog. As he approached the docks he saw several boats that had arrived overnight. He inquired and found a paddle steamer that was crossing to Dover around midday, conditions prevailing. He jogged back to the room to give Cheryl the good news. He found her gazing out the window and forlorn.

"Cheryl love. I have good news."

She went to him forcing a smile. "Tell me, quickly."

"I found a paddle steamer flying a German flag that came down from Amsterdam last night and soon as it's loaded, will leave for Dover. They take passengers and I paid for two seats."

"What about the fog?"

"I asked a lot of questions and the fat little captain gave me good answers. He has a compass and has crossed many times in fog if it doesn't lift. Fog also deters the Prussian Navy from coming out."

"How big is a paddle steamer and it's German?"

"It also had an international flag because it carries mail. The captain spoke French well enough that we understood each other." He paused to answer her question. "This one is about twenty to twenty-five meters. It looks sturdy and has seats below deck. It shouldn't take more than an hour. We'll be in Dover for afternoon tea and berry scones."

"You paint such a sweet picture, Ben darling."

"I'm sorry for coming this way. I should have known my parents were not here. I felt since I was close I should check out the house to see if there had been damage from any of the battles. They were fought nearby. The caretaker may need to get in touch with my father. Please forgive me for a bad decision."

She touched his face. "It wasn't a bad decision, it's bad conditions."

"My darling wife, so understanding. How could I love you more?" He paused. "If we had gone straight from Paris the Channel trip would have been longer and the waters through there can be wicked."

She fell into his arm and tightened her eyes to hold back the tears. He held her close for comfort, but he felt he had failed her.

ᔓ

CHAPTER SEVENTEEN

ᔕ

*F*or the last time, they packed their smelly and wrinkled clothes and headed to the wharf. They wore their riding clothes for warmth. On shore in June it was typical, sunny with a cool breeze, but in the middle of the Channel it was always cold.

"Oh, for a bath and clean clothes," she expressed to Ben.

"Tonight. We'll take a bath together and get in my soft bed. That's a good thought to keep in mind while we're crossing."

Cheryl thought as she smiled, hot shower that so recently she rushed in and out of, would sound so wonderful.

As they walked Cheryl wanted to tell him in the future there would be a high-speed rail underneath the Straits. She had decided to tell him nothing about the situation that she was in. He would not understand. It would create a tension in their lives that could prove unnecessary. One day I'll just be gone. Then again I could live my entire life in this time and place. It bothered her beyond reason, but that was the decision she made and was going to let it be.

As they neared, the heavy breeze brought a mixture of smells that overwhelmed the olfactory lobe. Dead fish, perspiration, smoke, and other odors emanating from produce stacked along the wharf. It was a stench without a name making it necessary to breathe through the mouth.

Many different types of boats were in this large Calais harbor. Sail boats, large and small with their rigging reaching tall. Large steamers, their smoke stacks standing alone. Some were going up the coast to Belgium and the Netherlands, others down the coast of France and onward. They carried grains, bales of skins, wool and even livestock. Men were tossing sacks of produce onto the ships, calling in tandem with each throw. Voices in different languages calling loud and others speaking softly to each other. A cacophony of sounds that rose and fell like the tide.

"Some of these goods are bound for America. Passengers too. Someday we'll be on one to visit your America." Such a preposterous statement, my dear man, she thought.

Further on down the pier Ben stopped in front of a small steamer that was being loaded with sacks of mail. "This is it." He smiled at her as if he was offering a great discovery.

"Oh. It — looks sturdy," was all she could say. It was large enough and okay for a short trip across the narrow strip of water, but she knew it was not always gentle.

Two young families were also waiting to board. Cheryl thought they were immigrating to a new home and appeared to have just enough baggage to start over. Four adults and six children looking to be under ten years of age with wide eyes full of wonderment. For the children it was an adventure, but for the parents much apprehension had to fill their hearts.

Cheryl clung tightly to Ben as they tread the steep gangplank. Moisture and footsteps, over time had made it slick. Ben said, "We'll go below and claim a seat." They were settled when the two families joined them for the crossing. Ben helped them with their bags and their smiles and nods showed gratitude. Cheryl reminded him of his hand.

She smiled at one of the mothers and wondered where they were from and where they were going. The bits of language she could detect sounded Eastern European. Taking steps into the future takes courage beyond imagination, especially in these times, with little communication or medical possibilities. My trip from Paris to London pales to what they have undertaken. I have Ben to lead me into the future, if there is one here. If I ever get back to my time, I will treasure every moment of electricity, a hot shower and my microwave.

ഗ

Dover came into view. Cheryl had been anxious to see the White Cliffs, but she was in no condition to enjoy this famous scenery. The waves still leaping, the crew gave the engine a burst of steam and the paddles struggled into calmer water. With a bump and a thud the steamer hit the dock. The boat had defied the cruelty of Neptune and delivered the crew and passengers safely to the English shore.

It was not just the fog they had faced, but an unnatural storm that had given them a frightening and harrowing ride across the Channel.

About twenty minutes into the ride, the steamer gave an abnormal swing that got Ben's attention. He had crossed at Calais and further down the coast many times and nothing more to remember than smooth to extremely rough waters. This abrupt swing felt different and he warned Cheryl, "Brace yourself. I don't like the feel of this."

"Your expression tells me there could be more and worse." He hardly had time to nod yes, when another bigger wave struck the side. Everyone grabbed something to stay upright. It was turning ugly fast. The rolls of water got bigger and cracked as they made their impact, sending the boat right, then left and right again. Waves slapped the stern and smacked the bow. The boat pitched and tilted with the rhythm of the monstrous waves that were ear splitting and thunderous. Ben feared the next one was going to take them over and they all would drown in this cabin as one. Being hit by another wayward boat and crushed to death was another real possibility.

While the storm was raging outside, inside the cabin there was a different kind of storm. The children were crying and gagging as their half-digested meal filled their mouth and sprayed like actor's spit, only heavier. One of the mothers and all of the children needed help. There were not enough arms to hold their little heads or to keep them from being tossed about.

Ben could taste the juicy flavor of bacon and oatmeal in his warm mouth, but he swallowed hard and managed to keep it down. Cheryl was not so lucky. She could feel her breakfast coming and could not stop it. She hung her head and there was nothing to catch it, except the floor. With each wave her stomach lurched and emptied until there was nothing but thin yellow bile curling in her mouth. As she heaved she could feel as if her stomach was shriveling and collapsing in on itself. Her ravaged body felt like a shell. Nothing inside, just skin covering the bones. Although she had presence enough to know it was just a feeling and baby was still there along with the stomach and gut. Ben had braced himself and held her with one arm through the ordeal and with the other held a young child who had been tossed his way.

When the steamer stopped completely Cheryl slumped in her seat, her eyes closed and her face gray. It frightened Ben. He looked around at the other damages and it was not a pretty scene. Vomit everywhere, on sleeves, down the fronts of the coats, in hair. His boot had not escaped the spew. The stale air and shades of vomit in the small confined space was almost unbearable.

It was not long before the captain opened the hatch door and did not have to be told what he would find. The stench hit him hard. He apologized for Mother Nature, although no one gave him any attention, or did not understand his message in German.

Ben was trying to decide the best way to get Cheryl and their bags off the paddle steamer. He went on deck and let his eyes search the area. Not too far was a spot that resembled a park and it had benches. I'll take her there and come back for our bags.

He sat beside her when he returned. "I don't think I have ever been so sick for so long. It seemed like the whole trip," she said in a weak and almost inaudible voice.

"The children were sick too and one of the mothers. They had their hands full."

"I could have helped if I hadn't…" Her eyes closed and her head fell to the side. Ben knew he had to make a decision quickly, go on to London this evening or get a room.

"Cheryl love, can you walk? The station house is not too far."

"I'll try." She managed to hang on to Ben as he carried their bags. It was a short walk across the cobbles, but he was in constant fear that she was going to lose consciousness. To their benefit, the last rail was leaving for London in about an hour.

They were on it and Cheryl's limp body fell asleep in Ben's arms. As he pushed her hair back from her face, he thought, how fast she looked emaciated.

∽

They arrived at Sheffield Station just before dark. Cheryl had slept all the way. Her clothes smelled of vomit, dark circles under her eyes and mussed hair was the way she was going to meet his parents, although she was too weak to care. Ben didn't care either for he loved all those unsightly features. He was concerned about her well-being and their baby.

Ben found a hansom cab and said emphatically Burlington Row 55. My wife is sick, can we please hurry?" The driver hopped on the high seat and urged the horse into a steady clip.

Another thirty minutes and they were home. "Cheryl love we're here. Sweetheart, can you hear me? We're home."

"I can hear you. I lost my stomach not my hearing," she mumbled.

He jumped from the cab, and said, "Please wait till I get someone from the house." He ran to the porch, tried the door, locked, he slammed the iron knocker several times that said urgent. He knew one of the family members would answer the door, because their two servants would be in their quarters on the third floor this late in the evening.

His sister, Beth, was the closest to the door and opened it a crack and peeked out. She screamed, "Ben!"

"It's me, Beth," he said quickly, and gave her a kiss on her cheek. "I need help."

Their father, who was in the library nearby, heard her and ran thinking she was faced with a burglar. A large image shadowed the door way and he almost ran back for his pistol, when he realized it was Ben. "Oh god, boy, you're here. We have been so worried about you," and ran fast to get to his son. "We didn't know all winter if you were alive or what. God heard my prayers and brought you home."

Ben was trying to tell Beth something, after a brief hug, about someone in the cab. She did not wait for more information, but ran to the cab to see for herself. She looked at Cheryl rolled in a ball on the seat. She gasped and put her hands over her mouth. She ran back into the house just in time to hear Ben say to his father, "I love you and I have to get my wife."

Beth, eyes wide and astounded said, "Papa, his wife! She looks like a street woman from the East End! She smells awful!"

The carriage driver had their bags on the green when Ben got back. He pulled Cheryl up and into his arms, while his father and sister looked on in horror.

"His wife?" his father exclaimed as Ben rushed past him. He went straight to the lift and closed the door and up to his bedroom and laid her on his bed.

He helped her out of her foul smelling clothes down to her chemise and gently laid her back on the soft pillow.

"This is such a relief," she whispered. "Burn those clothes."

After Beth called her mother, she went to Ben's bedroom and paused at the door. "Beth, would you please bring a bowl of warm water and a cloth."

Suddenly his mother rushed in, her arms flailing. "Bennie. Oh Bennie! What's going on?"

"Mother, is that all you can say." He gave her a big hug and a kiss on her cheek.

"Your wife! When? What's wrong with her?" her expression was of disbelief. "Oh Bennie! Why didn't you tell us?" Her arms up as if she were surrendering. "We didn't know if you were alive." Both hands going to her face. "Bennie, why is your hand bandaged? Oh Bennie, say something."

"Mother, easy. We just came from a war zone and a harrowing trip across the Channel. We don't need this..." He stopped short of saying drama, realizing she was shocked, relieved and surprised all in the same package. "I will explain everything. It seems you didn't get my telegram I sent just before we left Paris saying we were on our way." He paused. "Not unusual. Paris is still in a mess."

"No! No! We didn't receive anything," she said, in a quieter voice as she pulled a handkerchief from her pocket and dabbed her eyes.

Beth arrived with a bowl of warm water and a cloth. Ben washed Cheryl's face and her arms. She was not unconscious, nor was she totally alert.

"Cheryl love," he said, as everyone looked on in a trance. At last they knew her name.

"I'm okay," barely audible and laughable had it not been so serious.

"I'm not so sure. Can you sit up?" She managed to sit and swing her legs around. He realized she was a little exposed, so he covered her shoulders and legs. She forced her eyes wide and looked at the people staring at her.

"Cheryl love, meet my mother Rebecca, my sister Beth and my papa William." He looked at Beth. "Where's Reggie?'

"My husband is at club tonight," she answered softly. "Had he known you would arrive he would have been here. But he will be here any time now."

Cheryl managed a smile. "I'm so sorry that I have to meet you like this. I've been very sick. It is a pleasure and please forgive me for looking so bad" Her voice weak but they detected an unusual accent.

Ben sat down on the edge of the bed with her and motioned for the others to sit too. He filled in the details about their trip from Paris and the Channel crossing. "I'll tell you later about our meeting and our wedding and the winter, the war. Our friends are okay. There is a lot." He paused and everybody waited. "And the best news of all, I am going to be a father." Beth gasped and put her hands to her face. Mother's mouth dropped open and eyes grew large. Father was stoic for a few moments, and then said, "I am going to be a grandfather." A tear welled in his eye.

When the tear was wiped away, the mouth closed and eyes relaxed, Ben asked if someone could bring Cheryl some hot broth.

By then Mrs. Johnson and Henry, their servants, were on the scene and Mrs. Johnson offered to get the broth and more food. "Food would be too much, thank you. Just a little broth for her stomach. We'll have a good breakfast tomorrow. Right now we need to wash up and get some rest. You have no ideas how much vomit there can be in such a small space and a short span of time."

Ben's mother and Beth were holding back at the thought of such a scene.

Mrs. Johnson returned with a large cup of beef broth. As Cheryl sipped slowly, the family decided to say good night "Bennie, we'll let you sleep as late as you want. We'll keep breakfast on the sideboard late."

"Thank you Mother, and good night all."

Cheryl did not want food or broth, but as she took more sips the warmth felt good in her body.

When she finished they went to the water closet. He helped her with the last few pieces of clothing. "Sit here next to the wash stand and I will wash you."

The warm cloth slid smoothly across her body. "It feels so good to be pampered." He dried her and then gave himself a once over.

"That bath I promised will have to wait until tomorrow, but there's a soft bed waiting."

"I hope you aren't feeling sexy. I'm too weak."

"I know darling. Do you want your gown?"

"Not that either, it's so filthy, I'll sleep without anything like you do."

"I have no objection." They went to Ben's bedroom and snuggled close, while sleep quickly crept into their bodies.

ᔕ

CHAPTER EIGHTEEN

ᔕ

The sunrise that streaked into the dusty sky or the heavy fog that hid the buildings was lost to Ben and Cheryl their first two weeks in London. Far below their bedroom was the kitchen. The aroma of bacon and fresh baked bread floated easily into their window. It was not enough to rouse them from their soft clean bed. Because of the war, the trip from Paris and the baby they were permitted the luxury of sleeping late. Breakfast remained on the sideboard for them. But family was still around, Mother and Beth always, often Beth's husband and Papa.

There were questions demanding answers. Cheryl was not interested in gossip. And Mother making plans for her son and his wife. The cook's inattention to the empty bread basket and the cold pot of tea sent the message they were disrupting her important schedule. These assertions and silent actions were an assault on the senses even in the late morning.

Ben had a galley kitchen in his section of their home. Cheryl decided for everyone's convenience to have breakfast, lunch and afternoon tea in their suite. Extra pans and dishes were added to the scant few already there. Ben arranged for a block of ice to be delivered daily. He liked the idea, but his mother did not.

They were home at last and both wanted a small feeling of independence. In the morning lingering over tea and *The Times* was a small luxury they needed. Cheryl wanted to boil their drinking water, and have vegetables that were not overcooked, or have a candlelight dinner with Ben. I want to be with him every moment I can. Often she flashed a mysterious stare at him. Oh Ben, if only I could tell you and you would understand. He knew her eyes were often speaking to him, but it was like an ancient script on parchment, he could see but not read.

The physical luxury was about all the family indulged Ben and Cheryl. They gathered each evening for dinner. The men discussed business, there was some gossip, household and social happenings interested everyone. Mingled in the conversation were innuendos directed at Cheryl. It would be better if you were not a foreigner. You speak strangely. Perhaps someone could talk for you. Bennie your sister wanted to have the first grandchild. Bennie you must get her some respectable clothes. Soon she can't go out. Alone these statements seemed innocent, but when Cheryl started putting them together, she realized that she had not been as accepted as it first appeared. Hoping the attitude would pass and not wanting to upset Ben, she ignored them.

Cheryl was gaining her strength and wanted to

see London in 1871. Ben took her to the new Brixton Market that had opened last year. The red berries and all shades of green vegetables delighted her sense of vision. Gazing down the aisles of produce, she reflected, how eternal is the market.

She was also pleased to find plain clothes. Two colored blouses and two skirts were immediately in her bag. She did not need a morning dress, a walking suit or a day dress as fashion dictated. There would be social engagements, musical evenings and Christmas, so she consented to have a few dresses made for these special events. With the help of the seamstress, they designed a few dresses that she could wear late in her pregnancy.

She also had to remember not to speak out of time. There could be a lot of questions that she would have trouble answering. She had to think hard about dates, but she remembered that the Science Museum was older than 1871 and requested a visit.

At the museum she was appalled at the crude instruments used to invade the body. An apparatus with a hand crank that turned a wheel was used to penetrate the skull, and the amputation kit with its jagged saws and picks or whatever they were. Advertised as new, she didn't want to imagine them being used. A sobering thought and soon to deliver her own child.

In her study of science she had never given much thought to older instruments of medicine, but these objects were eye opening. Weighing thoughts against reality, perhaps, somehow I can help bring some of these devices along in time. After baby, if I am still here.

As they rode home in the carriage, if I'm still here, kept running in her mind. Thoughts of being torn away were ever present, but life had been so overwhelming the last weeks they, for once, took second place. It would soon be summer, and she suddenly realized there had been no indication or any sense of her colleagues bringing her home. The concern was one sided, her side.

What should I be looking for, beams. That was a joke. Something physical. Maybe I should try ESP. Send a message. That's a laugh. She did not know what to expect, only if true to holography my image will return and leave nothing behind. The silence was disconcerting and frightening.

She squeezed his hand and gazed into his eyes, "I love you Ben. Finding you is the best in my life and always will be."

He acknowledged with a contented smile and a quick kiss. Never in a million years would he understand the meaning of her words.

Cheryl tired easily and Ben's piano practice kept them from going out every day. As the weeks rolled on they visited the British Museum, the National Gallery and other places she was interested in seeing. It was exciting for her to compare her time with the time she had been propelled into. Even with the enjoyment of seeing the famous landmarks, her unpleasant thoughts always invaded her senses. What if I hadn't met Ben or Jacques and his friends hadn't taken me in. I'd be wandering the streets of Paris and the reflection horrified her. I could have ended up in a worse situation than being here, Germany during World War II or a Roman harem. Another thought even worse, the possibility of having to leave Ben behind. I don't want to. I love him too much. It would be a hurt compared to death. Cruel and unusual punishment without a crime. Although if I go home now will I be able to take my baby with me, or would it vanish as my image vanished. Regardless how much she wished, she had absolutely no control over her desires and she sadly realized that fact. When alone, she hated the mental invasions and frequently chose gossip and embroidery with Rebecca and Beth in the morning room.

ᔓ

The family's large, gray stone home was surrounded by about two acres of gardens and lawn. Many evenings Ben and Cheryl walked among the evergreens and dogwood bushes. The flat stone path guided them past the summer flowers. The fragrance of yellow and red roses, pink carnations, meadow rue with its tiny pale green leaves and other colors and shapes were in abundance. The colors would brighten any day or rekindle hope. Statuettes, sundials and benches spaced around completed their park like area.

Inside Ben's mother had collected, over the years, French Baroque furniture for their home. Ornate with scrolls and curlicues, it fit well in this large structure. Window decoration, tufted chairs and sofas, and rugs held deep burgundy and greens of nature in the fall, as the colors flowed from room to room. There were shared spaces, such as living, dining, library and others, but each family had a private suite.

Cheryl suspected Ben had not decorated his area of the home. It was not feminine, but colorful and a little ornate. His rooms at Jacques were the colors of late autumn, soft browns, with a dash of bright colors.

He had explained one day that he had bought and arranged the furniture. His space here was comfortable and she molded into the surroundings.

What Cheryl liked most in their home was the music room referred to as Ben's piano room. It was decorated in shades of blue. An extra-large oriental rug covered the floor. Ornate book shelves held Ben's leather bound volumes and folders of music. The wall was ringed with artwork from the period just before and including the Impressionists. Ben's rosewood grand piano sat elegantly like a diamond on a velvet pillow, directly in front of three tall windows that formed an arc. An afternoon breeze often glided easily through the long sheers.

One day after Ben had practiced and as he lay with his head in her lap, she asked, "Tell me about the paintings. Where did you get them?" She knew they were masterpieces and would be priceless in the future.

"My mother, over the years traveling with my father, purchased most of them. I bought a few in Paris. That one," he pointed above the sofa, "I bought from Edgar. He is so happy the war is over so he can get back to painting." Cheryl knew he would do hundreds more. She especially loved his blue dancers, yet to grace the art world.

Her question was all Ben needed. He got up, took her hand and walked to the end of the room. "This is a Delacroix, Eugene. He was French, but spent some time here in England and Mother bought it at a small shop here in London. His paintings are so dark, not just color but the impression. This bowl of flowers you would expect bright colors, but they too are dark. He was capturing a different mood. Just like music, every composition has a specific personality. We have two others, one in my parents' suite and the other down the hall."

"Just the opposite of Renoir," as she pointed to the next one. Oh, how would I know? Ben said nothing.

"We all love the Renoirs. Mother bought them in Paris, The reds, oranges and greens together are vibrant, yet there is softness about them."

Cheryl wondered which one he was doing when they saw him painting by the Seine. It's probably in New York or Washington.

"There are a lot of Renoirs in the house."

"I thought the one in your bedroom was."

"Yes, I bought that one myself in Paris when I first went there for recitals."

"I wasn't sure," Cheryl said, as they moved along.

"It's a Jean Baptiste Corot. This one and two others Mother got in Italy when they first went there on business. She liked the haunting feeling of his landscapes. It does pull you in — in a mysterious way. We all like the landscapes of Camille, too," as they gazed at the next one.

She recognized the Pissarro. "You speak like you know him."

"No, I met him a few times. Jacques and I occasionally went with Edouard to the café before the war, and he was usually there."

Three small Parisian street scenes hung by the door. "Can you guess?" Cheryl could not place the style. They were beautiful and colorful, but they could be by anyone.

"Edouard."

"Oh, I should have recognized them. I love his work." She paused. "And the colors from all the art work blends so beautifully with the other colors in this room. It is a wonderful place to play, almost spiritual."

"As I play Chopin and gaze at a Renoir they become one in beauty. I can see a little bit of Paris. It was beautiful once and a fascinating place before the war and will be again. There is another of Edouard's in the library and my sister and Reggie have two in their suite."

He turned and pulled her close in his arms and looked up and far away. "How we come by a canvas and a sheet of music is rather novel. Think darling, a little jar of red or green liquid and a few strokes placed here and there, can become a landscape or a vase of roses to live through the ages. And also a bunch of little, black elliptical shapes to become a symphony. Each having a different emotional impact on our senses." He paused. "How such unimaginable little things can become things of beauty. All this color and music leads to another thing of beauty, making love."

She cupped her hands around his dark brown beard and whispered, "First your music and now your words have put me in a very sensuous mood."

They walked upstairs and into their suite. Ben locked the door and thought I should get a Do Not Disturb sign, but then….

He unbuttoned her blouse and slipped it off her shoulders and fondled her full and firm breast as he kissed her lips. Her skirt and underthings fell easily and she sat on the edge of the bed and watched him undress. With the shed of each piece of clothing her heart beat faster.

Their love was slow and without effort it moved gracefully between their bodies. It floated up mountains, it whipped with the wind, and it drifted slowly as the moon and then the last rush to complete its journey home. In each other's arms they fell in a peaceful afternoon nap.

They woke later and found it necessary for a little more caressing and touching and soft words before dressing. Cheryl made tea and they sat at the tiny table overlooking the garden full of scarlet, royal and sunshine colors of summer. Holding hands, they thought, what pleasures of making love really meant, especially when their love for each other was so deep.

ᔓᔕ

CHAPTER NINETEEN

ᔕ

Lightning crackled silently and thunder blasted loudly in the dark morning sky. Rivulets and circles of water rolled down the window panes. The weather woke Ben. He quietly slipped out of bed.

He went downstairs to breakfast and joined Reggie and Papa for eggs, bacon and sweet cakes, Mrs. Johnson's specialty. Their conversation was casual and Papa told his breakfast companions that he and Rebecca would be leaving next week for Belgium and would probably be gone for about a month.

Ben told of his plans. Tomorrow he had an appointment with his agent, Sir Keller Prymn. "My hand is well and I spent all winter planning for this moment when I can get back to work. I feel like I am back in shape. Fortunately my hand injury happened while we were traveling, and I couldn't practice anyway. Practice is where I am headed now." He paused, "Where's Mother? Has she been to breakfast?"

"Yes, and already busy with her daily activities," his father replied.

Before Ben went to practice he went back upstairs with tea, rolls and eggs for Cheryl. She was up and they sat by the window as she ate. She said she was tired and wanted to go back to bed. He gave her a quick kiss and went to practice.

In his piano room, he went through his finger exercises and then to the sofa to choose new music and organize a recital presentation. Not long after he heard footsteps. He knew it had to be his mother.

She noticed that Ben was alone, and just what she had been waiting for.

"Oh, you *are* alone. I don't want to intrude."

"Mother, you would never intrude. Please sit."

"It's nice to get you alone. She is always underfoot. Where is she?"

"I took her tea and rolls, but she was still tired and wanted to go back to sleep."

"She couldn't get up and make you breakfast. Wasn't that the purpose of stocking your kitchen?"

"Mother, there was breakfast down here, or I am perfectly capable of making my own. She is going to have our baby and needs her rest. She knows what is best for her."

"I don't know how she knows."

"Mother, in America she is a scientist and studied the body."

"What was she doing in Paris?"

Ben had not explained her complete story to the family. He wasn't sure he knew all of it himself. "She was in southern France teaching and felt threatened and came to Paris on her way to America. That's where I met her. That I spoke English, I knew she needed my help and we fell in love."

"I believe she told Beth she was lost and ended up in Paris."

"Well, that is about the same thing."

"Not exactly Bennie. She told William she might still be going back to America."

"Papa must have misunderstood. She has no plans to leave. We have talked about visiting someday."

"She also doesn't seem to understand she can't go out when she gets bigger with that child."

"That child is my son or daughter and your grandchild. She is not ashamed of our baby and neither am I. She will go out when she wants to."

"Not in my presence. Bennie, you have changed so much since we last saw you. I do believe it's all her fault. There is something strange about her. I don't understand you don't see that."

"There is nothing strange about either one of us. I just went through a war. She just went through a traumatic escape from god knows what. She still fears she is being followed. They told her not to leave. These are fears like the war that don't leave you immediately. She is my wife and I love her more than you can imagine." Speculating about the future, he continued, "When our baby comes, he will be ours to raise. He will complete my family just like me and Beth did for you and Dad. No handing him over to a nanny or nurse — I love you Mother and always will, but now I am Ben — not Bennie."

She stared straight ahead not knowing what to say. "Forgive me darling child. Everything has happened so fast. We were so worried about you all winter. I do want the best for you."

"And Cheryl and our baby." He looked out the window. "Mother the war left something with me, although I don't have a name for it. Finding Cheryl and falling in love helped me to slowly put it aside. On our way here we witnessed a young man shot in the back by a Prussian soldier. I saw people near starvation. I killed two Prussian soldiers that we found inside the city. I killed another as he stared directly into my eyes. He had a knife against Jacques' neck. I felt it too, icy and razor sharp. I pulled the trigger and he fell at my feet. We didn't have street fighting until the French troops and disgruntled citizens took up their cause of dissatisfaction with the armistice. That's when Jean-Pierre got shot just trying to get out of the way. They were completely innocent, thankfully it wasn't worse and he's well now." He shuffled his music in discomfort. "Cheryl's escape was awful for her too, and she still isn't ready to talk about it." He looked at his mother and tears were streaming down her face. "I'm sorry, I didn't mean to upset you, but only to help you understand what we have been through."

"I just can't imagine. We'll do our best for both of you." She rose and laid her hand on his shoulder.

"Tomorrow I'm going to see my agent and start scheduling recitals. My hand is well and I've been practicing. I feel I'm ready to start my life again after carrying a rifle all winter."

Their talk lasted longer than both planned and was more confrontational than either expected, but in the end he had helped his mother understand his winter at war.

ಌ

The next day after breakfast Ben dressed, kissed Cheryl goodbye and was on his way to meet with his agent. Later he was going to have lunch with Reggie at his club.

The day was brighter than yesterday. The scattered clouds shared the sky with the sun. Yesterday Cheryl had not felt well, or was just tired, and left their suite only for dinner. Feeling much better today she decided to get some fresh air and exercise before joining Ben's mother and Beth in the morning room.

The room overlooked a small area of the vast garden. They watched Cheryl as she exited the side door and leisurely looked at the new carnations, roses and a few others flowers along the path. She started to walk faster to give her body some much needed exercise.

Beth looked up from her embroidery, and watched Cheryl as she moved quickly into the distance. Suddenly Cheryl disappeared from view.

"Oh! — Mother! I was watching Cheryl and she just disappeared before my eyes."

"Elizabeth, that is impossible! She was quite a distance. You must have looked at your work when she took a quick turn."

"No Mother, she was there and then she wasn't!"

"Hush, such silliness."

ಌ

Cheryl was dazed as she sat on a bench in

another part of the garden. She felt empty and confused. She looked at her surroundings. I don't remember that sundial. I was walking among the flowers. Did I wander over here in a stupor? She turned slightly and was relieved to see Ben's house. She was afraid to get up for fear of passing out again. She stood up and felt okay after taking a few steps. She walked back into the house and went to the morning room.

Beth immediately asked her, "I saw you one moment and the next you disappeared. What happened?"

"Oh… I must… there are a lot of tall flowers out there."

"See darling," Rebecca said. "Now, no more."

Cheryl instantly knew and it hit her hard. She picked up her knitting and was trembling so badly she could not slip her yarn or get her needles to function. She quickly put the bundle down hoping neither had noticed she was upset.

"You hardly did anything and you're going to quit," Rebecca said.

"I know but I believe the walk made me dizzy, and I am going to excuse myself and rest." Cheryl left without further explanation.

She fell on their bed, her head in her arms, breathing hard and fast. It wasn't her imagination. She knew her lab had at last found an equation to move her around. They probably don't even know that it's affecting me. What is going to happen to my baby? Oh, please not now, if ever, or let me be alone when it happens. They can think I was kidnapped as I've alluded to. She waited for something to happen. She wanted to cry but the tears would not come. The only thing she felt was the fear she had no control over.

Hearing footsteps brought her out of a light sleep. Oh god, where am I? She turned and looked up and saw Ben leaning over her. Relief ran through her body. He was her protector and love.

"Cheryl love, Mother said you didn't stay long and appeared unwell. I rushed right up here. Darling, what's wrong?"

"No! No Ben, I felt a little weak after I walked in the garden and wanted to rest."

"You look a bit pale."

"I'm all right. How was your meeting with Sir Prymn?"

"Wonderful. I didn't know what to expect after not being here all winter. He said they all understood that I was trapped and was concerned about my well-being. He offered congratulations to us and our baby. He scheduled three recitals. First at the Gallery in two weeks and a reception after. I can't wait to introduce you to a lot of nice people. Too bad Mother and Dad won't be here, but Reggie and Beth will be. Then at the Vista the following Saturday."

She gave him a congratulatory hug and warm kiss. "I am excited for you. At last you're getting back to where you want to be."

"That's not all. One bigger one at the end of September at St. James Hall. There are about twenty-five hundred seats."

"Ben, I'm as thrilled as you are. Did he mention the continent?"

"Yes, he'll start working on that, starting with Vienna. He also wants to schedule one at Oxford soon. He has to get in touch with them first. And Paris again."

"Speaking of Paris, you have a letter."

Ben offered highlights as he read. "Jacques and Elise got married two weeks ago. They opened the store. Henri and Janine went home. And Renée and Jean-Pierre are with her mother and making wedding plans. The garden is growing. They have a new family member."

"A baby! No, it can't be."

"Fanny, a briard. He writes she is darker than Jacquie and more independent."

"Jacques is happy. He has his two loves, Elise and a new doggie."

He continued reading. "The peace agreement was finally signed. But the last week of May was about the worst of all of this. There were fires all over the city and an awful lot of people killed. None of us left our building for the whole week. We thank God that it only lasted a week. It was absolutely horrible. The store is keeping Elise busy. Here darling you can read it, although that's about all the news." As he handed her the letter, he continued, "Sounds like we got out just in time."

As Ben read the letter, Cheryl's incident in the garden slipped out of her mind momentarily. She had hoped Beth or his mother would not say more.

ೞ

After dinner Ben and Cheryl relaxed on a bench in the back of the garden, although she had hesitated when he suggested a walk. He held her hand in her lap. The sky was cloudless and the sounds of the city were far away. Cheryl wanted time to stop. I can't imagine being anywhere else but with Ben, forever. Forever had nearly vanished before her eyes earlier in the day. It could and probably would happen again. Fortunately she had only been sent to the other side of the garden. Next time it could be to anywhere or to any time. Fear raked and scraped her mind. I don't want to leave Ben and our baby. Please God hear my prayer.

Ben felt her hand trembling, and asked, "Are you cold?" And he glanced her way and noticed she was white. "Cheryl love, you're pale. Do you feel all right?"

"I'm fine." She thought it sounded convincing, but she had to get her mind directed to another path.

"I am so excited for you that you can, at last, express your love of music. How did you know at a young age that piano was going to be your life?"

"I'm not sure. It has been with me for so long. I believe a governess who traveled with us when my sister and I were young set the foundation. She was musical and would tell us stories that were full of music. I remember they were about fairyland. There was always a piano in the fairy house and they sang and danced. She played piano and sang little nursery rhymes for us. One day I wanted to try to play and she let me. Then she taught me more and convinced my parents that I had talent and they started formal lessons. Here I am today."

"She sounded like a perfect governess. Any other one might have missed your talent."

"I certainly believe that. After formal school I studied with Koenig. He helped me understand the secret emotion that each composition might be holding. Like Chopin's Revolutionary Etude — it rolls." Cheryl smiled knowing which one he meant. "So when you play, make it roll. Others skip along or dance smoothly. Each piece has its own personality, in part or whole, and the one who plays has to find that message in order to interpret."

"Ben darling," and she squeezed his hand, "you have so opened my eyes to the world of music. And think, it touches only one of our senses, hearing. Many others take several to express themselves. Painting you can see and touch. My dress you can feel and see. I've been so wrapped up in science all of my life, and its ever changing challenge is so very interesting. I get excited when new concepts are released in science, at least for me, but it lacks the emotions I found in music, your music especially. If I had never met you I probably would have missed a part of life that is so beautiful and touches my soul so deeply."

"I too am very thankful to have music in my life. It takes me into a heavenly glaze. I live on a different plain. I almost see music." He turned and gave her a quick kiss on the lips. "You have taken me on a different plain as well. All the music in my life, I discovered, was only half of me. You and your love have filled the other half and now I'm complete."

"Ben, you fill my life with yourself and brought music along. You are my all."

He shook his head, smiled and laughed. "About the best thing I've heard about myself, I will accept."

She shivered slightly. "Cold. It's pushing dark. Let's go in."

"Okay, but I love these moments with you."

As they walked back to the house she savored the warmth of his hand in hers. Her thoughts were of all the wonderful things he had been to her. His patience, concern. His expression of love for her. How much she loved him. And one day just without explanation having to leave him behind. She suddenly broke into a sob and her breath caught. Ben was startled and turned to her. "Oh, Cheryl love." And he took her in his arms and held her close, waiting for her sobs to wane.

CHAPTER TWENTY

ᔓ

Sunshine peeked shyly through the cracks between the drapes into their bedroom. Bells on the ice and milk wagons created a rhythm as they started and stopped at the homes along Burlington. The horses whinnied to each other in recognition. The most enticing was the fresh air that carried the aroma of bacon and baking sweet cakes up and into their bedroom window.

"My sweetheart, we have to go to breakfast today. It's a sendoff for Mother and Dad on their business trip."

"I'll make it," her head sunk deep in her pillow.

"I have enjoyed sleeping late too. It's a welcome after last winter. He rolled over and faced her. "I know we have to get going, but let me hold you for just a moment or two. It helps my day to begin in the right way." She stretched her arms to receive him and they lay close, no words needed to express their love.

Ben made tea to help the waking process. Dressed, they joined the family in the breakfast room.

Mrs. Johnson outdid herself today. Beef slices, mutton in cream, and strawberries were presented with the bacon, eggs and apple sweet cakes. The conversation was light and pleasant.

William expressed, “I hope the weather is as good in the Channel as it’s here. Then we hug the coast to Belgium where the waters aren’t rough at all.”

Cheryl said, “I hope for you too. That’s where I lost my strength.”

Ben added, “It was one of the worst crossings I’ve ever had.” He looked at Cheryl, “I’m so sorry you had to experience it.”

“Our boat is a large steamer not a little paddle boat.” Ben’s father added humorously.

“Dad, we wanted to get home. We had already waited five days in Calais, and our room, not so pleasant. By now the Prussian Navy should have gone home. Are you going to Cambrai?”

The thought of Cambrai and her near encounter with the Prussian soldiers lived quickly in Cheryl’s eyes and Ben saw it happen. He took her hand and changed the subject.

“Not this trip, since you were there recently.”

“Dad, you and Mother will miss my first recital, but hopefully you will be back for the ones in September.”

“Oh Ben, we have the privilege of hearing you every day,” his mother added.

He realized she had called him Ben. Maybe our little talk did sink in. “Here at home I start and stop, repeat passages over and over, people coming and going. It's much better to sit and listen all the way through in a classical environment as beautiful as St. James Hall. The red and gold ceiling and, the little sparkling gas jets suspended like stars hanging in the heavens. It's a wonderful mood for the artist and the audience. Posters and announcements went out the day after I was at Sir Prymn's."

"We got them at the bank and the club. And at the club there was a lot of talk about attending," Reggie added.

"That's good to hear that I haven't been forgotten. The Gallery and the Vista seat only about two hundred or so, but St. James Hall seats about twenty-five hundred," Ben added. They continued their conversation until Henry announced the carriage had arrived for Mr. and Mrs. Rutherford. They all walked to the foyer and hugs and kisses were exchanged and they were off.

Ben went to practice and Cheryl curled up with an art book she found in their library. "You will be able to get a lot done with this early start."

"Tomorrow I will do the same thing and then if you would like, I'll take you and Beth to the market."

"I'd love to get some more fresh vegetables. I'm sure Beth would like to go."

Ben continued to practice and Cheryl went for a walk in the garden by herself. She wondered if the garden had anything to do with her receiving the equation. Not possible and she tried to forget the thought.

The next day was another with desirable weather. Feathery clouds floated in the deep empty sky. Ben finished his practice and they were on their way to the market by mid-morning. Beth's trips out were mostly with her mother to visit and take tea. She was excited to go with Ben and Cheryl.

High season and the market was filled with vegetables and fruits of all kinds. All three quickly had several bundles. Ben was a few steps ahead of Cheryl. She was paying for a bundle of asparagus when she made a low but desperate call. Ben turned around just in time to take two big steps and catch her in outstretched arms before she hit the floor. She stared at him as if she did not know him or where she was. She appeared to be near passing out. Ben picked her up and carried her to a grassy area and sat her on a bench. Beth quickly grabbed all the bundles, and followed him.

A crowd quickly gathered with advice. Raise her arms, pat her on her back. Someone brought a wet cloth and Ben put it on her head. Another brought a glass of water. She blinked several times, shook her head, smiled and took a sip. All life stood still waiting for her to respond.

"Cheryl love, what happened?"

"I don't know — did I pass out?" Thinking of her baby, "Did I fall?"

"No, I turned just in time to catch you."

She sat for a few more moments. "Oh… Ben… I think I'm okay."

Ben looked at Beth loaded with their purchases, said, "I believe we have enough and should go home."

When they arrived home Beth sorted the bags and Ben put theirs away.

"I want you to rest. I am taking a pillow and coverlet and you can lie down on the sofa in the piano room. I want to practice but I want to be near you. Maybe you can sleep if my playing isn't too loud."

She insisted she was okay, although she thought of their baby and rest would not hurt. She was glad her mother-in-law was not there to see her stretched out on the sofa in one of the main rooms of the house. She closed her eyes, but thought interfered with sleep. Concerned at what had happened wasn't some bodily condition. It was her lab tinkering with her being. As her thoughts blurred and Ben's music ebbed and flowed from her consciousness, she slipped to the edge of sleep.

Later, she sat up and Ben went to her side. He saw that mysterious stare again and it troubled him. Is something happening to her mentally? He knew of depression in pregnancy and other changes in a woman's body, but not enough to know what was normal or expected. Maybe my father can enlighten me. It would be better to asked mother, but that could be delicate.

Cheryl felt better when the four gathered for their evening meal. Reggie had banking news that interested no one, but they listened politely. They discussed where Mother and Father might be at this time. Beth expressed how glad that Ben and Cheryl were here. Last year she was alone all day and some of the evenings when her parents were away on business.

"After dessert Ben suggested to Cheryl. "How about a stroll along the street and see if any of the neighbors are out. There is a lot to see in our garden, but the street will be a change of scenery, since I suggest you not go out there alone." He asked Reggie and Beth to join them but they declined for personal time upstairs.

Cheryl was willing and Ben got her shawl and draped it around her shoulders. He couldn't resist a quick kiss.

It was that comfortable silence they enjoyed as they slowly passed the old trees, the gas lights and the stone mansions similar to theirs.

"Darling Ben, always know that I love you now and forever will, regardless of what happens."

That startled him although he did not show it outwardly. "Cheryl love, why are you talking this way? It disturbs me."

"Having a baby in the mid-nineteenth century is a risk."

"Have you not felt him moving?"

"Oh, I have and tonight when we are trying to sleep he will be up and moving around."

"Then darling, what's bothering you? I've felt this for several weeks."

"It's hard to explain. I don't understand why I have been passing out."

That confirmed to Ben that it had happened more than once. "Darling is there something physically wrong that I should know about?"

"I'm not sure."

"Tell me," he stated emphatically, but with love.

She thought, if only I could. But it's best that I don't. We'll just let fate play its hand. "Nothing that I know exactly. I'm thinking what could happen. I keep thinking about the officials at school, with their threats."

"Oh, Cheryl love, I will protect you. Just don't leave our property without me. Do you want to carry my pistol when you go in the garden? Maybe I should start again."

"No." And she found a smile.

"Please let me know if you are ill then we can get the doctor. Promise me that."

"I will."

They reached the far end of their street near the cathedral when they decided to return. They walked back in the shadows of dusk. Just before the door Ben turned, "I'll go to the ends of the earth for you, body and soul."

"I know and I love you for that and everything else that you are." She gazed into his eyes and he saw that the mysterious stare was absent.

The next day Ben was practicing and Cheryl was in the library when Beth joined her. Cheryl's bag lay open on the library table, and a small rectangular-shaped gadget with a shiny black face was exposed.

"Cheryl, that thing is humming! What is it?"

Cheryl gently pushed the off button and started to push it back in her bag.

"May I see it? Why is it making that noise?"

"It's just a thing I brought from America. It doesn't work anymore." She pulled it out and held it so Beth could see it.

"How do you use it?

"It is used in science experiments as a reflector, and you have to be near a tower in the science lab for it to work. I can't show you because it's broken. I dropped it several times. That's why it only hums." Cheryl knew her explanation was not very plausible. It was all she could come up with quickly. It concerned her as much as it had Beth. They must know I have my cell, and in the lab are using it somehow. I'm not thinking clearly and that's not possible. Yet it frightened her. She knew she had to hide it in the back of her linen chest and hope it stayed mute.

ಌ

The day after, Beth found Ben in the kitchen, coaxed him into the garden and although reluctantly, told him everything that she thought strange. She always has her bag. That weird humming device. Her disappearance in the garden. Her being upset after returning from the garden.

"She has said she still fears they might come for her. I cannot understand that. She doesn't understand that either or she doesn't want to tell me. Maybe it was something clandestine and they think she knows more than she does." He looked into the sky shaking his head, confused. "Maybe she has her bag for personal stuff if she is kidnapped. She is living with something that I believe is worrying her. Beth, it disturbs me too, but I'm sure it will work out. I just wish she would confide in me more." Ben kept seeing Cheryl's eyes and that message he was missing.

The dinner topic was mainly about Ben's recitals. "After the Gallery performance there is to be a reception. That was nice of them to plan one," Ben offered. "Then the next week-end at the Vista Circle, as it's named, the platform with the piano is in the middle and the seating all around. You are close to the people when you play and I like that."

"After you get started, you will not even know they are there," Cheryl said. "You will be in your own world as you play."

"True."

"I am so excited for you Ben. We waited for so long for this to happen again. We were so worried all winter," his sister said lovingly. "We were ecstatic when we heard about the armistice, then we heard of street fighting. We were awfully worried. Mother was frantic at times. Every morning we would get up thinking maybe we would hear today."

"I felt bad because I knew you would be worried, but only important messages were going out. But then if I hadn't been there I would never have met the love of my life." He paused with a smile for Cheryl. "I'm looking forward to playing at St. James Hall. I played there two years ago, remember Beth. This will be a perfect launch back into my career. Sir Prymn wants to schedule a recital at Oxford the last week of October, but I didn't promise because you probably shouldn't travel that distance. And I don't want to leave you." He gazed lovingly at her.

"Ben, you're so sweet, but just getting back to performing, please don't pass up such a wonderful chance. How far is it and how long would you be gone?"

"Oxford is about ninety kilometers and I'd be gone no more than three days."

"That's not long, please accept. Your parents will be back by then and if they aren't Beth is here, Henry, Mrs. Johnson. I'll be fine. I would like to go, but there will be other times." Her thoughts seized her, other times, could be in my future, 2018.

"If you are sure, I will tell Sir Prymn to schedule. Then until after the baby comes, I will stay in London to be near you. There will be the holidays and there will be playing, singing and eating. It won't be a dull time."

CHAPTER TWENTY-ONE

ও

*T*he sun beamed in the robin-egg blue sky the day of Ben's recital at the Gallery. Last evening ended late so it made the morning also late. They had breakfast with Reggie and Beth in their robes. Mother would never have approved, but she wasn't home. It was always a more relaxed atmosphere when their parents were away. Cheryl noticed even Reggie and Beth were more openly affectionate when the parents were not around.

Ben practiced and then they both napped. It was going to be a long evening. After the usual light dinner of cold meats, salad and custard, they all went to dress.

Cheryl let Ben choose which of her new dresses to wear. "I like the medium green. It's just a few shades more than soft and wonderful with your dark blond hair. Is it linen?"

It's silk rayon. It doesn't hide our little one."

"Cheryl love, if you're comfortable, I'm

comfortable. You're radiant with Baby."

The carriage arrived at the determined hour and the four boarded and were driven to the Gallery. Arriving, they saw the Gallery garden filled with ladies in colorful gowns and their gentlemen in formal wear, greeting and conversing before the musical evening. Reggie, Beth and Cheryl joined those in the garden. Ben went to check the piano and then to the anteroom.

The candelabrum suspended from the ceiling was lit, and the crowd strolled in and was seated. Cheryl thought this room is hauntingly seductive. Even more so as she watched Ben enter and step upon the low platform near his piano He bowed, smiling all the way down and all the way up. The crowd was saying welcome back. They had not forgotten him.

He opened with the powerful Revolutionary Étude and made it roll, as he had described it, all the way to the demanding final chords. He paused briefly before the next and the next. He played with his heart as his fingers glided smoothly across the keys. He let each composition speak for itself just touching the keys in the right place. Once again Ben made those little black ellipses become a thing of beauty.

Afterward, he quickly found Cheryl, Beth and Reggie to join him in the reception line. He introduced Cheryl a hundred times, each with a little more love in his voice. A slight edge came off the delight when every woman glanced quickly at her growing belly. She realized it was novel to see a woman in public at this stage of her pregnancy. Maybe I can change this custom a little earlier than history has it and start a lot of gossip along the way.

Going home he received a loving kiss from

Cheryl as praise, "Sweetheart, you were wonderful."

"I played for you. You're my muse." She squeezed his hand and played her finger in his.

Beth and Reggie offered their words of praise. "Ben, my brother, I believe it was the best you have ever played. I'm so proud of you. Aren't we Reggie?"

"Definitely a beautiful evening. Monday at the bank I'll receive all the congratulations for you."

ശ

Reddish patches on the leaves, cooler nights, fog and mist pushed September into its place. The colorful flowers of summer were bygones. William and Rebecca returned with gifts for all. Clothes, small mementoes, packaged food. It was like Christmas without a tree. One item Ben especially liked was a little metal box with raised images of composers painted in bright colors with their names below the relief.

"Ben, your mother nearly ran me over getting to that box after she saw it. She knew you would love it."

"I do. It's a perfect size for special things," he said, as he ran his fingers over the images. "Beethoven, Schubert, Chopin."

Rebecca brought gold earrings and a matching necklace for Cheryl and a similar set for Beth. Hand embroidered evening gloves for both the girls that were made in Italy. Rebecca did not forget Mrs. Johnson, although she was not present.

Ben started to thank them both for the gifts, when his father interrupted him, and said, "That's not all." He reached under the table and brought up a canvas bag. He slowly unwrapped two bottles of Raynal French Brandy for Ben and Reggie. "Not for just after dinner. Remember that cough in the winter." Everyone laughed at William's subtlety. "There's one for Henry. I'll see that he gets it. And a few left over for Christmas."

"We all thank you. Glad you're home safely and are here for my next recital." Other thanks were echoed.

The daily routine soon fell into place. Reggie and William had their offices and clubs. Mother and Beth visited and embroidered. Ben practiced. Cheryl felt she did not have much to do, not even cleaning or tidying their suite. Baby would soon be her important new career, motherhood. She was working on making things for their baby, along with Rebecca and Beth. She had a little over two months to wait, but when alone her thoughts disturbed her. To add to the original she was concerned about giving birth in this time. Even reading a new Dickens novel didn't ease her mind.

Nothing had happened in a while that she felt was from her lab, which allowed her to relax. Maybe they have given up looking for me.

As the days passed her emotional state improved. She slept well and they loved often. A good appetite. She and Ben accepted several small social engagements. They prepared the room for the baby. Henry helped Ben with new white, linen window covering to make it brighter. Each time they shopped she added to the layette. The museums or the art gallery were on their schedule, time and weather permitting.

One day Cheryl was in the library when Rebecca casually strolled in. Cheryl asked her about Belgium and their business associates, the weather and overall was it a good trip. She mentioned how sad Paris was when they left, and in Jacques' letter he said everyone was working together for its recovery.

"And Paris, how *did* you meet Ben?"

Cheryl was instantly uncomfortable, because she was not sure what Ben had told her. "It was a group of people and he was there." Hoping she was vague enough she changed the subject. "Tomorrow is Ben's recital and he's so glad you're back. The one at the Gallery was so well received. He played his heart out. You could see and feel he loved every moment of it. He'll do it all over again tomorrow evening."

"And Ben tells me you are going."

"Of course I'm going. I wouldn't miss it. Why shouldn't I?"

"Well, we'll see," she answered cryptically.

"I don't understand Rebecca." Cheryl knew, but wanted to hear directly, not innuendos.

And she did. "Dear girl, you are getting big with child."

"And I am so happy about that. The doctor says I'm doing well."

"That's good, but you should not be seen in public."

"That's ridiculous. Where I came from women work until two weeks before their baby is born." Cheryl was so incensed she almost said even TV anchors worked when they are pregnant. That would have no meaning and she excused herself before she said something she would regret.

She did not say anything to Ben about her conversation with his mother. She did not want to upset him before his recital.

The day of his performance they had a light dinner together. Everyone was in a relaxed and happy mood. Ben was to leave early to select a piano that would be rolled into the circle. Cheryl was to come later with the family.

A knock on their door alerted Ben that his carriage was waiting. He kissed Cheryl on the cheek and said, "See you after and ride home with you."

"Good luck with a piano."

Shortly after Ben left there was another light knock on their door.

"Rebecca. Come in."

"No thanks, I wanted to tell you we will be leaving at seven-fifteen. No need to come down before then." She turned quickly and walked briskly down the hall.

"Thank you." She left so fast Cheryl wasn't sure she heard her.

Ready with her hair flowing, as Ben requested, and wearing her deep rose gown, she sat by the window waiting for seven-fifteen. A few seconds before, she took her evening bag and went downstairs. To her surprise it was all quiet and no one was around. No waiting carriage. In the library she glanced at the mantel clock, exactly seven-fifteen. She walked to the back of the house and Henry was just going upstairs.

"Henry."

"Yes ma'am. May I help you?"

"We were supposed to leave at seven-fifteen. Where is everyone?"

"They left earlier my dear." He looked bewildered. "And I heard the Mrs. tell Beth you had decided not to go, because…" and he dropped his head.

"Because my child is showing."

"Yes, not exactly those words but… oh please don't mention I said anything."

"Of course I won't." Even without Henry's pointed expression she knew she had been deliberately left behind. I didn't think her so devious.

As she walked back to their suite she wanted to cry. I wanted so much to hear Ben play at Vista Circle.

ഗ

Riding home with the family Ben was frantic. He kept questioning Rebecca and Beth, but the answers were vague. "Why didn't you go see if she was all right?"

"I saw her after you left and told her seven. She looked as if she wasn't ready to go anywhere."

"Mother, I don't like what I hear. All she had to do when I left was slip into her gown. Beth, why didn't you go check on her?"

Beth was bewildered and could not fit, what she thought were the facts, together. "Ben, I thought Mother knew. And we were rushed."

At home Ben bounded up the stairs two at a time and yanked the door open. Beth close behind. Cheryl was gazing out the window with a half cup of tea in front of her, still dressed.

"Are you okay?" his voice quivering.

"Yes, I'm fine," she answered abruptly.

Ben turned to Beth, "If I need you I'll call." Confused, she left quickly.

"I was frantic when I found that you were not with my family. Why didn't you come down?"

She stared at him. She had not planned what she was going to say.

"I did!" Reluctantly she explained, but left out what Henry had told her. I will try to deal with this by myself.

"Someone misunderstood the time you were to leave." The way he said that, Cheryl felt he was implying it was her.

"Ben — I — did not misunderstand." She was hesitant, because she did not want to put herself between Ben and his mother.

He paced the floor totally confused, but thankful she was okay. He finally went to her and pulled her up into his arms. "I am totally sorry this happened, regardless of who got mixed up. I was frantic riding home."

"I'm sorry too. I so much wanted to hear you and be there to support you. Your career means everything to me. I wanted to see Vista Circle and hear you play in the round."

"Oh, Cheryl love, you have given me strength and purpose. I was okay before I met you. Now I am exceedingly fulfilled. I can't imagine life without you."

His words made her heart cry, again. I hope he never has to face that choice. "Darling, I will do my best to always be with you."

"I'll speak to Mother in the morning and let her know to be more accurate next time."

"Tell me about the evening."

"I did a mix of composers. Different program than the Gallery. It was well received. Lots of congratulations, both for playing and glad that I was back. Let's put all this behind us and snuggle into bed."

Cheryl thought, I'm glad I didn't tell him everything, but in the future I'll go with him, if he must leave early.

ꕥ

CHAPTER TWENTY-TWO

ꕥ

*F*all is timeless, long ago as it is today and will be tomorrow. The green leaves of summer slowly changing to brilliant reds and golds, their encore before being lost forever as if they had never been. The biting rains and brisk winds often hastened the seasonable process.

The weather curtailed Ben and Cheryl's visits to the markets, museums, and even walks in their garden. They spent more time in the piano room. One evening, with the help of Mrs. Johnson, Cheryl surprised Ben with a candlelight dinner in their suite. The flame danced, the sunset beamed, and with each moment their love glowed until they gave in before dessert. They made love as the evening slipped to heavy shadows of the night and enclosed them from the world.

ꕥ

St. James Hall awaited the evening of Ben's recital. He felt honored to be playing where Clara Schumann, Paderewski, and other greats had performed.

The evening before, Ben announced at dinner he would leave early and Cheryl was going with him. He would escort her to their box seats to join the family just before he played.

Rebecca was appalled that Cheryl was so willing to go out in public when her pregnancy was so apparent. Her belly was not a round protrusion. The baby was long in her body. This permitted her to wear one of the new high-waist gowns one last time, although obviously a baby was underneath.

Henry knocked on their door, and called, "Mr. Ben, the carriage has arrived for you and your lady."

Ben opened the door. "Thank you Henry, we're on our way down." He turned to Cheryl, "I am so glad you're going with me."

Approving or disapproving of Cheryl's appearance, Ben's mother and father were there to see them off and they, with Beth and Reggie, would follow shortly.

Arriving at St. James Hall, Ben and Cheryl were met at the front by an attendant. Entering the hall Cheryl's hands went to her heart. The red and gold ceiling surrounded with ornate woodwork was breathtaking. Ben pointed out the bold relief of the composers, Mozart, Rossini, Haydn and others at the windows. On to the anteroom and to check the piano at the center of the stage. Cheryl, in her deep rose gown and hair free, stood in the arc of the grand piano as he played her favorite Chopin étude. A tear rolled down her cheek as his fingers sent pure love to her heart.

When he finished, she said, “I’m sorry, but you don’t know how much you have exposed my life to the beauty of these compositions. Hearing the rough stuff as you call it, doesn’t in any way deplete the beauty or emotion of hearing you in concert. In Paris and each time I hear you play, my soul opens wider and I love you more.”

“Thank you — Cheryl love, my wonderful wife. It’s so great to share what means so very much to me.” He took his handkerchief and patted her cheek and kissed her lips. “I love every cell of your body, as you say we have.” They smiled into each other’s eyes. “I’ll take you to the box now. Then get on with my debut after the long winter in Paris hearing gunfire, the mobs, seeing death and personal fear.”

Cheryl watched as he came on stage in his handsome formal attire and bowed to a full house that was offering their best wishes. She pushed all depressing thoughts of her misplaced plight out of her mind. All I have gone through and will in the future tonight will be one of the most memorable.

The passionate music and the elegant hall were one of grandeur. A contented smile never left her face. Her eyes never left Ben until the last note of his tempestuous encore, Bach’s Prelude from Prelude & Fugue no. 2 in C minor. The spirit of this prelude sent one last high throughout the audience that would last all the way home. There was no formal receiving line after the performance, but as they exited a spontaneous queue formed in the grand foyer to compliment Ben for a wonderful evening, some with many words of beauty, others just one chosen with care.

Before the last candle was snuffed in their bedroom, they discussed the evening and that it was a success.

"I made a few mistakes. I tried hard to be perfect, but that never seems to happen."

"I didn't hear any. When is anything perfect? No matter how hard we try and trying hard is the important part and then we have to accept the results."

"Yes. I did my best and that is all I can do."

They chatted about going to Paris again and a tour including Vienna. These two hearts were at peace and full of promise.

ଓଃ

The promising future and love of Ben did not completely assuage the boredom Cheryl was experiencing. She knew she could not do much until after the baby arrived. Then he would take a lot of her time. She wanted it that way.

She planned to go with Ben on tours, so a teaching job would be out of the question. I could be just a casual helper. We should learn German. We'll be going there this summer. And always the last thought, if I'm still here.

Ben was planning his trip to Oxford alone. There was rail service, and he could study his music in comfort or let the swaying of the carriage lull him to sleep.

The end of October the rains and winds had increased. It kept everyone inside. Winter was creeping in but not unnoticed. The hearths were often blazing to temper the cold. Cheryl wrote in her diary that she had started when they arrived in London. She recorded her stay in Paris, their wedding and other important events. Ben mostly practiced.

ഗ

The morning sky was glowing and it was so welcome. Today Ben was leaving for Oxford. As he dressed Cheryl packed his bag with the few things he would need. Three days were not long but she would miss him. While he was gone she wanted to go to the market, but that was not possible. She would have to be satisfied with a walk in the garden collecting herbs. The sun would dry out the grass and the trees would not be dripping.

The expected knock by Henry told Ben the carriage had arrived.

"Thank you, Henry. I will be down within moments." He took Cheryl in his arms and kissed her lovingly. "I'll be back before you even miss me. I will only play here in the city until next spring. Then we can launch our European tour. We'll take a nurse to help us with the baby."

"I'm glad you're going. I'd like to go and visit Oxford, but best I stay here. There will be other times when I am not so cumbersome."

"Walk downstairs with me."

At the door he gave his mother and sister a light peck on the cheek, but brought Cheryl's lips to his. "Bye love, see you in just three days."

Cheryl watched and waved as he bounded into the carriage with his leather case full of music and small bag of personal things. She said a few words to

Rebecca and Beth and went to her suite.

She read *The Times,* and oh, how she wished for a science journal. By the time I get back there will be hundreds of new concepts to read about and learn. Studying the changing scenes of science all of her life had left little time for reading art books or contemporary novels. No science journals to catch up on in 1871 provided time for the extra reading. The books available didn't provide the brain stimulation that she craved, but they kept her mildly entertained.

Later she joined Rebecca and Beth for handwork. She was beginning to like knitting and to watch her baby coverlet grow, even though it was lopsided. In a small way she was proud of her first attempt at making something. Thanks to Elise who had begun her knitting instructions a few months ago.

Dinner that evening was like many others, mutton, potatoes, lettuce salad and dessert. Cheryl declined a chat in the living room for a walk in the garden. She was glad it was spacious, because she was spending a lot of time out there.

Taking the stairs to their suite for additional exercise, she slung her bag over her arm and her light-weight cloak over her shoulders. Looking out the window, she mused, I think I'll go to the herb garden and pick herbs for my sandwich tomorrow. A sprig or two of tarragon, coriander, and a few tiny thyme leaves. Simply thinking about their aroma seemed to bring the fragrance into her sense of smell.

She walked energetically to the back of the garden where Henry had planted the herbs. She picked a bunch of dill and tarragon, drew them near her nose and took a deep breath. How wonderful. She bent over to add rosemary to the bunch and as she came up she staggered and not even time for a thought, everything of her being went black.

ꕥ

Ben had arrived at Oxford the day before and had eaten a hearty dinner and slept well. Today he would look over his music and eat light before his recital.

At his home in London, breakfast and lunch were bygones, and Cheryl had not made an appearance, although that was not unusual. They gathered for dinner and Cheryl did not come down. Beth decided to go to her suite. Perhaps she was napping and had overslept. She knocked lightly. No answer and again, no answer. She opened the door a crack and called, "Cheryl." No response.

She must be sleeping. Easily Beth tip-toed into the bedroom. The bed was neatly made but no Cheryl. Stepping into the center of their suite she called louder, "Cheryl, where are you?" The silence gave her chills. She thought, the water closet. She ran across the hall to find the door partly open and the room empty.

She ran downstairs and said to her parents, "She's not up there, how about the piano room or library?"

Her mother responded, "We just looked there."

"Oh lord, where might she be?" William expressed, his voice almost quivering. At once the four realized they had not seen her since the previous evening.

Mrs. Johnson was called but she had nothing to

add. She immediately went for Henry and they joined the search.

Together and separately they searched every inch of the house and garden. When gathered back in the dining room, Beth said she could not find Cheryl's bag, the big black one she carried everywhere. With that information they decided she could have gone out last evening and something had happened to her.

Everyone alarmed, Henry was immediately sent for the Metropolitan Police. Another hour passed before he returned with two officers. They were informed, and again the house and gardens were searched.

"We will look for her in every corner of the city." The police assured the family as they left to begin their search.

No one was ready to retire for the evening. Every few moments William would look out the front door and gaze up and down the street. Rebecca wrung her hands and paced. Beth sat calmly and in deep thought. Reggie continued opening every door, in and out, anticipating something could have been missed. Each speculated as to what had happened to her and where to look. Intermittently they grabbed a bite of food from the table. Rebecca was so upset she did not even notice the breach of etiquette.

The police returned near midnight without news, although they were continuing to search.

"We have to get word to Ben," Beth said.

"He will start home in a few hours," his mother answered.

"We should still inform him so he can get the first rail here," his father stated emphatically.

A policeman asserted, "We can do that, but it

would be morning and he could already be on his way home."

William decided to send the telegram should Ben delays his return for some unexpected reason, and a few hours could be crucial.

ഗ

Ben woke to a thunderous banging on his door. When he gained his senses he was concerned he had overslept and missed his rail home. Peeking out the door he saw the telegraph boy.

His thoughts were neutral for a moment, probably a congratulatory message or could it be bad news. Reading quickly, skipping over words but he understood the message. Bad, no it's horrible! He instantly feared for Cheryl and their child.

Thoughts ramped up. She had feared that someone would follow her. How did they know where she was? How did they get to her? She wouldn't go off our property. Someone broke in. They did. I know that happened. They broke in and kidnapped her. Last night. No one saw her since last night. Oh my god, she could be anywhere. A whole day, gone. Gagged, tied up.

He lost control of his mind and body. He was wild, crazy. He stuffed his bag without care. Music out of order he shoved it into the leather case. He ran to the rail station and boarded the carriage for home. His body taut and yet he fidgeted uncontrollably. I've let her down again. I should have stayed home.

The ride seemed long, but his anger and disturbing thoughts broken when he realized they were approaching London. He hailed the first hansom he saw and almost demanded they race to his home. He prayed with every bounce of the seat and squeak of the wheels, please, please let her be there.

He arrived and found his prayers had vanished with the wind, as if never uttered. Father, Mother, Beth, Reggie, and the servants were still in a panic. The police had been there and would come back when he arrived. He did not wait. He went to them, Father and Reggie at his side.

At the main division of Scotland Yard in the heart of London, Ben told the officials all he knew. She had escaped from a school in southern France and was in Paris on her way to America. She always feared she would be followed because they told her not to leave and if she did there would be consequences. Ben realized he had never pressed her for the name of the school. When mentioned she would become extremely upset. Oh, why didn't I find out where and the name. How foolish of me. Now it could be too late! He paced. He shook his head in despair as it ached. His heart pounded, stomach whirled, legs weak, his body was about to fail as one.

They assured him that every station in London had been informed of her missing. The officials had also sent telegrams to all ports where ships were leaving for another country. Rail service had been advised to watch for persons fitting her description. Hospitals were being checked.

She had been gone possibly twenty-four hours before anyone missed her. Ben felt it was too late for any of these checks to be effective. Any illicit intent could have already taken place. Kidnapping heading the list and after that he could not think about what might be happening to her. The officials appeared to be doing everything possible so they decided to leave. His father went home. Ben and Reggie rented a cabriolet and horse, and slowly drove through the streets. The squalor and stench was overbearing, but they stopped and talked along the way. No one had seen anyone strange or appearing to be captive.

Stopping in parks and wooded areas hoping for something, just any little thing, a hat, her bag, a shoe.

The next day Ben went to the station for news, and after, again, rented a carriage and drove the streets. In his sight were dirty hungry children, beggars with their hand extended for a coin. Rats scurrying across the cobbles. He stopped and walked dark dank alleys and shivered at the grotesque sights and putrid smells. He was sick at seeing what people had to endure, and for a moment he shared their helplessness.

Two days passed. Every night Ben had slept in a chair near the door. He changed his clothes only when his mother insisted.

The next morning early, Ben woke to someone banging the iron knocker. He jumped up and ran to the door. Hope squeezed his heart. His father was close behind. Opening the door he saw the telegraph boy. The police wouldn't send information this way. Blackmail, a ransom note. I'll pay anything, ran through his mind. Maybe it's from her. Frightened, yet he had to know.

He grabbed the piece of paper and read aloud. "Ben. Cheryl is here. Safe. Depressed. Kidnapped. Come for her, Jacques. Oh Dad, they took her to Paris. Jacques says she's safe." He covered his face with his hands and sobbed without shame.

"Oh — son, I am *so* glad she's okay, but I just

don't understand why she is so important they would kidnap her. Are you sure she is not a Prussian spy?"

His emotions were spread on his wet and reddened face and he wiped them away on his sleeve. More composed, he said, "I don't know how they got to her. I don't believe she would go out alone. Is there an opening in the garden wall where they could get in? She does go there. I told her it was safe. I'm leaving immediately. Send a message to Jacques."

"I'll have Henry check the garden wall, too," he called, as Ben ran upstairs, always two at a time.

William sent a reply with the telegraph boy and went to find his wife and daughter.

Ben threw a few pieces of clothing for himself and Cheryl in a bag and spent a few minutes in the water closet, which he badly needed. Thinking as he washed and packed, I'll go to Dover. There is always some kind of a boat to Calais. Portsmouth or Brighton, not so often. From Dover to Lille by rail and then on to Paris. With luck he could be there tomorrow or for sure the next day.

ಌ

CHAPTER TWENTY-THREE

ↄ

Ben gave his father a big hug, then a kiss on the cheek for his mother and Beth. Mrs. Johnson rushed in with a bag of sandwiches and sweet cakes.

"Thank you," and he also gave her a quick peck on the cheek.

And then he ran. His mind was so far away he did not even turn to wave. He was only looking forward to Paris and to Cheryl.

His family was bewildered as they watched the cab clatter down the cobbles and turn from view. Kidnapped. Why? They discussed different scenarios. Were they really married? Was she trying to go back to America? Why was the school so determined to have her back?

William restated his thought as he had to Ben earlier. Was she a Prussian spy trying to defect and they wanted her back. Was she trying to hide in Ben's care? Was the baby his? There was no end to their questions and definitely they had no answers.

In the breakfast room they continued their wild speculation. But mostly they feared for her and Ben's lives. They all felt something was wrong with this story, especially Beth.

The sun was bright yellow in the lower eastern sky. Perfect for a brisk walk to refresh the senses, but Ben was rushing to the rail station and arrived with only minutes before it left for Dover. Even though he had ridden in the carriage, he was breathless. As he rode he kept saying to himself, Cheryl love, I'm coming. I can relax until Dover. That didn't happen. His muscles ached from being so tense. His hands trembled. He thought about what his father had mentioned, was she a Prussian spy? No, she can't be, but all speculation is fair game. She has said nothing that would lead to that. She never spoke German. Will the officials at school ever leave her alone? His mind and his body were a tortured and agonizing mix.

At Dover he was in luck again. There was a large sail boat about to leave and he received permission from the captain to board. The weather was calm for this time of the year. The fall winds blowing in from the North Sea had not begun. Ben thought about their return trip. He had to get her back to London soon. Each day would take them further toward winter.

They glided into the dock at Calais and Ben was off to the rail station. He hoped, but he knew a train to Paris would not be leaving until morning. After getting the departure times for the next day, he found an inn for the night. He stretched out on the bed and for a moment he felt like he could unwind, but his mind kept going.

He decided to have dinner hoping the diversion

would ease his thoughts and distract his body. He picked at his food. After a fast walk he went back to his room hoping for sleep, but only dozed off and on throughout the night. Peace would only come when Cheryl, with their baby was in his arms.

The next morning he was at the rail station long before the train was to leave. Ben inquired, had the rails to Paris been repaired. They had. To Lille and then to his destination. He would arrive late in the afternoon.

What seemed like years to Ben, and then he saw the wooded area slowly turn from small villages to larger houses. He knew they were approaching Paris.

He hailed the first carriage he saw and again demanded they hurry. As they traversed the cobbles and neared Jacques' building, his heart was coiled and ready to spring. Thoughts spiraled out of control. Will she still carry our baby? Is her mind damaged from the trauma? How did they treat her? Did they touch her? If they did, my hands that make beautiful music will become weapons and send them to their demise.

The carriage turned into Rue-du-Chambert and Ben yelled to the driver. "Over to the right!" He jumped out and saw old Gezot's store open as Jacques had stated in his letter. He ran. He always ran and quickly opened the door and saw Elise helping two ladies and a dog nearby, a briard.

Elise saw Ben and dropped everything and ran to him, the dog at her heels. "Oh Ben!" and she hugged him and gazed pathetically into his eyes. "We are so glad to see you."

"How is she? The baby?"

"I don't know. She's so depressed she will hardly talk. She cries constantly. But she said she felt the baby moving, so that's good."

"Is she in my rooms? Does she know I was on my way?"

"Yes. We got your father's telegram. I'll go over with you."

The ladies in the store were stunned, their faces dropped and their eyes widened, realizing this was something of the utmost importance.

Ben and Elise went across the hall with Fanny in tow. Ben knocked and called, "Cheryl love." There was no answer. He slowly opened the door. She was not in the living room area. She had to be in the bedroom. He wanted to run, but did not want to frighten her. He slowly stepped around the corner and into the bedroom. She was lying on her side, her arm covering her face. He whispered, "Cheryl love." Even his soft voice startled her and he knew that was not good.

Elise left quietly, Fanny following her.

Cheryl got up as fast as she could and fell into his arms, her sobs out of control and her breath lurching. They held each other and wept. He for her being kidnapped and she for her lab messing with her being.

Finally he said, "It's all right love. I'm here and this will never happen again. I'm never going to let you out of my sight. Did they hurt you or baby?"

She managed to nod her head enough that he understood, no.

"It's okay." He kept her close and rubbed her back and neck. "You can tell me about it later. Now darling just know I'm here."

She stopped crying for a moment and looked into his face. He saw that stare that he could not understand. He thought, she's traumatized.

"Oh Ben, I love you — you will never know how much. Carry those words with you." She realized the lab had probably used the original equations that had sent her to Paris the first time, to propel her here again. An error, but it was evident to her, the lab was working with equations that were affecting her. She feared they were getting close to pulling her back. She feared she and Ben's life together could soon be over, and that made her senses uncontrollable.

"I know darling, let's go sit in the living room." She went to the sofa and he got a cold wet cloth, and then wiped her face holding it over her swollen eyes.

"That does feel good."

"Are you sure the baby is all right?"

"I think so. I hope. Feel," and she took his hand, "he's moving now." And she managed a smile. He placed his hand easily on her swollen belly and his eyes widen with love and relief.

He sat next to her. "Darling, I know you're upset, but do you think they are still in the area?"

"They're gone." She hid her face in her hands. "They let me go when they found out I was going to have a baby. They said they didn't want two, but would be back for me later. I pleaded with them to bring me to the park and I walked over to Jacques and Elise's."

"When did you cross the Channel?"

"I don't know. I was out most of the time." She started to cry again, knowing she was lying to Ben, but knowing she had no choice. "Please can we wait until later?"

"Of course we can."

He pulled her on his lap and she curled into his

body. She could feel his strong arms around her, which said protection, love, and all in between.

After a while she said, “I have to go to the water closet.” She got up and seemed weak and unstable, so with his arm around her waist, he guided her fragile body.

He then suggested they lie on the bed and rest. With the coverlet protecting them from the world, they drifted into a light sleep they both badly needed.

After the rest, he said, “I believe you had better eat. Me too I have hardly eaten since I got the telegram the morning at Oxford. Did they tie you up?”

“At my wrists and put my cloak over them.”

“You couldn’t alert someone.”

“I think I was out some of the time and dazed the rest. I didn’t seem to have a sense of anything.”

“Did they give you something to make you pass out?”

“No. I didn’t take anything. I think it was fright.”

“You have to eat to get your strength back. I also brought you some fresh clothes.”

“You are a darling. I’ve been taking these off at night. And I have my cloak.”

“They broke in, didn’t they?”

“I don’t know. Suddenly, one was in front of me and one behind me. It all happened so fast.” She buried her head in his arms. She felt better that he was with her, but terrified knowing her lab might propel her back at any moment. I can’t run. I can’t hide. Desire and hope were empty states of mind.

She took Ben’s hand and placed it on her belly. He felt the little bumps rising and falling. “It’s a wonderful feeling and so reassuring."

"Have you seen Jacques?"

"Just Elise."

"Go see if he's in the store. He's anxious to see you."

Ben went across the hall and Jacques was there. They greeted each other with handshakes and pats on the back.

"You don't know how glad we are to see you. We have been crazy with worry for her and the baby. Elise stayed with her at night."

"I couldn't leave her alone. If something happened to the baby in the night she couldn't get to us. How is she now?" Elise paused, "And you?"

"We're both better that we're together. She needs nourishment and rest."

"You *will* have supper with us," Elise stated emphatically.

"Yes. I will answer for her." Ben looked down. "So this is Fanny. She's beautiful." He rubbed her ears and she responded by moving closer for more attention. "When did you get her?"

"A few weeks after you left. Elise and I were out riding in the country and came upon a sign. We inquired and they had had a litter during the war so she was about eight months old. They were outside Paris but they had to keep quiet about the small animals, just in case. So we brought her home. She adapted well and really fast. She is our first baby since we got married." They all smiled at Jacques' affectionate statement.

After chatting briefly Ben went back to Cheryl. It wasn't hard to talk her into having supper upstairs. She thought of Lucie's warm bread.

Jacques and Elise could see the change in her in these few hours. Her eyes were still swollen from endless crying but she was smiling.

"We'll rest for a few days, but I want to get started before the Channel gets rough. Our ride over was awful. We want to avoid that again if possible." He gazed at Cheryl and read her mind in agreement.

"Have supper with us till you go." Elise stated. "Lucie does most of the cooking and bakes bread for here in the store."

The next few days they rested, and took walks with Fanny happily leading the way. Ben practiced. They enjoyed being with Jacque, Elise and Lucie. With their hearts content they made love.

As Cheryl felt better her concern was what she would tell his parents. He immediately quelled her anxieties saying he would handle that.

A few more days passed. The sunrises were brilliant and sunsets were golden. It was time to go home.

ᔓ

When they arrived at home in London everyone was waiting and waiting for an explanation from Cheryl. Ben said, "She was kidnapped. She was unconscious most of the time. She was taken by two men but they did not abuse her. They took her to Paris on the way south. When they found she was pregnant they let her go. They didn't want two. They would get her later. She begged them to take her to the park near Jacques and they were gone. She walked to Jacques' building and that is where I came in. If I find them, I will kill them. No time for explanations. She still is absolutely terrified and needs rest. That is all I know. That is all she knows. I don't want this discussed here again." His every word carried a strong emphasis.

He picked her up and took the lift to their suite.

ℴ∽

CHAPTER TWENTY-FOUR

*B*en and Cheryl had arrived home before the harsh, North Sea winds aggressed the waters of the Channel. The hearths blazing and central heating would be turned on as the season moved toward snow. The rooms were warm but the atmosphere was cold. The family wanted to hear in Cheryl's own words about her ordeal. Ben would not let them talk to her about it or ask questions. She was home and well, and that was the most important part. He felt there was nothing more to be said.

Days when the sun was bright and the wind blew elsewhere, they went shopping to complete the baby layette and purchase Christmas gifts. When Ben wasn't looking, Cheryl managed discreetly to buy gifts for him.

She had to do this with some secrecy, because she could not go out alone.

Ben planned a mini-recital and social evening

for his close friends at their home. He had not seen several of them since they had returned from Paris the first time.

Mrs. Johnson prepared small meat sandwiches, dainty cakes, fruits and nuts. Pink punch and mulled wine were a choice at the end of the table. Not yet a holiday gathering, pinkish water lilies and purple anemones floating in a large bowl of pale water decorated the table.

The small group of guests arrived near the same time. Ben and Cheryl greeted them at the entrance. The ladies and men were handsomely dressed, although not in formal attire. Cheryl was introduced, and after cloaks and hats were taken they gathered in the piano room. Everyone wanted to hear about Ben's winter in Paris, their wedding, and other ordeals that had circulated as rumors. They were also excited about the baby. Several of the friends had young children.

Ben was willing to talk about topics other than the war. He was not excited about reliving horrible memories of killing or fear at a social evening, and did his best to deflect the subject. Cheryl noted his reluctance and suggested he play. Afterward she guided everyone to share Mrs. Johnson's delicacies and hoped the theme of war would not be resurrected.

Reggie and Beth had joined the group. Mother and Father had popped in to say hello and then walked down the street for an evening with their neighborhood friends.

The next Saturday Ben and Cheryl were on their way to a musical evening at the Wellestons. A violinist, flutist, and harpist would join Ben in playing together, and they would also perform separately.

Cheryl asked, “Is their music room large?”

“Yes, it’s a small ball room. I expect there will be a lot of people. Everyone in their family plays an instrument or sings, and they are patrons of the arts especially music. It is a delight to be invited and I know you will enjoy it, too.”

As the traditional Christmas carols and Bach’s “Sheep May Safely Graze” were played, Cheryl’s thoughts blocked out the music. One more time she hoped, so strongly, that her lab would concentrate on the holidays rather than an equation to get her home. She knew her hope wasn’t a choice.

The last Sunday in November was Stir-Up Sunday for English families. It was a fun day at the Rutherford’s, when everyone gathered in the kitchen to prepare sweets for the holidays. First was plum pudding. Nuts had to be shelled and chopped. Dried fruits, peels, and suet cut into tiny pieces. Mother donned an apron and measured flour and sugar. Aroma of cloves, nutmeg and cinnamon filled the air as Cheryl measured each carefully. This is the closest thing I’ve come to scientific preparation since I’ve been here.

Father portioned the brandy, as he sneaked a sip or two. Reggie prepared the pans. Mrs. Johnson put all the ingredients together, mixed and poured into the shaped tins for the two hour steaming. The process began all over again for almond cakes and gingerbread.

Happiness floated around the kitchen with the aromas of what they were creating. These pastries would be served during the holidays and in baskets and stockings for the children at the orphanage.

The preparations and having people around cleared Cheryl’s head of her bad experience and anticipation. The long day ended with a light meal that included Henry and Mrs. Johnson.

ꕤ

December eased in with light snow in its wake. Ben and Cheryl spent a few days writing Christmas cards to his friends and to those supporting his career he added special thanks and apologized for being absent the past winter.

Rebecca and Mrs. Johnson were planning the holiday festivities. Tomorrow they would decorate.

A large tree was brought in and placed in the entrance way. Another rather large one for personal gifts was set up in Ben's piano room. Smaller ones were placed in most of the other rooms. Henry and Ben brought boxes and boxes of decorations from storage.

The family placed tiny mittens, toys, dolls, garlands of pine cones and berries on all the trees. Candles were also positioned strategically on the larger trees and would be lighted on Christmas Eve. Small vignettes of pine branches filled with ivy, holly, mistletoe and red berries were everywhere. Cheryl wished for a CD of Christmas music to add to the festive aura, but there was only light banter and laughter.

Family guests arrived from far off that would be staying until after the Twelve Days of Christmas celebration, which was January six. Reggie's mother, who was alone, Rebecca's Aunt Cassie also alone and William's younger brother, Nathan and his wife, Ann. Cousins, who lived closer, would be coming only for an evening.

One afternoon Rebecca, Beth, and Mrs. Johnson prepared baskets and stockings for children at the orphanage. The next day Beth, Cheryl and Ben delivered the presents. Their little faces were bright when they saw the treasures. Cheryl's heart broke. These beautiful children without even one parent. And that could happen to my babe if I get pulled home. I may never know my child and her heart cried. There would be Ben to care for him, but that was little consolation to her as a mother.

For a while Cheryl felt no indication of being disrupted, and she thought, at home, perhaps they *are* concentrating more on Christmas.

One day before their first holiday evening at home a weird feeling came over her. She felt a little dizzy, and her hands were shaking. Her fear was exceptionally strong that something was about to happen. To relax herself, she sat down by the window and gazed into the dusk and watched the old lamplighter. He hobbled up the street with his pole over his shoulder. Stopping at the lamps, he touched his pole to the jet and a flame was born.

She smiled and thought of Robert Lewis Stevenson's poem, "The Lamplighter." "…the sun has left the sky. It's time to take the window to see Leerie go by…With lantern and with ladder he comes posting up the street." She had memorized many of these little verses and recited them when she needed solace or was deep in a science project and needed a break. There had been so many other things invading her mind for some time she had not thought of the verses.

Seeing the lamplighter her thoughts traveled to these little lines that had eased her senses many times and had just called upon it again. As she watched him suddenly his image was jerked across the street. Cheryl's hands went to her mouth and she gasped. For a moment it simply startled her, and then she knew, her lab was near but just missed the point. I could be next.

Ben noted her distress, and asked, "What happened? What are you watching?"

"Leerie fell and it surprised me. Oh, he got up and looks okay." It was all she could think of so quickly.

"Who's Leerie?" Ben went to the window and gazed out. "He fell. Are you watching the lamplighter? Is he okay? Some of those guys are not too young."

Composing herself, "A poem in a book of verses that I started reading and memorizing when I was very young. Seeing him jogged my memory. The lamplighter in one of the poems was named Leerie." A book that would be published years from now. Ben wondered if it was in their library.

"You look pale. Do you feel okay?"

Determined to enjoy the evening, she answered, "Yes, I feel wonderful. Want to get ready?"

Ben glanced at the mantel clock, walked to her and took her face in his hands. "We have two hours. Time enough to make love. We'll probably be too tired after."

"I agree." She rose and took his hand.

Dusk was out the window and held them close for their love. Afterward they rested and dressed for the evening.

७३

Friends arrived to enjoy the camaraderie, good food and embrace the holiday spirit. All the doors were open and Ben's music floated from room to room. It was a long evening as anticipated, eating, singing, Ben playing and stories. It was late when everyone said good night and Merry Christmas. William and Rebecca saw the last of the guests depart and waved as the carriages rolled away.

The next day everyone slept late. When awake the day was slow and without substance.

Ben's mother found him in the kitchen later in the morning getting a snack and decided to approach the subject of the baby.

"I believe your baby is coming soon. Should you take her to the hospital?"

"I know she is uncomfortable, but she says she feels fine. I'll ask her if she feels ready to go."

His mother told him, Aunt Cassie was in a dither and felt the baby was going to come any time. She had worked in a hospital year's back.

"I do commend Cheryl because she has been to all the gatherings. I was wrong about her going out. We did get some looks, but she didn't seem to mind. You just don't see women in public as they get bigger."

"Mother, she is a strong lady. She knows all about science and the body. You should hear what she tells me. I tell her science is as foreign to me as music almost is to her. So we're learning together what make the other go. So I trust her to do the right thing."

"That's good. I just don't understand. William was talking about a business trip to America next year. From what he hears, the disruption from the civil war has settled and he wants to expand his market base."

"If you do we'll go with you. She hopes her grandmother is still alive. I think I'd better check on her. I've been down here a long time."

"Does she have parents?"

"No, she said both died years ago, and she lived with her grandmother."

Upstairs Cheryl was making tea. He sat with her at the table and thought this is a good time to talk.

"Cheryl love, our baby is near coming. Do you want to go to the hospital?"

"Not yet. I do believe he has dropped, but I will wait until I start having labor pains."

"Will there be enough time to get to the hospital if it happens in the night?"

"Oh yeah. First babies always take their time. Hours and sometimes days."

"Our guest ladies and my mother are watching and getting nervous."

"There will be time. Ben, please go with me when I go into labor. I know they will give you a hard time and you will probably have to break the door down." She gave him a pleasing smile. "Also I do not want ether or chloroform. I know this is the latest pain reliever, but no! This is why I want you there. They might do it anyway if you aren't watching."

She shrugged her shoulders. "Also darling, this is not a pleasant thing to talk about, but we have to." Her tone frightened Ben. "Should I not be able to deliver naturally, you have an important task, which is another reason I want you there. If they cut me open to deliver caesarean sometimes they don't sew up the uterus and a woman bleeds to death and they wonder why she died. Also, it's a practice to take out the womb, and then I would not be able to have more children. So tell the doctor, scream at the doctor or even grab the cat gut and sew up my womb or you won't have a wife and the baby won't have a mother."

She could see Ben was white and frozen. "You are scaring me, badly," he said quietly.

"With love I mean to. It's that important."

"Did you discuss this with the doctor?"

"I did and he was kind enough to listen, but I couldn't read how he took it. It makes perfect sense. I don't understand why it hasn't been thought of before. Hopefully I got through to him. He's not an old fogy that might think women are oversensitive or crazy. Hopefully I created some thought."

"Ask him again the next time you see him. I'll go in with you and talk to him and watch his reaction. Darling wife, I will tie myself to you with knots that can't be undone until after it's all over. I won't let you die, not like that."

Cheryl knew she had impressed upon Ben the importance, if cut open, what was necessary, and she knew at all costs he would see that it was done.

ꕥ

There were several more social evenings with friends, when the family went together and sometimes separately.

One evening music was heard floating up the street. A small string ensemble was playing on the corner. Ben and Cheryl along with Reggie and Beth dressed warmly and walked down and joined the listeners.

Another evening Ben welcomed a group of carolers into their home to warm by the hearth and have a sip of Raynal. Cheryl was concerned about inviting strangers into their home until Ben explained he knew several of the girls from music classes and programs.

After the sip that warmed all the way down the group gathered at Ben's piano and happily sang "Holly and the Ivy" and then in a more prayerful mood, "Silent Night." Their voices filled the halls, the rooms and even floated up the stairs. Moments that touched the hearts of everyone listening.

Social gathering and musical evenings set the mood for the important days yet to be celebrated.

Christmas Eve at the Rutherford home was for guests in residence and several cousins and their families who lived across town. There were twenty around the table, decorated with holly, ivy, asparagus ferns, and red berries. They began their feast with caviar sandwiches and deviled oysters. Creamed sweet breads, cold turkey and salads followed as the main course. At last, for dessert they would have their plum pudding and sweet cakes they all worked so hard to make on Stir-Up Sunday.

After they sang carols in the piano room, William read the Christmas story in St. Matthew. With reverence the evening closed.

Christmas breakfast started early with baked apples, meats, omelet, griddle cakes and other tasty items that Mrs. Johnson prepared. Then it was time to go to the Christmas service. The Altonbourne Cathedral was at the end of their street. A ten minute brisk walk. Everyone decided that a walk would enliven their spirits.

Cheryl looked at Ben. “I can walk but I will have to go slow.”

“You have a perfect excuse to stay home and I with you.”

“No. It’s a special occasion.”

They all bundled in high boots and wool cloaks and began their trek. Ben and Cheryl lagged behind and he tried to convince her to turn and go home, but she declined. “We’re almost there.” He could see that she was struggling and held her close.

Inside she was relieved to sit, but realized she should have listened to him. She appeared relaxed even though she felt distressed. The sermon will give me time to take the pressure off, literally. A few pains wove in and out of her belly, not severe, but enough to get her attention. I have no recourse but to sit here and wait my fate. Oh God not here! She prayed silently.

She tried to settle her mind by listening to the bishop. He was so far into his theme that it was not making sense to her. She sat quietly with her hands folded in her lap. Ben seemed to be settled and giving his attention to the message.

After greetings and Merry Christmas to everyone, whether they knew them or not, they started home. Cheryl was one happy girl when the big stone house come into view. She had not disturbed the birth that she so feared the walk might bring on.

At home they exchanged gifts. Roman coins, silver pins and studs, leather folders for stationery, china and crystal were among the gifts. Reggie’s mother and Aunt Cassie had many pieces of handwork for the ladies. For the men they monogrammed handkerchiefs and neck scarves. They also had knitted small garments for the baby soon to arrive.

Cheryl had managed to get a silver paperweight for Ben's music when it was laying on his piano. One day it had blown all over and needed to be weighted down. Something more personal, she presented him with monogrammed cufflinks.

After the gifts were given and received with love, it was time for Christmas dinner.

The food was placed on the gorgeously decorated table with greens and reds of the season. Mrs. Johnson had prepared, at Rebecca's request, roasted goose surrounded with every vegetable in the market. Plum pudding, lemon creams, jellies and bonbons completed the meal. Finger bowls at each plate were filled with scented water, signaling Christmas festivities were over. By then Ben could see that Cheryl was totally stressed and insisted she nap. She agreed. He excused both of them and they went to rest.

The day after, the Twelve Days of Christmas began and would end on January sixth, and at that time all of the guests would leave for home. These days honoring the saints were not officially celebrated at the Rutherford's, but a few evenings they gathered in Ben's piano room to listen to him play or to sing carols.

One evening Cheryl read poetry and another Beth read psalms. Cheryl thought, the food and gift giving had been nice, but this was a more spiritual way of celebrating love.

In between the Twelve Days celebrations, the family had a New Year's Eve party. As the clock neared the hour, everyone gathered at the open front door to wait. They were quiet and listening for the bells to send their missive. When they started ringing all over

London, it was the new year, it was 1872. For the moment Cheryl was overwhelmed by the combinations of those numbers. Ben took her in his arms and kissed her long. She forgot everything as she always did when he was so close. Finally Ben's father tapped him on his shoulder so they could receive good wishes from all.

ꕥ

CHAPTER TWENTY-FIVE

ᔓ

The last few days the snow drifted gently, resting on the bushes in a protective way. The temperature also fell. The last evening before the house guests were to depart talk was casual and reminiscing. William and his brother laughed about incidents from their childhood. Aunt Cassie related some of Rebecca's incidents from her earlier years that she wanted to forget. They wanted to hear about Cheryl's trip from America to France and the American Civil War. She managed a few ordinary experiences, and convinced the family where she was, things were rather boring and uninteresting.

As the hour crept toward nine o'clock, Cheryl said, "I'm very tired. I hope you will excuse me. But I will be down to have breakfast with all of you and to see you off. It's been a wonderful season and very special, and know we'll have many more. I have loved meeting all of you and sharing the holidays. Ben, you stay," she said, as she lightly touched his shoulder. "Good night all."

Her leaving opened the discussion among the women about the baby. Cassie and Rebecca just knew she was about to deliver.

"Ben you seem so relaxed," his mother addressed him.

"Not really Mother, but she assured me there would be a lot of warning pains before the baby actually arrives. And that hasn't happened yet. I am nervous as any first time father would be. Nervous. I am extremely anxious for her. She explained all of the possibilities that could happen. Some were horrible." Rebecca, Aunt Cassie and Reggie's mother knew specifically what he had not put into words.

Not much later everyone retired and the house was as silent as a breath. Ben slipped in beside Cheryl. She groaned a little. He kissed her on her forehead, rolled over and was asleep in a flash.

Outside, there was a peaceful silence as snowflakes continued to land softly. Dawn was on the edge in its quiet way.

Cheryl turned over in her warm bed, and a sharp pain ruffled through her body. Oh, that didn't feel so good. As she lay quietly another severe pain struck. Oh no! Oh! Yes! She held her breath then relaxed. Several more pains shot through her within the next few moments. Oh no! This is not how birth usually happens. Then she felt the warm gush between her legs. Oh god, my water broke. Too late for the hospital.

"Ben," she whispered desperately. Nothing. "Ben," she called a little louder.

"What?" he finally answered, sounding grumpy.

"I think… I know our baby is coming." And with more emphasis, "Now!"

He leaped out of bed. Naked.

She pushed the coverlets back and sat up to show him she was all wet. "My water broke," she said, as she lurched with another pain.

Ben started for the door.

"Put some clothes on." And she had to laugh.

"We have to get you to the hospital!"

"My dear husband, there is no time. It will be born here and probably very soon."

"Why didn't you tell me," he said rather loudly.

"You act like you didn't know," and she had to laugh again. "It just happened about fifteen minutes ago."

"I know you're excited, but please get dressed and go." He was trying but not doing too well. "You're making me laugh in spite of my pain. Get Aunt Cassie. She worked in a hospital and I can tell her what to do if she doesn't know." She paused to accept another pain. "Your pants Ben, your shirt is not enough and hurry!"

Ben rushed to his parents' suite and his mother went for Aunt Cassie. William sent Henry for the doctor. Mrs. Johnson arrived with clean bedclothes and provisions for a birth. With the help of Aunt Cassie and Ben's mother they prepared Cheryl as best they could.

Ben was also back and he held her hand and talked to her. Cheryl said, "The pain has subsided and I feel a tremendous amount of pressure. He's ready now." Even in this state of birth, Cheryl felt relieved knowing the baby was going to be born, now. No cesarean, no forceps, just a little pain and it would all be over.

Aunt Cassie said, "Ben dear, it probably is time for you to wait in the hall."

"No! I'm staying. I promised her I would not leave her, and I intend to keep my promise."

His mother and Cassie gasped in unison.

Rebecca took Cheryl's other hand and rubbed her arm while Ben was on her other side talking and caressing her face. Cassie positioned her legs.

Cheryl squeaked out, "So much pressure. My body is expanding. I need to push." She rested for a moment and then pushed again.

"Oh honey, he's coming, keep pushing! Push hard!"

Gripping Ben's hand one more time she pushed hard and the baby slid out without cause. Cassie turned him over and patted his back and he took his first breath.

Just then the doctor rushed in ready for action that was all over.

Cassie with tears in her eyes, said, "We did it, but I am so glad you are here." He cut the cord and had her push for the afterbirth. It was all over before anyone could get concerned.

Rebecca took the baby and with Ben, they washed him with the warm water and cloth that Mrs. Johnson had brought. After the doctor checked him over Rebecca swaddled him and handed him to his father. "My son, *your* baby son."

Ben held him and the tears rolled down his face as he gazed at the tiny bundle. He touched his puffy cheeks and ran his finger over his pinkish lips. "He's so beautiful. Our baby and she didn't even have to go to the hospital. I was able to stay with her. God answered my prayers. She told me all of the difficulties that could occur and it scared me. For her especially."

While they were caring for the baby, Cheryl was also being washed and the bedclothes changed again.

Ben walked over and sat down on the bed next to her. She smiled at him, and said, "I heard, you gave me a baby boy. Remember, I said the man determines the sex of the child."

"I do," he said proudly.

She reached out her arms to receive the tiny treasure that was not so tiny. She cuddled him. "I suspect he weighs about seven and a half to eight pounds."

"Will you translate that to kilograms?"

"Little over three and a half kilograms."

The doctor stepped in and explained breastfeeding. "Your milk will be in soon and your little one will tell you when he is hungry." She was going to breast feed for at least a month until they could get fresh milk daily from a quality source. The doctor just stared at her holding her baby. He sensed something different about her. He was thinking about how she had been so specific about her birth. How would she know about sewing up the womb? He had heard of this new procedure rather than taking the womb out. My god it's so reasonable. But wanting her husband with her. Unbelievable.

"My dear lady, you are a miracle to deliver so fast. He's a nice baby, big, well formed."

"Oh Dr. Kirk, you don't know how glad I am too. I expected to be in labor for hours. I could have ten children like this." She saw Ben's eyes widen.

"I deliver most of my babies in the hospital, but

you did well with these wonderful ladies," he said, as he looked at Rebecca and Cassie.

Rebecca looked at Cassie. "You and Cheryl did all of the work."

"Well, I believe all is well here. I will be back every day as long as you want me to make a visit." With that the doctor exited the bedroom.

Ben's mother came to his side and placed her hand on his shoulder. "Congratulations to both of you. He's a beautiful baby. Cheryl you were so brave and I am so glad you didn't have a long labor. We'll leave you three alone for a few moments and then there's a bunch of people waiting outside the door."

Alone they gazed into each other's eyes that were overflowing with love for each other and their baby, cuddled in Cheryl's arms. Ben moved closer to her, and said, "Cheryl love, my darling wife, I can't tell you how much I love you. I will have to invent new and special words for that meaning so you would know how much you are to me. My body and mind spills over with love. There are no words to express how deeply I love you."

"Oh Ben, yes, you have made my heart completely full of love for you. You are my heart. You gave me our baby with pure love," she said as she lightly touched his face. He kissed her. Their tears of joy and love met and mingled and one dropped on the baby's tiny cheek. She smiled, but another side of her heart cried.

Ben pulled back and touched the baby's little nose. "Did we decide on Andrew?"

"It's close to my maiden name and it's a nice name."

"Andrew it is. He will no longer be just Baby."

Ben reached for a cloth and wiped her face and then his. "Mother said there are a lot of people waiting outside that door. Do you feel like seeing them?"

"Yeah. Invite them in. I'm fine. Tired and a little sore, having no medication I'm alert. — Are you all right?"

He shook his head as he walked toward the door. "Now I am."

Their bedroom was filled with joy and congratulations. Ben's mother hugged William and said, "We are grandparents. A baby in the house is so grand." A tear fell from William's eye.

"We'll have to do this too," Reggie said to Beth as he gazed lovingly into her eyes. Her return look, what do you think….

No one went home that day. Baby Andrew's arrival was the grandest celebration of the holiday season.

ॐ

CHAPTER TWENTY-SIX

ဢ

The snow fall ceased, the streets were cleared and the carriages rolled again. Everyone went home with a bit more joy in their hearts. They had been there when baby Andrew was born without prolonged anxiety. He brought a happiness and energy into their home that had been dormant for too long.

At the office William bored everyone by talking about his new grandson. They all listened and smiled and knew some had already been guilty and others would someday also be bragging. Upon arriving home, he would request time with his grandson. He would usually take him into the library and they would rock and talk. One day Ben heard his father singing to him. Baby Andrew was staring so intently at his grandfather that Ben wished to know his son's thoughts.

Holding him was also a delight for Rebecca. It had been a long time since there had been a baby in their home. She hoped for more and soon, especially that Beth would give them a baby girl.

Every day Andrew grew and changed. His eyes wide with discovery and his coos and bubbles represented contentment. His blond fuzz and his warm eyes, already evident, were a gift from Cheryl. But it was obvious he was going to be big like his father. He was long, especially his fingers. Ben knew his tiny hands were destined for the piano.

He did not want for attention. Ben and Cheryl were primary, but when they napped or went out, Beth was the little mother in waiting. Each day when she held him or bathed him she wished for a baby of her own and decided to try a little harder to conceive. She knew Reggie would not object. Andrew was nearby when Ben practiced and at dinner. He was a happy baby.

Cheryl felt wonderful, physically. She exercised daily and tended their suite. The man and the baby in her life whom she loved so dearly also kept her busy. She liked being a wife and a mother.

The domestic activity helped keep her mind from being overwhelmed about thoughts of her lab. She had a strong premonition they had given up trying to find her. She had not felt any peculiarities since watching the lamplighter, which was over two months ago. If I do get plucked back, I am going to with every part of my mind or equation, find a way to return. Ben and Andrew need me and I so desperately need them.

She fought with herself. Should I write a letter that he would find someday, explaining everything? I know he would not understand the holography bit, cars and electricity were still far away, but I could just write scientific. Twice she had actually started writing, but after a few sentences had torn it to shreds.

ၹ

This particular day Ben arrived home after spending the morning with his agent. First a kiss for Cheryl and then baby Andrew.

"We're going to have a busy spring and summer. I've been scheduled for several summer festivals on the continent."

"Great. Where?"

"Three in Paris, Berlin two, Vienna two and three in Salzburg. All music festivals except Paris where they are just salon recitals. We could be on the continent all summer."

"I'm excited. I'm excited for you."

"First they want me to come back to Queens College. I didn't commit because I know you want to visit Oxford. I wanted to make sure you felt well enough to travel. You must go to the college with me this time. And Andrew a little older would always be better."

"That's wonderful. I'm fine. Anytime. Should we get a nursemaid now?'

"Yes, as soon as you can. I'll talk to Mother and she can help us with arrangements for you to meet a qualified girl who can travel with us. I'll ask her when I see her. Probably at dinner tonight."

Over the next two weeks Cheryl interviewed several girls and made a choice. The girl had home experience and had worked in a hospital caring for babies. Cheryl explained she would only be needed when she and Ben had to go somewhere together. The baby would not be pushed off on her as the primary guardian. Cheryl thought going to Oxford would be a good short trip before the continent. Before final acceptance, Cheryl had her care for Andrew one entire morning and liked the way she handled him, with care and assurance. Allie Pearson was hired.

ൾ

Ben's recital at Queens College had been scheduled and they were to leave the next day. Cheryl and Allie packed things for Andrew. He was still breast feeding, but she planned to stop as soon as they returned from Oxford. Arrangements had been made for milk to be delivered daily from a nearby farm. Bottles had been obtained and Cheryl had explained to Ben they had to be sterilized and a proposed feeding schedule.

Arriving at Oxford in the late morning, they were met by an attendant from the college. He escorted them to their hotel and then asked Ben to accompany him to the hall where the recital was to be played the next evening.

Cheryl said they would get settled and she would be ready for a tour of Oxford when he returned. A cradle was brought into Ben and Cheryl's room. With clothes and baby things organized, Cheryl decided to go to the apothecary she had noticed next to the hotel. She told Allie she would not be gone long.

She stepped outside, took a deep breath, and realized what a beautiful day it had become. The warm sun was calling for a short stroll. She had not had any moments alone for many, many days.

Which way? She looked up the cobbled street and saw a cluster of evergreens. A park and she headed in that direction. She walked in and followed a path that took her in and out of small patches of early flowers just beginning to peek from the earth. She slowed her step to enjoy the early presentation of spring. It had been a troubled fall and winter and she looked forward to better times. That was not always within her reach, but being optimistic was.

She strolled past the bushes that were trusting life one more time. The evergreens were coming from the dark shades of winter and over their tops was the old city of Oxford. Today I'm going over there with Ben as my guide and it brought a quiet thrill and a dainty smile. She looked up at the taller trees and realized she could not focus her eyes. She blinked and they were still clouded. She sat down on the nearest bench, gazed into the distance and tried to see if anyone was around. She saw no one. As she was staring ahead her vision darkened, her mind faded, her body went limp and she barely had enough consciousness to think. No! — No! They're sending me some….

ᔕ

After playing the piano, Ben hurried back to the hotel to take Cheryl on a tour of the city. He had also planned a romantic dinner at a nearby restaurant. It would be their first evening out in months.

When Ben reached the hotel, he took the lift to the third level and hurried down the hall to their room. Opening the door he found Allie rocking Andrew and singing to him.

"Hello, Mr. Ben," she said, hardly missing a tone.

He looked around and abruptly asked, "Where's Cheryl?"

"She went to the apothecary. She said she would not be long."

"How long was that?"

"Maybe two hours."

"Two hours! That's a long time. Please Allie don't leave this room." He turned and started to leave. "The apothecary. Next door." He was gone before she could answer. The fear that he lived with every day clasped his heart. How would anyone know she was here? How did they get into our garden? Please dear God let me be overreacting.

He did not wait for the lift, but took the stairs, two at a time, as his heart jumped frantically with his body. Outside and two steps he checked with the clerk at the store and he did not remember her. Out in the street he saw the same evergreens that had drawn Cheryl earlier. They did the same for Ben although he ran. In the same park he continued to run from section to section and it did not take long to know that Cheryl was not there. He ran further up the street, looking, and then back down, passing the hotel. Not finding her in the area, he had an awful feeling that something tragic had happened. She would not just wander off in a strange town. He knew his worst fear could be reality.

He went back to their room. She was not there and he told Allie to pack up they might be leaving very soon, possibly on the next rail home.

He went to the police station and reported her missing. Explaining the past circumstances, he felt that she could have been kidnapped again. He stressed the police hurry because they could not have taken her far.

The officials took action immediately. Messages were sent to every station in Oxford, every rail departure and every platform from where coaches were departing for short distances. Ben explained that Scotland Yard in London knew of her situation and would take action immediately. They were notified by telegram as Ben waited.

All law enforcement in the surrounding areas and in London were informed. Ben knew the next move was to get home, and to get Andrew a wet nurse or started on milk.

He sent word to cancel his recital. Then he went to the stationhouse to check the time for the next rail leaving for London. He had two hours.

In a rush back to the hotel, pain flashed through his chest and his breath would jerk. He knew he had to keep his body and mind from failing until he could get Allie and Andrew home. But knowing Cheryl was in grave danger and time was absolutely critical nearly broke him.

At the hotel he found Allie had honored his request, and had packed and was ready for travel if need be. They left the hotel with Ben carrying their bags and she Andrew. They walked to the rail station.

Allie waited inside the stationhouse where Andrew was getting cranky. He was hungry. She gave him her finger to suck on and that worked for a while. She asked the station master if there was a lady in the back. He said he would get his wife. Allie asked her if she had some sugar water for Andrew. She was happy to help and gave Allie a small bottle ideally enough to pacify him until they reached home. She offered milk, but Allie explained he had only breast milk and there had been an accident. At home there would be milk and they would start upon arrival.

Ben's anxiety was relieved somewhat by pacing on the platform. He was constantly checking the large clock inside to see if the hands by some bit of magic were moving faster.

Finally they were on board and on their way. There were no stops until London.

He was absolutely frantic all the way, thinking with every bump of the carriage what if they don't find her this time. He tried to explain to Allie without going into details, but he could see that he only frightened her.

They arrived home in the late afternoon and Ben rushed into the house with Allie trailing with a crying baby. He pushed the door open with force as if behind it he would find Cheryl.

Beth ran from the library. "Ben, why are you home? You just left this morning."

"Cheryl disappeared! I fear she has been kidnapped again. I'm a mess."

"Oh, no," and she started to cry.

"No time for tears, Andrew needs a bottle as soon as you can get it. Everything is upstairs. Did we get milk?"

"Yes. Fresh today."

"He hasn't been fed since late morning. Allie got some sugar water and has been giving him drops, but he needs milk. Get it for him. Allie can help." He barked orders. "I am going to the police station. Take care of him."

His mother came rushing in and heard enough

of the conversation to know something terrible had happened.

"Oh Bennie, not again," her voice tearful. "But we will take care of Andrew."

Ben left in the same carriage that brought them from the rail terminal. The distance to the station was short, but the ride was long. He thought this cannot go on. We can't live like this. They have to catch the culprits and end this fear. Why would a school be so determined to get her back? If a school, it had to be a clandestine place and she didn't realize that until she got there. Is she a Prussian spy trying to defect?

At Scotland Yard, they told Ben they had sent telegrams to all ports, where ships departed for other countries, Dover, Portsmouth, Brighton and others. West to Wales and north to Scotland had all been informed. The fingers of information were spreading fast. Ben sent a telegram to Jacques. If they were taking her to southern France again, she might be able to escape and make her way to Jacques and Elise.

The evening grew late and nothing more could be done tonight. Ben went home. He checked first on Andrew. Beth and Allie had been giving him small amounts of milk and he seemed to be doing fine. Rebecca suggested a wet nurse and Ben replied, "Whatever."

Beth said, "He can sleep in our room tonight and until she's back and you feel better. I'll have Reggie bring his cradle in." Ben did not argue.

ഗ

Ben went to Scotland Yard the next day and the

next. Each trip gave him time to think about what he didn't want to, but it was propelled into his mind automatically. Were they hurting her? Forgive me God, but I'll kill them with my bare hands. He clutched and twisted those potential weapons of choice. Whatever it is let me go for her. Tears would always run down his face before he arrived. Each day as he ran into the building, his prayer was that she would be standing there and he would rush and take her in his arms. But each day his prayer went unanswered.

At first it all made sense. She had been kidnapped again. Thinking deeper, something seemed to be amiss, but he could not see through the maze of his emotions for a coherent answer. Again he blamed himself for leaving her alone at Oxford. I let her down. I should have been there to protect her. I didn't think she would go out.

His body was out of control. He kicked at whatever was near. His step was heavy. He snapped at his family. He ate little and slept less. His mind was crammed with horrifying thoughts. Where had they taken her? He had read what they do to people who defy authority. Disfigurement. Isolation. Were they beating her? Starving her? Raping her? Each thought made him wild, but together they made him insane.

ග

Spring announced itself with gentle winds. New shoots were breaking into the light. Buds on the trees were being advanced by the cheerful sun and warm days. Henry and his helpers were raking, cleaning and planting in the Rutherford gardens.

Baby Andrew was growing. Ben offered fatherhood only when his mother insisted. He was being cared for and Cheryl was not and that was where his attention lay. He was spending most of his time at the metro police stations around London. He walked along the Thames looking for a body, talking to street people, and inquiring in shops, had they seen anyone in distress. He had sent telegrams to Jacques several times and contemplated going over. He went to the ports south and to Dover several times.

At first his activities bothered his family, but they slowly understood he had to explore all the avenues until they were exhausted. They left him to what his day would bring, for they knew he was not himself and would not be until Cheryl was found. Their hearts were heavy and they felt totally helpless.

Eventually he ceased going somewhere every day knowing that time was running out. He had lost interest in everything that was important to him. He slept during the day in a chair near the front door and paced the floor at night. He ate only when his mother placed food in front of him.

He questioned himself. Have I displeased God that he would take her away? I only loved her. She is the light in my life. She completed me. I would die for her and probably will if she is not found. Was she here to just give me a beautiful baby boy? Cheryl is love and without Cheryl there is no love. Questions without answers like night without a day. His hope was falling like a stone in the water.

His despair was slowly turning to resignation to… But what distressed his mother to tears, was that he had not touched his piano since his return from

Oxford. She worried his mind was damaged, and he would never again be himself. Her love for him was unconditional, but it had not helped him through this horrible nightmare. Love had not conquered all, even a mother's love. He was sinking farther away each day. He was headed for the cliff of depression and the chasm below awaited him body and soul. Her scream for him to stop had been swallowed by the wind.

ᔕ

Spring was on the fringe of leaving, but it had a few showers yet to release. Ben was in the library watching the drops hit and wiggle down the pane as his mind searched for Cheryl.

He was brought back from his faraway place when he heard the iron knocker on the door, banging hard. Ben ran and so did his mother. A messenger boy handed him a summons from Scotland Yard's main station He was to come immediately.

"The carriage is waiting for you," the young boy said.

"Do you know why?" Ben asked abruptly.

"No sir. I was just sent to tell you to come."

Ben felt urgency in the boy's voice. He knew they had found her, but was she alive? Was he being called to claim her body?

"I want to believe she is alive," he said to his mother, with a slight smile and thinking she could read his other thought. "Whatever, this might be the end." He did not wait for hat or wrap, but ran to the carriage and the horse pulled away.

His mother with tears running down her face

and Beth sobbing, they held each other, knowing this could be the final chapter that Ben had been waiting for. "Let this be a happy ending," Rebecca said. "He is such a good person he doesn't deserve this horrible situation."

The summons had seemed so definite and urgent, his body and mind were out of control by the time he reached Scotland Yard. Hoping for a good outcome, but knowing there were other options. As usual he ran into the station. Quickly his eyes scanned the room, no Cheryl. It has to be a body. His heart dropped.

"Mr. Rutherford, that was quick."

"I understood there was some immediacy in the command."

"I suppose in telling the boy and in making him understand I created a sense of urgency. I do apologize. I hope I didn't take you away from something special."

"Finding my wife is the special activity in my life. Is there new information?"

"Nothing new, I am sorry to say. Although we had a message from Paris a few days ago and they are closing the case. We also received a message from Berlin and the Prussian Command says they have no women spies. Our office addressed Paris' decisions and opted to demote the case of Cheryl Rutherford to inactive. I am sure you know what that means. We just keep hitting walls everywhere we looked. With all my heart I did not want to deliver this message." He paused, but he could not look at Ben, for he knew he would break. "This has been a long ordeal and was sad for everyone who has worked on the case." He knew how large the hurt that Ben was carrying. "Should something new occur we will activate it immediately. Time has just run out for us to find her."

Ben knew eventually this would happen, but hearing the chief's words devastated him. His heart stopped. I am going to die. He knew he had to leave before he fell completely apart.

"Thank you for all you've done." With those abrupt words he rushed out and was immediately in a carriage on his way home.

He rode in a stupor, gazing out the window, yet seeing nothing. He could not think and he was glad because, his thoughts made him crazy.

His mother and Beth heard the clopping and the rattling of the carriage as it crossed the cobbles nearing their home. They rushed to the door, anxious. He opened the door and they saw his ashen face and hollow eyes, no words were needed.

He went straight to his piano room and softly closed the door. He opened the windows hoping she would drift in on the gentle breeze, and then again he knew it was a silly thought. Or maybe I can send a message out on the melody I play and it will reach her, yesterday, across the ocean or into the future. I'll play for you one last time. Listen to the love in every tone. I am sending every feeling out to you on wings of love that I've ever had, have now, or will have ever again.

His fingers reached for the keys and he played from his heart. As he played he spoke to her. "Our love was so strong how could we be separated. You are my étude, my sonata, my waltz." He paused. "Where are you darling? Please send a message and I'll be there. I'll watch for you out the window. I'll look for you in every crowd. Without you I am only half a life."

Images of their life together flashed through his mind. I feel her soft body as if she were here next to me. That first time I looked into her eyes and hers answered back. The first time I made love to her. I wanted her to know how my heart felt, she did and she replied with love emanating from every part of her being. Cheryl, your love brought out the last bit of emotion for me to express my music so completely. "Listen darling."

He played her favorite Chopin étude, closed his eyes and let his hands fall into his lap. No breeze glided in the window. In the stillness his psychic drifted deep among the stars. He waited and then he felt a strong cold whiff. It hovered near "Oh! — No! — No! — Cheryl love! — What did they do to you?"

His body instantly flamed and tears flowed down his face as a stream moves after the rain. He sat silent for moments just feeling her. An ethereal calm came over him, an aura. Tension and stress fell away like the withered petal falls. His heart beat was a whisper. Then he spoke to her. "Every song I play will be a love song for you — I will be the best dad that I can be. When I look into Andrew's eyes I will be looking into your eyes — When I speak to him I will be speaking to you. When I hold him I will be holding part of you — I will go on but I will only be half a person — This moment I've found peace knowing that you are not in prison or being tortured — I know you're frolicking in eternity with your science book, analyzing the rainbow. Eternity, what a big place — Do they have those black holes that you told me about? They say there's no sorrow or death, is that true?" As he spoke he could hear his beautiful music suspended in the room as the stars hang in the heavens.

He rose and walked effortlessly into the hall. His mother and Beth had not gone far, and asked.

His eyes had softened, but his voice was far away. "She died. Her spirit just came to me."

ഗ

CHAPTER TWENTY-SEVEN

ෆ

The morning sun starting its climb was casting a long shadow on the hospital floor. The hum of the monitor and the drip of the IV were steady, anchoring Cheryl's lifeless body to the outside world. Words dissolved before reaching her, so Zach held her hand and tried desperately to connect with her psychic. He had been at her side since he first heard of the accident, six days ago.

When she had first arrived at the hospital the doctors, after learning the details, ordered an MRI to check for brain damage. No damage was observed, but there was unusual activity centered in the limbic system, especially the amygdala and hippocampus. This puzzled them and the decision was to observe her closely. She was placed in intensive care and wired completely for monitoring, and an MRI was ordered for each day. After six days the results showed no change.

Since Cheryl was in intensive care, visitation

was limited to Zach and her mother. Zach stayed all night and his father brought a change of clothing and other necessary items. Her mother was there only throughout the day. She needed to share her time with her husband as he recuperated from a heart attack.

Colleagues and friends were informed of her condition daily. Dr. Seigbahn came to the hospital and talked with Zach and her mother several times. He was deeply concerned, because Cheryl was an important part of his dedicated science team and he also had enjoyed their casual chats from time to time.

This was day six that Cheryl had been in a deep coma, totally unresponsive to voice or to touch. With no signs of waking, it was beginning to cause great concern. This was an unprecedented circumstance that made everyone extremely anxious. What effect would the beams have on her brain when she woke up or long term. She had been an unintentional guinea pig.

They were just bringing her back from her early morning MRI when her mother arrived. The attendant said to Zach, "I believe I saw her lips moving but no sound came out."

"Oh god, that's a good sign." Zach was animated and excited. "This could be the first sign of her waking." He bent over her and started talking softly. "Cheryl, sweetheart, can you hear me?" He paused, "Cheryl." He looked at her mother and said, "I'm going to keep talking to her."

Her mother also spoke softly to her, but still no response. The moments of excitement were dampened and only the hum of the monitor responded.

The doctor arrived within the hour and announced good news. "The unusual brain activity, in the limbic system, we've been watching has ceased. Also, I have been sitting with the doctors who were reading the results and making comparisons with her other MRI's and they assured me they could detect no damage to her brain. I can't be sure what this means, but we can hope she could wake up soon."

Zach told the doctor that the attendant thought he noted lip movement but no sound. "Perhaps she is trying to talk."

"If his observation is accurate, that is definitely a good sign. Watch her, talk to her and if there's any change, call the nurses and they will get in touch with me. I'm here all day."

Zach was holding her hand and after a time he was sure he felt a tiny movement in several fingers. He relayed the news to her mother.

After a while Zach definitely saw her lips move but heard no sound. He immediately called the nurse, and while she was there Cheryl's lips moved again.

"These are the first signs that a person is waking from being comatose. They usually wake slowly. A few movements and a few words at first. These are good signs and I will call Dr. Keppler. He has been extremely concerned about her because of the circumstances under which this happened."

Eventually her eyelids twitched, but she did not open her eyes. Zach was anxious and continued to hold her hand through the wires and speak softly. Over the next hour he could see more eye and lip movement and feel it in her fingers. Finally she formed a word ever so faintly, "Ben."

Zach heard it. But he did not interpret it as a name, just part of a sentence like where have I been.

"Ben, are you here?" Her words were faint, but he understood.

Then she spoke in French. Zach did not understand. Her mother added. "She was very fluent in French in high school, so maybe that's not so unusual."

Over the next hour she slowly regained consciousness and said a few more words. When she first opened her eyes she stared at Zach in a most bewildered and confused way and her lips formed Ben. "Honey, it's Zach. Are you with me?" She closed her eyes again and appeared to fall asleep.

Finally, she opened her eyes fully and spoke her first sentence. "Where am I?" appearing to know what she asked.

Zach said, "Sweetheart, you're in the hospital. Can you hear my voice?"

"Yes," and she tried to move.

"Be easy honey, you're all wired up. You have an IV in your arm, but I'm here and I'll help you." He touched her forehead lightly. "You're going to be all right. Relax now and wake up slowly — everything is okay — your mother is here." She tried to turn her head but only her eyes cooperated. She closed them as if to slip away.

She opened her eyes later, looked at Zach and called his name, and tears rolled down the side of her face onto the pillow. To hear her call his name brought tears to him and also to her mother. It was the reassurance they were anxiously awaiting.

"She knows you Zach. Oh Cheryl, you're going to be okay." Her mother wiped her face with a tissue.

As she regained her awareness of the external world her mind was also waking. Her first thoughts were faint, but of Ben. Who is Ben? Her mind heard gunshots, screams, a piano being played. She even imagined the smell of burning wax. It was a dream in her half-waking state.

She became more alert as the hours passed. Her doctor visited and said that she could be taken off the monitor, but for the remainder of the day leave the IV in and perhaps get some exercise. He also said he would leave ordered for her to be moved to a regular room, but he wanted another MRI tomorrow and Friday. If that MRI still showed no brain damage, he would release her to go home on Saturday.

Her mother knowing Zach had moved out suggested Cheryl go home with her. "Zach, you probably want to get back to work, but come over for dinner and spend the evening." They all agreed that was a reasonable arrangement.

Later Zach and her mother helped her walk. She was weak, but with a little effort she made it down the hall and back. While she was walking they moved her to a regular room. After they had got her back in bed, her mother said, "Since everything is progressing very well here, I will go home to your father with the good news."

"I'm so sorry I have worried you two, but seems there was an accident. Can one of you fill me in a little more?" She looked at Zach then back at her mother.

"I'll go now and let Zach tell you. He understands it better than I do." She kissed Cheryl on the cheek. "I'll see you early tomorrow."

Cheryl closed her eyes for a few moments and when she opened them, she smiled at Zach. "What happened to me? I remember being hit by light."

"Well, I don't understand fully, but Ned said when you entered the lab, that instant he sent an equation to move an image of a statue, they had in range, to the back room. He said it was an experimental equation, it went awry and hit you and knocked you out."

"Did my image go to the back room?"

"No, it just hit you and put you in a coma. But the doctors assured us everything appeared normal in your body. They felt if there was a problem it would show up soon, but it hasn't. Doc said he would talk to you later about the brain activity. So if you feel anything strange, tell him."

"Right now I feel fine, just a little weak and hungry." She gazed out the window and Zach could see her mind working, trying to analyze what he told her, the length of the beams, white or red or laser, how and if they crossed.

"Why don't you wait a while for such deep thoughts?"

She smiled and nodded.

"May I call Dr. Seigbahn or one of the guys or Kim and tell them..."

She smiled and nodded again.

Zach relaxed in the big chair and made several calls to report Cheryl was awake and lucid. Everyone was elated to receive the good news. Other than her parents, he was the happiest of them all.

After learning Zach had been at her side, day and night, she insisted he go home tonight and get some rest. Seeing that she appeared okay he did not need too much urging.

She was discharged Saturday afternoon. The

doctor's orders were to rest, eat normally, take walks with someone and come to his office at the beginning of next week for one last check before release. Zach took her to her parents' home, and he spent the remainder of Saturday and most of Sunday with her.

ꙮ

Monday Zach took her to the doctor. As expected he released her. "You may go back to work next Monday. A few more days' rest will not hurt to make sure you are acclimated body and mind."

On the way out of the doctor's office, Zach asked, "May I take you to dinner?"

"You may," and she squeezed his hand. "Then I'll go back to Mom and Dad's for one more day."

"It's a little early for dinner. Is there somewhere you would like to go before?"

"Not that I can think of. Let's go down to the pier and walk, then have dinner at the Oceanside."

"I like that."

As they walked along the pier, things had a double meaning for Cheryl. Her mind flashed to giant steamers and large sailboats. Then they were gone and she saw only fishing boats and dinghies. The sounds of voices shouting and yelling, but it was Zach talking about the boats.

Inside they started with a glass of wine followed by scallops and mixed vegetables. As they ate Cheryl kept gazing out the window for something or someone. Zach noticed her strange attention, but thought it a reaction from her coma. She seemed to be enjoying the food and they chatted comfortably, but Cheryl felt uneasy about her being. Finally she cast it off as a result of the six days confinement. Zach did not.

On Wednesday evening after dinner, Cheryl thanked and hugged her parents for their love and care, and Zach took her to the apartment. They talked for a while and their relationship entered into the conversation, "Cheryl, I want you back in my arms. I realized while you were unconscious that I would be devastated if you never woke up. I hope you can come to the same conclusion. I love you Cheryl as I did before and this made me realize I always have." He kissed her lightly.

"Zach, I know and I love you too, but let's give it some more time. We have been through a different experience the last couple weeks. You have been anxious and that could prompt thoughts that could be different in a month. I haven't been able to think about anything. I've been so far away. You understand don't you?" She said, as she looked lovingly at him.

"I do and will give you all the time you need. I can't imagine you being so gone from the world."

"I can get my head going during the day and you can come over for dinner and we can spend the evenings together and watch television, if that's okay. Would you please bring me the latest *Science* journal tomorrow?"

He thought, she's normal or very close. "I'll be here with the latest journal and I'll bring a take-out for dinner. I don't think there is anything in your refrigerator but ice cubes."

ᘓ

The next day she felt lonely. She rearranged a few things filling the space that Zach had vacated. She cleaned the bath and moved the dust cloth back and forth in the living room. My gym bag, what happened to it? My new sweat pants and jacket. Kim's book, shoes, my cell. It probably got lost in all the chaos or stolen. So much time has passed they're gone. I have to replace these things before I go back to work. Looking in her refrigerator, Zach was right, just ice cubes. I have my purse and Zach said my car is here. With all of those thoughts she decided to go out and get the necessities and groceries.

Her thoughts were not only what she was going to buy, but Ben kept appearing to her in her psychic. Who is Ben? Just a name. From high school. There was only Zach in college. Someone I don't even know. The silent voice was so persistent, words vanished, just a presence and it was beginning to haunt her.

Zach arrived early Friday. He informed her, "The gang from your lab wants to come over for a welcome back and they will bring everything to eat. Around six."

"Oh gosh, that's great," and she grinned sheepishly. "I went out today."

"You did! How did it go?"

"Perfect. I'm just like always and I don't know what the fuss is all about."

"My dearest, you were in a deep coma and that's what the fuss is about."

"I know, but I'm all right now."

"I think you are." And he gave her a big hug and a warm kiss just as the doorbell rang.

Kim and her husband, the guys and gals from

the lab and a few from other departments arrived with food. Kisses and hugs were freely offered. They told her how much they missed her and how glad they were that she was coming back to work.

Jeff added, "Especially the report Dr. Seigbahn wants. It took all of us."

Everyone indulged in the food and enjoyed the casual conversation. The guys couldn't apologize enough. All three felt culpable for what had happened. It was a joint action of ideas and performance. Cheryl assured them they bore no responsibility. After all it was an experimental lab.

As they were talking and laughing, Cheryl had a flash back of a group around a large table having their evening meal and speaking French. She dismissed it as an idle thought and projected her mind back to her friends.

"We're going to make this a short evening," Ned told Cheryl. "We just wanted to have a few personal moments with you before you came back."

The group picked up on the cue and one by one said good night. Zach stayed. They cuddled on the couch and talked about various things, but nothing romantic was suggested by either.

Zach soon said, "Time for me to go, too. Dad thinks he has to wait up for me. See you tomorrow."

ග

She had not slept well last night. Today in the early afternoon she almost fell asleep while reading. Giving in she decided to soak in a hot bath and then nap before Zach arrived. She started her bath. The sound of the water sloshing from the faucet hit her psychic with a thud. A boat being tossed like a toy. I was so sick and Ben holding me as I vomited. We were crossing the English Channel and a storm hit. She got into the tub, and lay back on the quilted cushion to let her thoughts continue. They dimmed and she just enjoyed the warmth on her body. She closed her eyes and imagined being all alone in the universe. She floated as the music surrounded her, and she tumbled with the allegrettos and ran with the allegros. Free and alone in the vast blue.

She soon realized she was in the bath tub and the music was coming from a radio in her bedroom. Oh, but it was a nice imaginary trip. The water cooled. She toweled dry and slipped into the bed for a nap.

Her sleep took her to Paris when she first arrived. She saw the young people that had taken her in, Jacques, Elise, Janine. She felt the fear of the Prussian soldiers. The surprise that Nikki had betrayed her friends. Edouard's paintings. And Ben.

She woke later and smiled, her dream was not about to end. Ben was my husband and our baby, Andrew. The war. Finding myself in Paris and Ben coming for me. I was ecstatic when I saw him. Everything — everything. Another life was before her and she was in it, vivid and real, as the music from her radio.

ᔕ

CHAPTER TWENTY-EIGHT

ꕥ

*T*he events of the past several weeks should have been well on their way to history, but they were not. She felt excellent and vibrant and mentally primed, yet she felt like a third dimension had been added to her person. Incidents that she was experiencing would launch her mind into another time and place. Even so real she dismissed her perceptions as fantasy. Then she speculated, am I hallucinating — I'm not seeing images.

It was Monday morning and she was going back to work. She met Kim at Billow's.

Cheryl's first words were, "Catch me up on all that I've missed."

"You were the topic of the week. I'm not sure much was accomplished. Every time Dr. Seighbahn came in we were hoping for news. He was in a terrible frenzy. We all were."

"Zach said he called him, sometimes twice a

day. He came to the hospital and talked to Mom and Zach. I didn't know he was there. They told me."

"He told us of his visits and always wanted us to tell him if we heard anything." Kim paused, "Are you sure you're okay?"

"Absolutely — positive. Let's go on over."

"Please, may I check on you later?"

"Yes, my dear friend."

They walked into the big room and balloons were released and a big cheer came from all. Dr. Seigbahn rushed out of his office with a bouquet of red roses for her. He followed with a few words of welcome back.

Accepting the roses with a big smile and her eyes, she thanked him and then turned to the group that was huddled close.

"I want to thank you all for the cards, the flowers and most of all your prayers as I lay there in that stupor. A few stopped over last week at my apartment and I told them they bore no responsibility for what happened. It was a routine experiment gone wrong and that's not so unusual. When did we ever get it right the first time?" That brought a few chuckles of understanding. "I just stopped in the lab to say have a good week-end and it turned into a drama. With that I say I'm feeling great and even feel like a third dimension has been added to my mind." She turned to Dr. Seigbahn and continued, "We'll have to explore and name it." Her attention went back to those around her. "Thank you all for your kindness."

The group slowly dispersed and Cheryl turned to Ned and others on her team. "Do you all have time to meet now and discuss what happened while I was absent? It seems convenient we're not exactly in the middle of something."

"Yes. How about the conference room and I'll get my note book," Ned replied and the others acknowledged.

Gathering at the long table everyone had their notes in front of them. Ned started. "We were all in here Saturday with the men from the U.S. Accident Prevention Board and the police. We were just answering questions and didn't have a chance to discuss among ourselves why this happened. So Sunday we all came back to strategize before we got our computers back. They took them away Friday. We thought maybe Monday morning they would be back and we wanted to be ready to work. Jonas, want to talk about the equations."

"I'll do that." He pulled out a sheet of paper from his notes and gave it to Cheryl to follow along. "Together we had written a digital time equation that represented holography, in several sets to send a statue in the middle of the lab, allowing five seconds for its image to reach the back room. When it hit you we knew something terrible had gone wrong. We panicked. I'll skip to Tuesday, but we were all crazy till we heard you woke up and was all right."

"Did you feel anything," Iris asked.

"No. I just saw and remembered the light beams and then I was out," Cheryl answered.

Jonas continued. "We got our computers back Tuesday afternoon and the information from the hard drive, all on paper, which was the key to what had happened. Getting our computers was like getting a car for Christmas."

"Birthday, wedding, Christmas all in one," Ned helped him, along.

"We went to work immediately," Jonas went on. "The first thing we did was compare the original equations that we put in with the information the hard drive gave us. We were shocked about the difference. There was an error in the first parameter that sent everything after that askew, so the remainder of the sets would be off and they were exaggerated till the end. The first error causing the beams to reassemble was the one that hit you." Jonas just looked at the paper, with hundreds of symbols, letters, numbers organized into equations and formulas and shook his head. "Okay, ah — Jeff, pick up here."

He also was in a state of awe but began. "After looking at it in its entirety we realized we had several possibilities. Even with that, we decided to put our original equation in the computer in reverse. We did not get anything. Although, before that we did a couple short one, but nothing happened."

Cheryl thought, was this the reverse equation when I remember being sent from London back to Paris and Ben coming for me. The short ones when I was in the garden. She was feeling all too close to her previous thoughts.

"Then we took our original equation from the first error and drew a diagram, measuring all angles, beam intersections etc. and wrote a new equation following the hard drive information, into six sets. We had no idea what was in it but we entered it and got results."

"How long did it take you to write the new one," Cheryl asked.

"It didn't take long because we had the information, we just had to organize it. We entered the first set and got results. Man were we happy."

Cheryl could see the relaxation in his face, and asked, "What were the results?"

"The pictures that were transmitted looked like the middle of an earthquake or a war zone. Some buildings were in rubble. We were able to move around the area like moving around Google Earth and we caught a quick glimpse of a horse and carriage, but then the set ended." He paused again, "Ned, what was next?"

"I believe it was the traveling scene. It appeared from out of a window of a train or car. We could just see a county side going by and a forest. Margaret, you want to add?"

"Okay." And she referred to her notes. "Next we were baffled because all we could see was a roaring ocean. Waves lapping against something. It could have been a boat or a cliff. It was a non-committal reference. Next was a very distinct, dirty city. Although nothing was familiar, but again we saw a horse and carriage." Margaret stopped, noting Ned's expression.

Cheryl began to feel extremely uncomfortable as she remembered her thoughts, her dreams, and her perceptions when awake. Similar incidents coming from two different directions seem to be melding into one. What she was hearing was all too real.

Ned sitting next to her noticed her discomfort, and asked, "Are you all right?"

She almost snapped her reply. "Of course, why wouldn't I be?" She knew her demeanor had been noticed and decided to relax herself. "I'm sorry, maybe I'm just tired, but I have rested all week."

Ned touched her arm. “That’s okay. You’ve been through a bad time. Do you want to wait to finish? There’s always tomorrow and we’ll be here.”

“No, it’s rather compelling.” She feared she knew just how exciting but no one else did.

Ned decided to end quickly. “The fifth set showed various things.” He turned to Cheryl. “We recorded all of this so you can look at them again, anytime. What this set showed briefly were gardens, a large gray stone house, once even a lamplighter, and with that, the horse and carriage gave us a general time frame. We still didn’t know if we were on the right track, but we kept going. At least we were getting something and that alone was encouraging.

“We put in the last set and found an old city, again. We googled around and found a park and saw a person, so we went in closer, casually waiting to see what the set would give us. Your image looked directly at us. We moved in closer to make sure, because this person was dressed differently than we were expecting to find. Although we tried to keep an open mind, but it was your image. I yelled, we found her.”

Everyone ran to the computer.

“I cried when I saw you,” Iris said.

“We backspaced to the beginning of the set and made a copy, then started the process of destruction from the beginning to the end. Coincidentally, we heard you woke up the next morning. Seigbahn went for champagne.” Ned finished.

Cheryl remembered the destruction process taking an effect on her in the park. Eyes blurring, sitting down on the bench and realizing what was happening to her being and wondering where would she end up.

Her thoughts made her anxious, but she tried to hide her feelings, and asked, "Were you here all night?"

"Yeah, we took turns, pulling most of a night."

She studied the equation, and then stated, "We do have to keep these, not in the computer, but in a vault somewhere." She forced a giggle under her breath and shook her head in dismay, thinking....

"Seigbahn already has a copy in his vault and at your disposal if you would like to review them again."

"I'm not sure that will be necessary. You guys seemed to have done an adequate job. Thank you. What else happened while I was gone?"

"Not much, but we did learn a lot just experimenting with the digital equations. We prepared a report for you. Seigbahn has a copy too."

They went over a few minor things that were of interest to everyone and then they all went for coffee continuing their talk of equations, beams or whatever new thought hit in the brain.

ᔕ

This third dimension, as she called it, that was invading her senses was becoming so overpowering she questioned, am I losing my mind. Am I delusional or hallucinating? Did they give me a hallucinogen in the hospital? Everything is so real but in the distance. And the results from the equation had confirmed too much. Was there more?

The days fell into a routine even though she carried these overwhelming thoughts that she could not understand. She and Zach continued to see each other, but they had not talked about living together again.

Their relationship was warm and loving although they had not made love. He wanted to say Cheryl, I love you, marry me, but he sensed something was bothering her, so he put his words on hold. His fear was that he was losing her.

This haunting life like dream that was playing out in her mind, caused her to think seriously, could I really have brain damage? That thought did not rest well in her psychic.

One evening alone after work and while she was preparing a salad for dinner, her favorite CD of Chopin études was playing. Zach had left it for her. The music allowed her mind to leave her body and travel in time. The sights and sounds were too realistic for comfort. Cheryl and Ben, I pronounce you man and wife. Congratulations Mr. and Mrs. Rutherford. Being pregnant and feeling pain and holding Ben's hand as she gave birth to a baby. Ben playing a recital at St. James Hall. Seeing him for the first time as he entered the room. Our bodies having such a strong attraction for each other. Romantic but oh so haunting.

She slept only a few hours that night and the next morning she went straight to the computer. She googled Benjamin Rutherford. She gasped when she found there was a real person, but her sensibility quickly told her that was a common name. There must be hundreds.

She hit the bio line. Scanning through, she read. "As a youth he was educated in Paris and London. Studied piano with the famous Alexander Holstein in Paris and in London with Basil Koenig. The young pianist had been caught up in the Franco-Prussian War of 1870 and 1871. He had been trapped in Paris during the Siege and had to put his career on hold. After the war he and his wife made their way to London where they took up residence and he gave many recitals. One child, Andrew, was born to young Rutherford and his wife Cheryl."

It could not be more explicit. She knew. She turned cold and she felt her heart almost stop and her breath seized and pulled in. Her whole body and mind was being taken into the past right before her eyes. Startled, her body in a spasm, she covered her face with her hands and her voice wobbled, "I can't believe it! I can't believe it!"

She was afraid to read on, but it was too compelling, "In March 1872 his wife disappeared. Much effort in England and France was devoted to finding her. In 1871 she had been kidnapped and was found in Paris. It was suspected that she had been kidnapped again and was either killed or died in prison somewhere in southern France. Over time the incident was filed both in Paris and in London. The mystery of her disappearance was never solved. In the ensuing years, Rutherford gave recitals in London, Berlin and Paris. His health gradually deteriorated and he died in 1885. He rests in Kensal Green Cemetery in the suburb of London. Son Andrew and his wife Elizabeth are buried nearby. Future generations of the Rutherford family immigrated to the United States in 1934."

Cheryl was so shaken that she could hardly move. Her head whirled and gait was unsteady as she stumbled to her bedroom. Grasping the pillow and burying her head just in time to catch the tears. What happened? Looks — like — I lived a — short life in the hologram state. It had all come together, what her team had told her, what her mind was telling her and the Internet. It is not just a story it had actually occurred.

Suddenly it was easy to remember, how she loved Ben and Andrew. I had such a short time with them. Andrew grew up without a mother and me without my husband. Oxford. Beth and Rebecca. Ben made love to me with such passion. Her tears dried, but her arms still wrapped tightly around the pillow she stared into space. How can I ever be normal knowing this? I can never tell anyone. They will think I am crazy. A burden I have to bear alone.

She lay still but her mind traveled. They do not know what they did to me in the lab and they never will. That equation with its radicals, integrals and fractions holds a part of my life in a different time.

She went to the big window and gazed across the avenue into the park. She wiped her face on her sleeve. She wondered, what was Ben's life like through those years. Did he remarry? Internet didn't mention that he did. Was he active in raising our child? What was he like? His father was a good man, a gentle man, a caring man. Another unjust event in life happening to a good person, but this was not like any other. We were cheated out of our love. What I know I will never reveal. It will live strong and each day I will add a little more until it's complete. It will be like a film that I can run over and over. She smiled.

ေ

CHAPTER TWENTY-NINE

Spring was not arriving easily. No flowing in on gossamer wings. For Cheryl it resembled a Shostakovich symphony. Abrupt changes, descent into beauty, haunting shadows and a prayer.

When spring found itself, the pleasures were well worth the wait. The white daffodils and the pink tulips were a soft welcome. The birds were coming home to nest in the backyards, one more time.

Cheryl's mood brightened with the light of day, but was lost as night crept into her soul. She was lonely even in the presence of Zach. Her remembering was growing stronger and her psychic pressed her to know more, even though she knew it was dangerous. It was like the strings of gravity pulling tighter inch by inch. Is this my own personal emotion or my science person talking?

My personal side, I know what I read and I know I lived it. The group of friends. Making love to

Ben the first time in the moonlight. I remember the overwhelming love I felt and his love that flowed to my body and soul. It was so natural and then we rested in each other's arms. She closed her eyes to be completely with him, to feel his body. To be cradled within his very self.

The treasured thoughts lingered long, but then her other mind slipped into her consciousness. I am a scientist and know how holograms are supposed to work. Should I relate what happened to me those days that were really years? Probably not. It's too early in the scientific scheme of things. It would be like finding our likeness on Pluto or proving that the theory of our universe is a hologram.

She wondered if other people were experiencing what she had and too afraid to air it publically. There could be thousands of experiences, war and greatness. There could be different lengths of time. Even before time or into the future. These thoughts put her mind in a state of awe.

Mine is so personal I will never share. Others can put their love story in a book, but I'm going to keep mine in my heart.

After much thought, she decided to do a genealogy search of the Rutherford family. She knew she would never get over the shock of reading about herself, her husband and their short life together.

She told Zach she had to catch up on what she had missed at the lab and needed a quiet evening. It wasn't science, but genealogy, and she wanted to be alone.

There were many websites with information. She made notes and organized them. It was near midnight when she took her notes to the couch to read them. Andrew born January 7, 1872, in London. Married Elizabeth Jorgenson. Three children, Andrew Jr., Lucy and George. Andrew Jr. was an accomplished pianist like his grandfather. Won a scholarship to Juilliard and his sister Lucy accompanied him to America. They arrived in 1934. His son was John Andrew and his son Benjamin George Rutherford II, also a pianist, but had chosen to become a professor, where he is presently, Eastman School of Music in Rochester, New York.

The overwhelming information made her unable to focus. She seemed to lose her senses, and mental numbness whirled in her brain. But soon she was laughing, energy returned, and her senses flowed. These mixed emotions finally settled into a feeling of peace, all within an hour.

They were not just names on a page. They were a part of her. She was part of them. She and Ben's spirit lived with them through the generations, as if she had walked by their side. Our love was sacrificed to produce this wonderful line of people. It had been written in the big book and we fulfilled destiny.

Now I have to meet Benjamin Rutherford II.

ὧ

Another week passed and she tried to function normally. It was hard, very hard. Almost to the brink of not caring for what was around. Zach. Her career. She hadn't called her parents as often. That frightened her, because these were the people she loved and they were her world. Now I have another world. Do I feel this way because it's new or stronger? Is it my love for Ben? I love Zach, but if compared, pale. Ben went through hell for me. I had no control and perhaps should have told him? He never knew. Now I have to stop questioning whether I was right or wrong, it's over.

ᔕ

Spring had finally decided on a theme. The days were full of sunlight and the nights were cool. It was preparing to turn over its fickle personality to summer.

Cheryl contacted Benjamin Rutherford II at Eastman and they exchanged several letters and a few e-mails discussing their genealogy. She wrote that she had business in Buffalo in June and the cities being so close, would it be possible to meet with him. He answered, yes.

She flew directly to Rochester. Telling him she had business in Buffalo would make her seem less anxious. She planned a quick trip, but further reading about the city piqued her interest, so she planned for four days.

In her rental car the GPS guided her to the Strathallan Hotel near downtown Rochester. Noting that George Eastman House was nearby she put on her Easy Spirits and enjoyed the fresh air as she walked along tree-lined East Avenue. Her previous assignment at Colburn did business with Kodak and sadly thought of the company's decline. No thinking about business, this is a mini vacation for me.

Entering the main entrance at the back of Eastman House she noted a display of posters advertising old movie films, but chose to examine the house first. After viewing the two large front rooms, she climbed the wide staircase to view photographic exhibits, old and new. After reading each carefully, she descended the stairs and as she did, imagined how it had been in times past. Ladies in their long colorful gowns, partners in black and white entering the front door to attend a ball.

On her way to the back entrance she stopped at the garden. It was small, but tulips of red, salmon and pink stood tall. After a quick peruse of the posters and the gift shop she felt an overall satisfaction.

Walking back to Strathallan, she thought of the Rutherford home and gardens. The paintings, what happened to them? It was late in the afternoon. In her room, she showered and slipped into a dark blue dress and went to the lounge for an early dinner. As she sat alone realizing she might appear to be bait. Her thoughts, I should have had room service.

She ate quickly and back upstairs kicked her shoes off and grabbed her science journal.

Friday her GPS guided her first through the Eastman School of Music's campus downtown and a drive around the old Victorian neighborhood, passing by the Rutherford's home. Then on to the University of Rochester's River Campus. She knew of the research done there and was impressed at its size and so many beautiful buildings. It roused her thoughts, if I decide not to stay with Colburn and Zach and I don't get back together, this would be a wonderful place to work.

She drove on to Mt. Hope Cemetery nearby, parked, got out and walked, walked and walked, passing Frederick Douglas' and Susan B. Anthony's resting places. She had heard of the cemetery and how beautiful it was and now she knew. A canopy of green hovered over the stones that identified lives that had been. She stopped several times resting on a bench contemplating the many things that had happened to her recently. Unbelievable but real.

From the peaceful surroundings of Mt. Hope, her next venue was the noisy and active Eastview, the classy-upscale mall in Victor, part of the Rochester area. A flowered summer dress and a blue leather bag from Lord and Taylor were her only purchases. Window shopping was another way to enjoy the mall.

The next stop was the big grocery store she had heard so much about, Wegmans in Pittsford Plaza, also part of the Rochester area. Impressed beyond belief at the selections of cheeses, fruits, fresh baked breads and the aromas pulling her through the store. She decided to pack a foam container with her dinner instead of sitting alone in the lounge. Always wondering why a grocery store would be a tourist stop, now she knew.

Another full day was waning and driving to the hotel, her remaining schedule ran through her mind. Sunday visit the Memorial Art Gallery and hear the Italian Baroque organ, but importantly tomorrow the visit with her ancestor.

Saturday early she phoned Dr. Benjamin Rutherford and was invited to his home for dinner. His wife had insisted. Cheryl accepted.

In her little black dress and white jacket, she looked as if she had stepped from the pages of the latest *Vogue* magazine. She knew just where to go, because she had driven through the warm and receptive neighborhood yesterday. The old Victorian homes had long tales to tell. The gaslights embellished the streets just like old Paris.

She was at peace, and ready to compare genealogies. As she took her last step onto the porch the door opened. Ben and his wife were there to meet her. She looked at him and was shocked as if lightning had struck her. He was an exact image of her husband, just a few years older. Short brown beard, tall.

For a moment she thought, after all the emotional preparation I had put myself through, my soul just shattered. Seeing such a perfect likeness, it was almost impossible to hold back. For her it was only a little while since she had left her Ben and inside she was still grieving. Later she could not remember those moments, but apparently survived without embarrassing herself.

His eyes widened and were full of surprise also, but he took her hand. "It is so good to meet you. I really feel I have known you all these years." He turned. "My wife, Isabella." She offered a warm welcome although calmer than Ben.

Inside their home a grand piano and other beautiful period furniture graced the large living room. An orchestration of operatic arias was circling around the room, holding emotions close to the heart. There were additional words of welcome from Isabella to their home and the city.

"Sit here Cheryl. I believe this old furniture is not only handsome but comfortable," Ben said.

"The dinner is being prepared, but before I go help Sarah, I'm sure you would like some refreshments. Cheryl may I offer you a glass of wine," Isabella asked warmly.

For a moment she thought just what I need. A second thought flashed, I might undo completely and embarrass myself. “No, thank you, just water.”

“Perhaps with lemon and a pinch of sugar.”

“Lemonade sound wonderful.”

“Isabella love, a large one for me too, please.”

Ben’s actions were exactly like her husbands. Even the way he said love, I was never Cheryl, but Cheryl Love.

“How was your trip from Baltimore and your business in Buffalo?”

“Both were good.” She hadn’t prepared a discussion of Buffalo.

Thankfully, Isabella interrupted with frosted glasses of lemonade, a plate with cheese and crackers, and colorful veggie bites on flakey pastry.

Cheryl was having a hard time relating to the present. Her mind kept taking laps back in time. All she could see and hear was the likeness of her husband, in this Ben. His voice, without the shaded English accent, had the same warmth, the same pitch, and the same passionate overtones.

She looked at his hands and wanted to hold them. She looked at his lips and wanted to kiss them. She wanted to stare into his eyes and say I love you. She told herself you have to get through this with some dignity. Calm — down. The music alive in the room did not help with her emotional control.

A few sips of lemonade helped cool her body and a few deep breaths helped order her mind.

“I believe Sarah needs my help in the kitchen. I will leave you two to your ancestors.”

Ben picked up the conversation. “I understand

from your letters you are a scientist and have a doctorate in that field. And I have to apologize, I am not very scientific. We live and breathe music in our home and work. Isabella is a very accomplished violist. We often play together. She is a member of the orchestra and teaches a few classes at the school. I've devoted my life to the piano just as my namesake did. Tell me about your scientific life."

"I work at Colburn Laboratories. We have several divisions of research that we concentrate on."

"And what division do you represent?"

"I am a physicist, but presently working with a group to develop uses for holography."

"Can you explain holography in a few simple terms for me?"

She laughed lightly and condensed the topic to a few words, enough for him to raise his eyebrows and stare into space for a moment.

"Interesting — but what got you into genealogy?"

An unexpected question and she had to think quickly. "My friend and colleague was telling me all the interesting things she was finding, so it piqued my curiosity. And this is where it led me."

"I found a lot about Benjamin Rutherford's lineage but nothing about his wife's."

Oh! Cheryl thought, I may be in deeper than I want to be. "I really didn't look a lot, just followed Ben."

"Andrew and Lucy were the first to come to the United States. He received a scholarship to Juilliard and she came with him. I believe I have heard through the ancestry tales that Andrew, Lucy and George, their brother, sold the painting the family had acquired for a vast sum, but stipulated they should remain in the old home as a gallery. That helped Andrew and Lucy afford to come and stay in New York."

"I didn't know that, how interesting." But she did know they had a wealth in art work that Ben and his mother had collected before the painters became famous.

"What happened to their brother George?"

"That's a mystery. It seems he went to Berlin and they lost touch and no one knows what happened to him. Things were not good in Germany at that time so perhaps he got caught up in, who knows what."

"You are from a long line of pianists. You must be very proud of that. Have you passed that talent to your son?"

"Jacob, plays piano well, but has chosen to be a journalist, and is presently in New York City. I wish he could have been here to meet you. Perhaps you will visit again when he can be here."

They continued to talk about stories that had come through the generations. Ben being trapped in Paris. His wife being kidnapped. This Ben's information was spotty, yet Cheryl knew it all and had to be careful not to reveal too much that she should not know.

Finally she asked, "What about your parents?"

"They lived here in Rochester. My father died two years ago and my mother last spring."

Isabella came in and announced, "Dinner is being served. Are you two talked out?"

"Almost," Ben said as he reached for Cheryl's hand and they crossed to the dining room.

Cheryl had been in and out of several states of emotion, but more relaxed now. She felt she could handle, emotionally, the remainder of the evening.

The dinner included roasted tenderloin, new creamed potatoes, asparagus, and salad with colorful vegetables. Cheryl complimented Isabella several times about her red table presentation and the luscious food.

After dessert Ben suggested, "Let's have our tea in the living room, Isabella, please."

As they were walking back to the living room, Cheryl asked, "Would you play for me? That would make the evening complete."

"I would love to, my dear. Do you have a request?"

"A Chopin would be fitting. My favorite is the "A-flat Major Allegro sostenuto."

Ben understood, her request being so specific and knowing it ended with such finality.

As he played he lost himself in his music just as Ben had so long ago. Her eyes had to leave him. She walked to the big window and gazed into the garden. And just for those moments she took the music and allowed herself to travel back to be with her Ben, whom she still loved so much, playing in his piano room.

Please don't let me cry. She tightened her fists as she brought them to the front of her body. Her face locked in a grimace. Her eyes sealed to hold the tears. Please just a little bit longer. She felt like she was grabbing for the last raft in the ocean of the universe. But she knew the end was coming, just as she had known her days with Ben would also have to end.

She turned just as his hands rose from the keys and he returned. He smiled at her. It was her husband's face she saw and that was almost the final rush that released her emotions, but she managed to hold them within one more time.

She returned the smile. “Beautiful. Beautiful as… as beautiful as I have heard…. Thank you so much.”

“My pleasure, my dear.” Yes. Yes. He thought.

He took her hand and half guided her to the chair. “Let’s enjoy our tea that Isabella just brought.”

He did not sit down. “Well, this has been a wonderful evening with you, Cheryl, but I have one more thing to show you about our common lineage.”

He left the room and returned with an old, small metal box.

Cheryl gasped softly and touched her face lightly. The box his mother brought him from Belgium. This is too much to hold. She tightened her whole body, because her emotions were everywhere, her toes, her fingers, her heart.

He sat down and placed the little box on his lap. “As I said my mother died last spring and she gave me this not long before.” He paused to run his fingers over the raised images of the composers as she remembered Ben did so long ago. “Surprisingly, I had never seen it or heard of it. Mother said Lucy brought it when she and Andrew Jr. came to America.”

It helped her that Ben was doing all of the talking. She knew she could not.

“The stories that came with it, that it contained stuff our grandfather Ben, had sealed away and all those years had never been opened. My mother said she wasn’t sure anyone cared to open it, because they thought they knew what it contained. On the other hand, it was sealed so tightly that probably no one could get into it very easily."

Cheryl moved idly in her chair.

"Last winter I kept thinking it could hold clues to my ancestry and with much effort I managed to get it open."

As he opened it now with ease, her stomach whirled. *I wish he had shown me this before I ate.*

"Perhaps you would like to read this article from *The Times*." He handed her the yellowed lace-like paper about Ben's recital at St. James Hall.

She tried to hide her trembling hands as she took it and pretended to read. *I don't have to read, I was there.*

He pulled out a ring. "I don't know about this."

His wedding ring. I gave it to him. She took it and fondled it with love that did not go unnoticed.

"Well, and down here at the bottom I found this. I believe you left it behind, Grandmother, or Great-grandmother." He held up her the cell phone that she thought had been lost. "Please tell me how this happened. Oh, please.... I was looking for you as you were looking for me."

Holding his ring to her heart and staring at him, she could no longer hold back the tears that had been so waiting all evening.

"One last thing, this little portrait, without question of you. Signed, Edouard, 1871. I knew you the moment I saw you."

He paused and almost in tears also, "All evening I have watched you and it is so evident the love you shared with Ben. I believe it is you who should have this little box that your husband so carefully packed and perhaps hoped someday you would find. But it found you."

He placed, with care, all the treasures of yesterday that was so long ago, back into the box and closed it and handed it to her. "You have many more years to treasure these and with the greatest of love I pass it along to you, Cheryl, my Great-great-grandmother."

ꕥ

EPILOGUE

ɞ

*T*he big plane with Cheryl aboard landed in London Tuesday. She knew before she could put her heart to rest, and her body together, she had to be with Ben one last time. Maybe somewhere in eternity he is watching.

She followed the grassy path, having less footsteps now, to the older part of Kensal Green Cemetery. She did not need a map. Her heart sensed the pull. As she got closer she felt that cold whiff of his spirit meet her, as he had hers in his piano room, so long ago. He's not just watching, he's here, and she smiled.

She stopped in front of his monument. Benjamin George Rutherford 1840 - 1885.

"Hi darling," she said aloud. "I loved you then and I love you now and all the times in between. I had no control over what happened. I wish you could have known, but trying to understand would have been painful. Maybe my decision wasn't right but.... You obviously were the best dad you could be. Love. Music and beautiful people were born through the ages. I just left your namesake and I was proud of him. He was truly so much like you. He played for me and I was hearing you and feeling you." She stopped talking when her thoughts were traveling faster than her voice could speak. Floating through time and stopping at so many wonderful happenings to relive… to feel.... This is so like losing the love of your life to death. It leaves you so helpless.

She sat down on Ben's grave, pulled up her knees and buried her head in her crossed arms. To run through my beautiful life with him would take days and days. I have only a few hours. I have to be selective today. Recitals. The music you brought to my life was a treasure that will never stop giving. You made life gentle, loving, positive. The war did affect you, but you were slowly leaving it behind. How did you die? Was there someone there to hold your hand as you slipped away? It should have been me with gray hair and sensible shoes.

She sat quietly. I hope these will not be the only moments I have with his spirit. She rose and looked at the smaller stone beside his. Cheryl McAndrews Rutherford. No date, just a name. "He thought of me until the last. Our love had been true, pure."

She rose and walked around touching the stone of her son that she never really knew, although, the memory of his tiny face and big brown eyes was forever cast in her mind. The sun was warm and the air fresh. The silence in this resting place was as in death.

She lingered and did not know how much time

had passed, but she could see that the sun had reached the distant roof-tops and tall trees.

"It's time to go." And she touched the ground where he lay resting in peace. "My body will rest here beside you someday and then my soul will find you in eternity. It's goodbye for just a little while."

ɞ

ACKNOWLEDGMENTS

My son, Joseph, was first to read and find typos and misspelled words. He also offered suggestions and ideas to the story line.

My son, David, was helpful with additional ideas and structure.

Janet Ragaisis, my friend, read my manuscript twice and offered suggestions and pointed to little slips.

Ruth Thaler-Carter, professional editor and writer, copyedited the final text and her suggestion gave this book its last and best scrutiny.

Thanks to all for giving their time to my book.

Composers and their music mentioned for the beauty that has lasted through the ages and continue to reach into our hearts.

Quote from Robert Lewis Stevenson's *A Child's Garden of Verses.*

And never to forget life's experiences and imagination.

Mary Ann Nocera

The author lives in Upstate New York

Other books by the author:

After Sunset - 2013

Freddy's Book - 2015

Heart to Heart - 2015

www.ingramcontent.com/pod-product-compliance
Lightning Source LLC
Chambersburg PA
CBHW030027180626
46810CB00001B/252
9780692910658